TEXAS GUNDOWN

TEXAS GUNDOWN

JASON MANNING

Texas Gundown
Copyright © 1990, 2016 Jason Manning
This edition published 2018
All rights reserved.

Cover design by Matt Forsyth

ISBN-13: 978-1-68068-122-2

to
CAROL

CONTENTS

COMANCHE KILL

C ale McKeller watched the chestnut look one way and then the other, up and down the gulch. He'd been right—the Indian party was closing in from both directions. He had to do something. He couldn't keep still by his cookfire any longer, waiting for the arrows to fly.

Putting his coffee cup down, he rose and commenced to walk slowly toward his gun. He heard the first hostile sound, the crack of a twig beneath a hastily placed foot. He tried to prepare himself, but almost jumped out of his skin.

The Comanche broke cover, running at him hard through the stand of cedars dead ahead. Cale dove for his Winchester, grabbed it, and rolled into a fighting stance. He saw the warrior lunge, knife upraised, dark face a mask of savagery, and brought the gun down. The barrel caught the attacking brave solidly upside the head and he fell forward. Cale levered a load into the breech, aimed from the hip, and fired, hoping like hell that he hadn't bent the barrel. The warrior was scrambling back up when the bullet hit him at the base of the skull and put him down forever.

Chapter One

On about sunset, Cale McKeller urged the leggy chestnut he called Beau to the rim of a sandy cutbank and sat his sweat-stained saddle to gaze down at the activity below.

The site was a good one for the business at hand, tailor-made for holding together a mixed herd of two thousand beeves—a wide-open little valley cut through dead center by the shallows of Lodgepole Creek. There were cutbanks east and west, steep and high enough to discourage the most determined longhorn. Or at least slow a *ladino* down long enough for a cowboy to drape a loop of hard-twist around its neck. There was very little brush in the valley, and if there was one thing a longhorn knew, it was the use of brush to elude capture. Cale had seen wily mavericks crawl on their bellies through the seemingly impenetrable *brasada* thickets to escape a range rider, hiding in brush pockets no taller than a half-grown youngster.

The chuckwagon, remuda, and night camp were situated at the south end of the valley, while the branding fires were a long half mile away to the north, downwind of the herd. Longhorns were *not* made more cooperative by the stench of burnt hide.

Spring had come to the hill country. Bright green patches of new grass were coming up through the tan matting of dead stuff. The post oaks were budding, the early flowers abloom. Cale let his gaze drift away across the hill country. This was Cyclone land. Miles and miles of it. He had never been able to shake the feeling that it was more land than one man had a right to own. Maybe it wasn't as large a spread as the one Captain King had carved out of the old Santa Gertrudis land grant down near Baffin Bay, but it was certainly large enough. Every last rock, tree, and beavertail cactus was Cale's by birthright. And no one knew how many cattle, exactly. It was going on a year now since the death of his father, Sam McKeller, and he still could not muster a single solitary spark of pride in the ownership.

Cale flexed his shoulders, wincing. He was bone-tired from doing his share of the work from dawn to dusk—or "can see" to "can't see," as the *brasaderos* called it. The problem was he had never really taken to range work. He'd been born to it, but never liked it. Which was one reason he had joined the army at an early age. Life in the cavalry was as hard as cowboying, but in different ways— and those different ways had naturally suited him. He had spent most of his horse-soldiering years campaigning against the Sioux and Cheyenne on the Northern Plains. A tall man, he was wide-shouldered and narrow of hip, and seventeen cavalry years had left him whipcord lean and whang-leather tough.

It had left him with infallible weather sense, as well. He looked up through drifting yellow dust at the darkening sky. Not a cloud in sight. But he could feel it. Bad weather coming.

Hearing the hoofbeats of a horse, he turned in the saddle to watch Frisco come up alongside. Francisco Madrigal was the Cyclone foreman. His father had been *caporal* before him. Old Joachim had been Sam McKeller's most loyal *vaquero*. Since the very beginning, when Sam had boldly staked his claim to this corner of the traditional hunting grounds of the Penateka Comanche, Joachim had sided him. Sam and Joachim and a few others, mostly Mexican cowboys, had brush-popped wild Spanish cattle and turned the Cyclone into a working spread by driving the first herds to Louisiana on the Opelousas Trail.

Checking his dun mare, Frisco hooked a leg around the bisquit of his saddle, took a ready-made cornhusk cigarette out of a pocket, and lit it. It was his custom to roll a half-dozen smokes every evening for the next day's consumption. Cale sometimes wondered why the young *caporal* rolled his cigarettes in *hoja* and not store-bought papers, but never enough to ask.

Frisco said, "Another day, another dollar, boss."

"Don't call me that," snapped Cale. "How many times do I have to tell you?"

With the quirly dangling rakishly from his smiling lips, Frisco scanned the dusk-darkened marking ground—the two thousand or so cattle, the twenty-odd men, the four branding fires, the supper smoke rising from the belly-cheater's cookfire down by the chuckwagon.

"The work is coming along. We will have Señor Snyder's herd ready for him in a few days."

Cale watched him suspiciously. "Are you fixing to start on me again?"

"*No comprende, jefe.*"

"You know exactly what I mean, and don't call me boss in either lingo."

"They are your cows. If you want to sell them to Señor Snyder for half what we could get if we pushed them ourselves, it's up to you."

"While you're at it, don't forget to throw in the part about how my father always took his own herds to market."

Frisco flashed a mitigating smile. He had an easygoing nature and a kind of roguish charm. It was hard to stay mad at him. He was also a top hand. The men all liked him and did what he told them to. As far as Cale knew, none had objected to his taking over as foreman. Born and raised on the Cyclone, Frisco was as much a part of the ranch as the land itself.

In his dress and gear the *caporal* looked every bit the *gringo*. He did not care for the flashy garb and silver trimmings on tack that so many *vaqueros* favored. From a distance he looked like an Anglo cowpuncher, with his red bandanna, flannel shirt, and leather vest, shotgun chaps over trousers tucked into high boots. But Frisco could not escape his ancestry when it came to bladed weapons. He carried a big belduque in his left boot. The knife was as wide as a cavalry saber, and near half as long as any "wristbreaker" Cale had carried in the service.

"Dammit," said Cale, "I don't know why I keep explaining myself to you. We've got a contract to deliver two thousand head to Snyder, and that's all there is to it. He's paid a fair price for the herd. He takes upon himself the cost and risk of pushing those cows to railhead. So we only see half of what we might get at Trail's End. It's money in the bank. Besides, we have a rustler problem, remember? We'd do better to stay close to home this year."

"That's it, you see," said Frisco amiably. "Your father never had a rustler problem. Not for long, anyway."

Cale's temper was as short as flea hair. Through gritted teeth he said, "I inherited rustlers when I inherited this ranch."

"*Es verdad*," agreed the *vaquero*. "When your father died, the buzzards of the two-legged variety *did* begin to fill the brush."

"Fine," said Cale, as if that was the end of the discussion.

But Frisco went on to say, "Some of the men think we should deal with the rustlers first, then the herd."

"We're going to deal with them—after the contract delivery date. Snyder takes a herd early in the season or not at all."

"But if we cleaned out the nightriders, we could take the herd ourselves," Frisco reasoned.

Cale glared at him. He knew that Frisco was right. The hard truth was this: Cale didn't care to push the herd north himself.

"But like I said," Frisco added, still wearing that happy-go-lucky smile, "they're your cows. I did not come up here to question your judgment."

"Huh!" Cale grunted, skeptical. "You sure fooled me."

Straightening in his saddle, Frisco pointed with his chin. "Looks like company."

Cale looked, saw a brace of riders coming south along the Lodgepole, kicking up a plume of dust that seemed to capture the last of the sun's light.

"That Palouse looks like Snyder's horse," said Cale.

"Pushing hard, by the dust," Frisco mentioned.

"Snyder's one to push hard. Himself, his horse, his men. Let's go see what brings him."

Two of the men working the herd were reps for Snyder. They were present mainly to grade the cows selected for the consignment, but did their share of the work. Like Cale, they knew the Appaloosa, and galloped out to say their howdies and report on the work's progress. When Cale and Frisco arrived, Snyder and his three cowboys were in a tight group.

Dressed in a dusty black frock coat and straight-brimmed black hat, Thomas Snyder was a thin, sallow man, his humorless face framed by a sharp goatee and trimmed mustache. He sat ramrod-straight in his double-girthed Texas saddle. Bony, long-fingered hands gripped the horn. A pious, puritanical man, he did not permit the riders in his employ to curse, gamble, or drink, and would not brook frivolity or laziness.

Cale put his tall chestnut alongside the Palouse and extended his hand. "Mr. Snyder. Come to look it over?"

Snyder grasped the offered hand in a perfunctory way, his black eyes piercing. "I've come to see you, Mr. McKeller, not the herd."

"What can I do for you?"

"I happened to be in Llano last night. The night before that one of your men apparently employed the services of a prostitute who plies her trade in one of the town's bit-houses. Word is he decided not to pay for service rendered, and used his fists on her when she took issue."

Cale gave Snyder a long look. This was the sort of shenanigan that Snyder most disapproved of, and it sounded as if he was blaming Cale for it.

"My men have standing orders," said Cale briskly. "No one takes time off in town until this job is done." After he'd said it, he wished he hadn't. It came across as though he were trying to get out from under the responsibility.

"The man's name is Yellen."

"Billy Yellen," murmured Frisco. "One of the line riders."

"McKeller, I have a reputation for honesty and fair-dealing, and for abiding by the laws of man and the Word of God. My men conduct themselves in a decent Christian manner, and I expect the same from all those with whom I associate. We have never done business before, you and I. I knew your father, but I don't know you. I've come here today to find out for myself just what you're made of, young man."

Cale bit down on his anger. He didn't like to be dictated to. But he had learned discipline and diplomacy as an army officer.

"Those orders I spoke of apply to all Cyclone hands. We have a problem with rustling in these parts, Mr. Snyder. Not just the Cyclone. Other ranches, too. We're getting hit hard. And with most of the outfit here, line riders especially have to be on the job seven days a week."

"I take that to mean you will fire this man Yellen."

Snyder's holier-than-thou attitude rubbed Cale wrong. He figured that all Snyder was doing was reacting to gossip. He would not be so quick to judge. On the other hand, if what Snyder related was true, then retribution had to be swift. If Yellen had broken Cale's rule, he had given the Cyclone a black eye in Llano at the same time. Llano was a tough town. There was no properly constituted law there, and the bunch that ran the tenderloin district would give Cyclone hands a rough time in the future if Cale let this go.

It was this line of reasoning, not placating the hard-nosed Snyder, that brought a curt nod from Cale.

"If Yellen did what you say, I'll hogleg him."

Snyder's eyes narrowed. "There is no doubting what he did." He turned to his reps. "Get back to work," he snapped, then neck-reined the quick-footed Palouse around so abruptly that Cale's chestnut jerked its head up and danced sideways.

Snyder and his escort went north, back the way they had come. The two reps rode south, returning to the marking ground. That left Cale and Frisco in the settling dust.

Cale took a deep, calming breath and let it out all at once. "Where's Yellen's camp?"

"Whitetail Meadow."

"Yellen." Cale shook his head. "Can't place him."

"Your father hired him a couple of years ago. I'd say he hasn't been up to Casa Piedra more than twice since you've been back. Line riders tend to be solitary hombres."

Cale nodded, grimacing. He had hoped to get back to Stone House—Casa Piedra, as it was known to many—tomorrow to pay Katy a visit. Now that he had traded his career in the army for the life of a rancher, his wife was his only happiness. He didn't like being away from her too long.

"Well," he said grimly, "I reckon I'll go pay Mr. Yellen a visit."

"Of course you'll give him a chance to tell his side of it."

"What do you think?"

"You're a fair-minded man, boss. I have always said it."

"How many times do I have to tell you?" growled Cale. *"Don't call me boss!* Are you hard of hearing, Frisco? If so I'll get you an ear trumpet."

"Dispense," apologized Frisco, suppressing a grin.

"Oh, I wouldn't bet my last silver dollar on it."

Cale left the marking ground that evening, putting some miles behind him before stopping for the night.

The next morning he shook out of his bedroll, put on his hat, and pulled on his long blue army-issue greatcoat. The night had turned bone-biting cold, and the hour prior to sunrise was the most bitter of all. He took his boots one at a time, turning them upside down and striking the heels hard, in case there were scorpions. The variety common to the Texas *brasada* were usually not as lethal as their *alacran* cousins south of the border, but plenty painful, which warranted sensible precautions. With his boots on he stood to strap the shellbelt around his waist, throwing a bunch of hopeful glances at the pewter-cast sky. The sun would be a late riser, and so Cale worked the brass buttons with stiff fingers and turned up the high collar.

He went up under the scrub cedar rimming the rocky clearing and fetched an armload of deadwood. Hollowing out the ashes of last night's fire, he built a new one. In a moment a wisp of smoke, flavored by cedar shavings, lifted into the frosty air.

The enameled coffeepot contained water collected the night before from the run down below. He broke the thin sheeting of ice on its surface with a stab of rigid fingers, then balanced the pot on the stones encircling the campfire. Waiting for the water to heat, a half-empty sack of Sultano in hand, he let his gaze sweep the brush on this side of the deep-cutting creek and the cactus-strewn slope of granite on the other. Threads of gradual, cloud-muted daylight cat-footed through the trees and down into the gulch. He saw nothing which gave cause for alarm. Heard nothing out of the ordinary, either. The fire crackled cheerfully. Eventually the coffeepot began to hiss and tap. Cale added coffee measured by the handful, producing a strong aroma that woke his appetite and got his stomach to knotting. Down below, the run played its music. Fed by one of the many warm springs in the region, it was draped with a low, creeping, cottony mist.

Up near the trees behind Cale the tall chestnut whickered gently, pleased to see Cale up and about, as comforted by camp routine as McKeller. In good spirits, Beau lay down clumsily and rolled over, thrashing this way and that, for his coat was changing, and the rocky ground felt good. Cale watched the chestnut's antics with amusement. Beau got up, shook vigorously, then strolled off a few yards to seek breakfast in the shelter of the cedar brake.

Sitting on his heels by a cheerful fire on a cold morning, Cale could imagine he was back on the Northern Plains, back with the Seventh, doing what he loved best. He couldn't shake the feeling that he had made the biggest mistake of his life a year ago, walking into Colonel Custer's study at Fort Abraham Lincoln and handing over his resignation.

Autie had scarcely glanced at it, looking up at Cale with his narrow eyes burning fiercely, as always.

"I will accept this with deep regret, if you are absolutely certain that it's what you want, Captain McKeller."

"It isn't a question of what I want. I'm the only son. There is no one else."

The man the Hunkpapa Sioux called Pahuska, the Long Hair, sighed deeply.

"Let's put aside formality, Cale." Custer rose from a small desk strewn with volumes of Napier's *History of the War in the Peninsula* and a riot of paper covered with his own hen-scratchings—Autie had spent the long, inactive winter months slaving over his Civil War memoirs. A fire blazed in the stone hearth. The country's most famous Indian fighter walked over and stared moodily into it, hands clasped behind his back. He cut a trim, dashing figure in his fringed buckskin tunic, long yellow hair curling to his shoulders, his recently acquired mustache covering a thin-lipped mouth.

"I believe this year will be a decisive one, Cale," he said softly. "I am confident that we will break the Sioux once and for all. It will be the biggest campaign ever mounted against an Indian foe. We'll strike into the heart of the Bighorn River country. I regret that you will miss it. You are a fine soldier and a first-rate officer. I have come to rely on you." Turning, he smiled wryly. "And why not? How long have we known one another?"

"Seventeen years."

"Yes. And served together most of that time." Custer looked up at the portrait of McClellan, his favorite general, hanging above the mantel. "But I won't try to dissuade you. We do what we must. I hope you and Katy will find happiness in Texas. I can tell you, Libbie will miss your wife's company. Our ladies have become fast friends." Coming forward, he extended his hand. "Best of luck, Captain. I don't doubt you're doing the right thing."

Cale clasped the hand tightly. "I'm sure that I am," he replied, his voice taut with emotion. Then he tried to ease the parting with humor. "Give Crazy Horse my best when you see him."

"Your best." Custer laughed sharply. "And my worst."

Cale remembered it vividly, as though it had happened yesterday. It had been difficult, leaving the Seventh, leaving Autie. A few months later Custer and the regiment had met disaster at Little Bighorn. The news had certainly convinced Katy that they had done the right thing. He kept a strong image of the way she had stared at him after hearing the news—that pale, horrified expression of one who has barely escaped catastrophe. But, try as he might, Cale couldn't shake the feeling that he had deserted Autie and his fellow soldiers. Not that he presumed his presence on the field of battle would have made any difference in the final outcome. He kept it from Katy—his conviction that it would have been better, somehow, had he died with the Seventh on that bare Montana knoll.

The lid of the coffeepot began to rattle in a rising cloud of fragrant steam, and Cale filled his tin cup with the thick brew. It was just to his liking, strong enough to stand a dead man up and walk him a mile. Way off to the southeast came a distant drumroll. Thunder. He could expect rain before the day was out. Cold wind, the last gasp of winter, was coming over the Staked Plains, colliding with moisture-laden breezes from the Gulf. A cactus wren filtered through the shinnery to his left.

Thoughts of all those dead men, their bones thick beneath the buffalo grass of the Yellowstone country, were strong in his mind. He also thought of Sam McKeller's bones, buried beneath Two Mile Oak, within sight of the Stone House.

Sam McKeller's death had left him with a ranch he had grown to resent as a young man. The Cyclone had been Sam's abiding obsession, the passion of his every waking moment. In Cale's eyes, the Cyclone was the thief of his father's affection.

Cale had been born in 1841, five years to the day after Texas won its independence in the marshy lowlands of San Jacinto. His mother was Swah-ya-wanna, otherwise known as Susanna, the Cherokee maiden Sam had lured—some said "stolen"—from the Female Seminary at Tahlequah.

When Cale was fourteen, a rough-and-tumble town cropped up on the Llano River, the Cyclone's northern boundary, and was named for the river it overlooked. Llano was wide-open from the word get and attracted plenty of tough men. The day after Cale's fifteenth birthday Susanna had run off with one of them, a frontiersman named Wolfhunter Geddes. Sam had been too preoccupied with putting another herd together for the market up at Sedalia, at the top end of the new Shawnee Trail, to spend time tracking her down.

In his nineteenth year Cale had left the Cyclone and found his true home: the army. That had been over seventeen years ago. A long time. But the way it came at a man, one year stealing by on the coattails of the one previous, it passed like a string of railcars behind a locomotive highballing down the backside of a long mountain.

His first cup of coffee consumed, Cale went over to rummage through his possibles and find something fit for breakfast. The search produced a small muslin sack containing a few old corn dodgers that promised to be as hard on the teeth as hardtack— what soldiers were apt to call "Lincoln shingles."

Carrying these back to the fire, Cale hunkered down once more, poured a second cup of crank. Beau had drifted downslope into his range of vision, and now the chestnut stopped muzzling a patch of bluestem to raise its head and adopt a listening pose, ears turning this way and that. Beau was a cavalry mount, a veteran of numerous excursions into hostile territory, and better than any watchdog.

Cale's instincts had been honed by a lifetime of warfare. It wasn't just Beau's attitude. Suddenly, and with utter certainty, he felt he was being watched.

There was no telltale sound. To go silent through the *brasada* was no easy task. The brush was thick in places, the grass brittle, the rock loose and shaly. Whoever it was knew the country and how to move through it.

There were still a few black bear in the hills, and a few big cats, and more than a few bad-tempered *ladinos* that could be as dangerous and aggressive as grizzlies. But Beau's reaction was an ironclad guarantee that Cale had two-legged company for breakfast. When animal predators got too close, the chestnut would fidget and whicker and generally raise a ruckus. But when predators of the human variety came calling, Beau got as stone-still and silent as a statue.

Cale took stock of his situation. Without solid information to the contrary, it was wise to assume that he was outnumbered. And if there were more than one, and they were stalking him, and they had any sense at all, they would come at him from different directions.

Apparently at ease, he stayed by the fire, sitting on his heels and working on a corn dodger, mentally measuring the distance to his Winchester repeater. The Model 1866 lay in its saddle boot, a long roll and reach away alongside his bedding.

Question was: Who was hunting him, and why?

Chapter Two

One observation provided small comfort. If they had wanted him laid out stone cold dead, seemed they could have done the job from a distance with rifles and some decent shooting.

Unless they were renegade Comanche.

Cale willed himself to stay put. It took some effort. He was happy to feel the weight of the Colt Cavalry on his hip, but he would have to sweep the greatcoat out of the way and the holster loop off the hammer before the short gun could be of much use.

There were several good reasons why renegades would be unlikely to try picking him off with a long shot. Reliable rifles were not easy for an Indian to come by, despite the best efforts of the *Comancheros* who still lurked west of the Cap Rock. Ammunition was always in short supply. In the final analysis, not many Comanches had the wherewithal to become even average shots with firearms. If they could ride down on their enemy, they preferred to use the lance or the bow and arrow; they were expert with both. And if not that, then they would rely on stealth to get them close enough for knife work.

Left hand holding the cup near his face, the fragrant steam warming the tip of his nose, Cale checked the brush on one side of the gulch and the rim of the rock slope on the other. To his right stood Beau, motionless but for the ears. Beyond the chestnut was a jumbled outcrop of rock. Good cover, but getting there meant a long run.

The coffee smelled good, real good. Cale wondered if he would live to drink another cup. Surviving the hell of half-a-hundred skirmishes and a dozen full-fledged battles had left him with a practical attitude toward death. Just another part of life. Nothing a man could do to avoid when the time came. That took some of the fear out of situations like this, and permitted a man of Cale's experience the luxury of looking at the problem objectively.

The more he thought about it, the more convinced he became that his visitors were Indians. He was inclined to discount the rustlers who had in recent months become a local plague. Bad as they were, nightriders were more likely to avoid an honest cowboy rather than trouble themselves with a bushwhacking. But any solitary white was fair game for renegades. The year 1877 found most of them on the reservation above the Red River in Oklahoma. Colonel Mackenzie had put an end to organized Comanche resistance three years earlier at the Battle of Palo Duro. But every now and then small bunches strayed off the reservation, looking to steal a few good horses, or dine on colt meat—a Comanche's favorite dish—or to catch a lone white unawares.

Cale watched the chestnut look one way and then the other, up and down the gulch. He'd been right—they were closing in from both directions. He had to do something. He couldn't keep still any longer, waiting for the arrows to fly.

Putting the cup down, he stood, moving without haste, and even had the nerve to pantomime stretching cold-stiff muscles. Then he strolled toward his saddle and hot roll, scarcely ten paces from the fire. It looked a whole lot farther. For once he regretted his habit of sleeping beyond the ring of firelight regardless of the season. Beau watched him, standing quiet, poised for action. "A damn fine horse," thought Cale proudly. "It'll be a crying shame if a renegade gets his hands on him. But then I won't be in any condition to care."

A step away from the rifle and a fair chance, halfway amazed that his ruse had worked, Cale heard the first hostile sound, the crack of a twig beneath a hastily placed foot. He had tried to prepare himself, but almost jumped out of his skin anyway.

The Comanche broke cover, running at him hard through the cedar. Cale glimpsed a deerskin war shirt, dark blue leggins, and beaded moccasins, all adorned with that long fringe the Comanche favored. No eagle feather dangled from the beaten silver disc in the warrior's scalplock, and no scalps decorated the war shirt. He was young and untried—but still dangerous.

Cale dove for the Winchester.

The warrior raised a shout. *"Keemah, tah-mahs! Namasi-kohtoo!"*

Cale hadn't spent his youth in Comancheria without picking up some of the lingo, and knew that the brave was calling on his "brothers" to close in quickly.

Falling on the sheathed repeater, Cale kept rolling, got a good grip on the bright brass receiver of the "Yellow Boy," and swung it sharply to shed the scabbard. He saw the warrior lunge, knife upraised, dark face a mask of savagery, and brought the rifle down, the barrel catching the Comanche solidly upside the head. The Indian fell forward. Bouncing to his feet, Cale levered a load into the breech, aimed from the hip, and fired, hoping like hell that he hadn't bent the barrel. The warrior was in the process of coming back up, but the bullet caught him at the base of the skull and put him down forever.

A guttural cry shattered the dawn. Cale flinched at the close and lethal whisper of an arrow that shredded the green boughs of cedar above him.

A second Comanche had crept through the cedar brake and positioned himself to grab the chestnut gelding. At the first warrior's shout this one forsook stealth for speed and came bounding through the shinnery with the fleet-footed agility of a deer. There was a lead-rope of braided horsehair in his grasp. Before Cale could bring the rifle around, the Comanche had reached Beau, and Cale held his fire for fear of striking the horse.

Snorting, Beau spun away from the loop as the Comanche made his throw. The rope fell wide of the mark, but the brave was quick-thinking and not easily discouraged. Before the chestnut could bolt away, he leaped forward and grabbed a fistful of mane. This provoked Beau into a violent frenzy. Snapping at its assailant, the gelding reared up on hind legs and twisted, trying to shake off the unwanted admirer. The Comanche was lifted off the ground, but hooked an arm under Beau's throatlatch and got the other hand over the chestnut's poll. His weight bore the gelding back down on all fours, and his copper-hued arms bulged with straining muscles as he attempted to force the animal's head lower still. Beau let out a high-pitched scream, misplaced a foreleg in a patch of loose grass-hidden rock, and went over sideways.

When Cale saw Beau go down he went from being scared to just plain boiling mad. He thought at first that the Comanche had slit the chestnut's throat with his knife. The next best thing to stealing an enemy's horse was killing it. And Beau was not one to submit meekly to capture. The chestnut was highly prejudiced when it came to Indians. In exchange for a stipend of cheap rye whiskey, an Arikara who occasionally scouted for the Seventh had promised Cale that he could turn the chestnut into a bonafide Indian-hater in a fortnight. This he had accomplished by slipping up on Cale's new remount at all hours and laying a willow switch across the animal's withers. It had not required much of this abuse to sour Beau on redmen in general.

Cale had learned the hard way that in a fight you were better off if you didn't get too riled and just kept your head. But he allowed his fondness for the gelding to blind him momentarily. Instead of fading back into the cover of the cedar he advanced into the clearing, cursing the Comanche horsecatcher in the brave's own tongue, and hoping for a clear shot.

As the chestnut toppled, the warrior released his grip and tried to land on the run, but for all his agility he lost his balance and fell, rolling downslope. Cale brought the Yellow Boy's stock to shoulder and drew a bead, and then Beau got back up into his line of fire. Stepping to one side, Cale sought a better angle, only to give up any such notion as two mounted Comanche suddenly appeared on the rimrock across the gulch.

Cale had already figured there were more of them—the horsecatcher had not been the one firing that first arrow. Spinning, he lunged for cover behind his saddle as two more arrows came flying.

He had tremendous respect for Comanche bowmanship. Most warriors were excellent archers, who could shoot so swiftly that they kept one arrow in flight all the time.

One arrow passed right between his legs, snagging in the long skirt of the greatcoat, breaking his stride. He stumbled and winced as another shaft passed right in front of his eyes. Falling on the saddle, he rolled, pulling it up in front of him. Two more arrows came, and he gasped as both struck the underside of the hull. One lodged solidly in the wooden frame. The other penetrated leather and clothing and pricked his skin between the ribs above his heart. A well-made arrow of dogwood or hickory could go right through a buffalo at fifteen yards. Cale counted himself a lucky fool that he was at least three times that far from the brace of Comanche archers.

Pushing with his legs, digging his heels for purchase, and keeping the saddle in front of him as a shield, he crawled hastily into the trees. A third arrow struck the saddle, another hit the ground so close to his churning legs that the point caught his pants. He found a shallow depression behind a half-buried spine of granite and rolled gratefully into it. Belly-down, he braced the Winchester across the saddle's seat.

Peering through the low evergreen boughs of scrub cedar, he searched for a target on the opposite slope. The mounted Comanches had disappeared. He scanned the clearing directly below him. Beau had vanished too, along with the Comanche who had tried to steal him. Cale doubted that the Indians or the gelding had gone very far. The dead brave lay ten feet away. Cale wasn't proud of the killing. He had shot the youth in the back. But a man who fought Comanche fair and square was tired of living.

Cale rolled over on his side, opened his shirt, and checked the wound in his chest. Hardly more than a scratch. But there was the possibility of poison to consider. Comanche poison was made by pounding deer liver into a paste and then mixing the paste with rattler venom. Tribal custom forbade the use of poison on war arrows. But Comanche culture had been disrupted by forty years of a losing war with the whites. Tribal law was no longer strictly adhered to. Especially by renegades. These days you couldn't expect a Comanche to fight fair, either.

Out in the middle of the clearing his campfire settled; a shower of orange sparks rose into a lazy blue ribbon of smoke. The coffeepot was still balanced on the rimfire stones, undisturbed. Cale had a sudden strong hankering for some java. His mouth was cotton-dry. His canteen was over by his bedroll. Closer, but not close enough. He wasn't going to lose his life just to wet his whistle. So he settled for plucking a handy stem of tanglehead and chewing on it.

There was no way of knowing whether they would try for him again. The Comanche was a pragmatist. Attacking him had already cost them one life. Would they risk greater loss to avenge the death of their *tah-mah?* Or would they play a waiting game, a test of nerves, hoping that he might try to make a run for it and break into the open?

He had decided to lie low all day if necessary when a shot rang out a hundred yards or so downstream.

This was followed immediately by two more reports, a Comanche cry of defiance, and then a fourth gunshot. Two different guns, judged Cale, one a revolver, the other a long gun. They spoke with different voices.

Again silence reigned. Cale waited. A few minutes later he heard the tapping of steel-shod hooves on stone. Deep in the brush to the south of the clearing Beau snickered, and then stepped out into the open. The chestnut's ears were perked forward. The gelding dipped its head a couple of times and gave a soft whinny. Cale was pretty sure then that whoever was coming up the gulch was not Indian. But that didn't mean they were friendly.

He heard the horse stop, and then a low drone of voices. He couldn't make out the words but he got the impression they were speaking English. He felt a little better about his future. They might be rustlers or road agents, but anything was better than Comanches.

A moment later he heard one man coming on foot through the brush, angling up the slope, and though he was trying for stealth he fell far short of the Comanche in that respect. Meanwhile one man on horseback proceeded up the creek. This one soon came into view, walking his dun mare into the clearing.

It was Frisco.

Cale got up and dragged his saddle out of the trees, the fear and tension draining out of him.

"Didn't happen to see any Indians out there, did you?" he asked, dropping his saddle by the fire.

"A few," replied Frisco, nonchalant. He leaned forward on his saddle horn, dark eyes taking in the dead warrior, the scuffed ground, and finally the arrow that yet hung in the lower reaches of Cale's greatcoat.

"How many is a few?"

"I saw six, personally."

"How many got away?"

"Six, at least."

"I thought you were a better shot," admonished Cale.

Frisco shrugged, as though what Cale thought regarding his marksmanship was of no real consequence. "Comanches are hard to kill."

"Well, I ought to be glad you came along when you did. They invited themselves to breakfast, but I didn't have enough to go around. And you know a Comanche won't go hungry...."

"*No tengo hambre*, anyway," replied Frisco. "But I could stand some coffee. We had a cold camp last night."

"Help yourself. Who's with you?"

"Tom Samples." Frisco dismounted, ground-hitching the dun, and commenced to digging in his saddlebags for a cup.

"What's he doing thrashing around in the brush? Hey, Tom! Come on in. No call to be bashful."

As Frisco settled to help himself to the coffeepot, Tom Samples emerged from the shinnery. He was broad-chested and auburn-haired, with a ruddy complexion and a surly curve to his lips. A Henry repeater was held in big, brawler's hands.

"Howdy, Tom," said Cale. "I don't think grown men should hide behind bushes unless they need to pee when women are present, do you?"

"Or," added Frisco, "unless they are set upon by a bunch of *Komantcia*."

Cale gave the *vaquero* a narrow look as he turned his back on Tom and sat on his saddle. He didn't need to see Tom to know that he had taken offense to his remark. Cale had meant to nettle him. In the past year Cale had managed to earn the respect of the Cyclone riders, if not their good fellowship. But Tom Samples refused to accept him. At the same time Tom had been cagey enough to avoid any blatant confrontation that could cost him his job. He wanted to stay on at the Cyclone—it had been his home for many years. Cale did his best to tolerate Samples's antagonism, but when he got to feeling irritable, as snappish as a coyote in a trap, Tom was the perfect target for insulting remarks.

"Looks like we got here just in time," Tom said, racking the Henry across his shoulders.

"They were already pretty discouraged," said Frisco between sips.

"We nighted not a half mile west," Tom told Cale. "Saw the smoke from your fire. Didn't know but that it might be rustlers."

Cale said, "The men who've been running irons in these parts aren't loco. Hardly the type to build an open fire on a high hillside."

"*Es verdad,*" Frisco agreed. "Their sign is as hard to find as bee tracks in a blizzard."

"Besides, I'd have thought you two would be too busy with the road branding to be out trailing nightriders." Cale challenged Frisco with a look that demanded explanation. He had left the *caporal* in charge of the marking ground. Typical of a longtime army officer, he was accustomed to having his orders obeyed or knowing the reason why.

Frisco merely smiled. "Well, you see, it is like this. An hour after you left a rider came from the Rocking Chair. The Comanches had killed one of Dusty Blake's men. Señor Blake sent riders out to warn everyone. I thought I had better come find you. Oh, I know you can take care of yourself, boss. You were born a *brasadero*. But *mi madre* would never forgive me if I let something happen to you. You know how she is. She thinks of you as a son."

Cale knew that was true. After his own mother's departure with Wolfhunter Geddes, his upbringing had been left to Esmerelda Madrigal, Frisco's mother and the Casa Piedra housekeeper. There were some who looked at Cale's dark complexion and jet-black hair and whispered that at least on one occasion Esmerelda had done more for Sam than keep house. Cale knew that was a dirty lie. But Essie did carry on sometimes as if he were one of her own.

"If you were going to go anywhere it should have been to Stone House," he told Frisco. "What with a raiding party running loose."

"When Blake's man was found they saw sign of only seven warriors. Now there are only six. Being so few they would not attack Casa Piedra."

That made sense to Cale, but he couldn't help worrying about Katy.

He pulled the greatcoat up between his legs and broke the head of the arrow from the shaft so that he could remove the thing without causing more damage to the garment. All Comanche war arrows had the point loosely attached and serrated, the better to detach and rotate in the wound, causing greater damage.

Shifting in the saddle, he felt the prick of the arrowhead that had pierced the hull; the shaft had snapped off during his hasty scurry for cover. He chided himself for having forgotten it. It would be a fine thing, he reflected, if the point *did* carry poison. He'd be a sight with his butt all swollen and festering.

"Let me borrow that pigsticker of yours," he said to Frisco, standing up.

Frisco tossed him his belduque. Cale had a clasp-knife in his saddlebags, but those were over near his hot roll; Frisco's toothpick was handier.

As Cale knelt to cut the point out of his rig he heard Tom say, "I'll go get my horse," but he didn't look up, for he figured Tom was telling Frisco. Samples rarely addressed him unless it was an opportunity for impertinence. Samples turned back into the cedar and Frisco strolled over to get a closer look at the warrior Cale had shot.

"Peneteka," he said. "Must have forgotten to sing his medicine song. Or got careless and laid a stick crossways in a campfire." He pried the knife from the dead youth's hand, turned it this way and that, admiring it. "He covered himself with beaver oil. Thought it would make him bulletproof. You'd think they'd know better by now. Or maybe he just missed a spot. Least we won't have to bury him. If we did such a thing his spirit would haunt us forever."

The arrowhead removed, Cale carried the knife back to its owner.

"I'm obliged that you came to warn me," he said. "But you and Tom can go on back now. I've been chasing Indians, or running from them, for a lot of years. I'll make out."

"I think I go with you. *Mi madre* would be impossible to live with if I left now and those Comanches decided to track you down and kill you. There is safety in numbers." Frisco returned his knife to its boot sheath and put the Comanche's under his belt.

"Hell," muttered Cale. "I've never been able to get you to do one single thing I said if you were set against it. Why should today be different?"

"If they killed you I would have to live with that on my conscience. Would you want me to endure such remorse? I must go. Not for you so much as for me."

"That makes a lot of sense. And I know Tom would be all broken up inside, too, if something happened to me."

"Don't pull the trigger unless you know your powder is dry, boss."

"What is *that* supposed to mean?" snapped Cale. "And don't call me boss!"

Frisco just shrugged, smiling lopsided.

Disgusted, Cale turned sharply away and grabbed up his saddle.

"Well, what are you waiting for?" he barked. "Let's get there."

Chapter Three

Wolfhunter Geddes sat with his back resting against the trunk of a live oak and watched a pitch-black night turn into a gray, overcast day. Eventually he saw the smoke from a dozen cookfires drift out of the chimneys of Casa Piedra and the adjacent *ranchito*.

He had been sitting there for hours, his new Sharps 50/90 Leadslinger, sheathed in a fringed and beaded buckskin scabbard, lying across his legs. Now, in the pearly light of daybreak, he got his first good look at the Stone House, and paid silent kudos to old Sam McKeller. Big Sam had picked a fine place to build his ranchhouse, out on that grassy plain. There wasn't a stick of cover for a quarter mile in any direction, except for one old wide-spreading oak way out by its lonesome to the southwest. There was a headstone under that oak, surrounded by a white picket fence. Wolfhunter wondered if it was Sam's head that stone was lying on. But he wasn't curious enough to leave his concealment just to find out.

The motte of oaks in which Wolfhunter maintained his vigil bordered a gravel creek bed, and was as close as a man could get without taking a chance at being seen. A sentry had been posted on the roof of Casa Piedra all night long. Sam McKeller was dead, but apparently they still did things his way. Wolfhunter reckoned he could have belly-crawled through the tall grass in the dark of night and slipped up on that sleepy-eyed guard and cut him from gullet to gonads without making a lick of noise. But he hadn't come to kill—leastwise, not Cyclone sentries. Besides, this morning he was feeling a little too old and sick to be going to such trouble just to prove he could.

Giving Casa Piedra and its outbuildings a long study, Wolfhunter decided that it hadn't much changed since last he had set eyes on it, better than twenty years ago. Wolfhunter narrowed his sunwashed green eyes. The older a man got the more he learned to appreciate life. Problem was, the older you got, the quicker the years sped past, fast as spooked pronghorn.

Casa Piedra was just that, a stone house. A square structure, built around a courtyard, with limestone and adobe walls that Wolfhunter recalled were at least two-three feet thick. The roof was flat, supported by heavy pine beams hauled from the East Texas woodlands. The walls rose three feet above the roofline to form a parapet. The windows were tall and narrow, and had long wooden shutters. A full-grown man would have to turn sideways and suck in his belt buckle to get through one. The house had been built around a well, and from where he sat Wolfhunter could see the tops of the three Spanish oaks shading the courtyard.

There were more buildings than Wolfhunter remembered. The *ranchito*, a dozen-and-a-half stone or picket *casitas*, laid out north of Casa Piedra, was bigger than some Mexican villages Wolfhunter had seen. These were the dwellings of the married *vaqueros*. The "batch" hands shacked in a stone bunkhouse to the west of the *casa grande*. Wolfhunter could also see a number of corrals and breaking pens, stables, a smithy, a smokehouse, a stock tank presided over by a Halladay windmill—not to mention a few outhouses.

As he watched, Wolfhunter began to see some activity. Most of it had to do with relieving bladders and gathering fresh water. He saw a few women out and about in the *ranchito*, and a pair of cowboys stirred out of the bunkhouse. The first went to the washbasin on a trestle table beneath the *ramada*, emptied it, and trudged over to the stock tank to fill a wooden bucket. He waved to the lookout on the roof of Casa Piedra, and the lookout waved back.

There were nine horses in the corrals, a tomcat patrolling the stable area, and a couple of dogs roaming the *ranchito*. But Wolfhunter had positioned himself downwind. A good breeze was kicking up from the north, carrying the scent of rain, and rippling through the sea of grass. The rotor of the Halladay was spinning up a storm.

Something besides wind rustled through the brush to his left. Wolfhunter listened carefully, and then relaxed. It was the coyote dog. He was certain, sight unseen. It certainly wasn't that pack of Penateka that had trailed him for a couple hundred miles. No self-respecting Comanche would make a racket like that. Oh, they were close, he knew that much. And in a way he was glad. The prospect of at least one more good fight pleased him.

The mangy yellow coyote dog broke into view carrying a possum in its bloody jaws. It lay down just out of Wolfhunter's reach, placed its mangled catch across its front paws, and looked at Wolfhunter.

"I'm confident you intend to share your breakfast with me," said Wolfhunter wryly. "As we have shared many a camp and you have such a generous nature."

Detecting the sarcasm in the man's tone, the coyote dog pulled back its lips and growled, down deep and low.

Wolfhunter snorted. "Piss on you, then."

He resumed his study of Casa Piedra and his speculation about the Comanche.

It occurred to him that he'd had no call incurring their wrath on this trip. He had come all this way to carry out Susanna's dying wish, not to pick a fight with redskins. No, he shouldn't have taken the time to dawdle with that Comanche girl.

"Hell," he grunted. "No use crying over spilt milk. Or spilt blood, as the case may be."

The coyote dog started tearing open the possum's belly with its teeth.

Wolfhunter chuckled, recalling with pleasure how the girl had struggled. A wild little punkin, for certain. The chuckle disintegrated into a cough, and the coughing fit became so severe that Wolfhunter had to lay his Big Fifty aside, roll over, and bury his face in the Navajo-made *bayeta* blanket on which he had been sitting. The hacking was so violent that it wracked his entire frame, and when finally it had passed, he was so weakened that he had to lie there for several minutes without the strength to rise. When he did manage to sit up, wiping blood-flecked sputum from his chin, he scanned Casa Piedra with fevered eyes, afraid that his coughing fit might have given him away. But there was no evidence that anyone had heard his hacking.

"Damn, Susanna," he gasped, resting his head against the tree trunk. "You better be saving me a place in Hell, darlin', for I have bought my ticket."

The coyote dog watched him with apathetic yellow eyes, as if it didn't particularly care if he was sick or not. The mongrel didn't need Geddes, and he didn't need it. But meanness, like misery, loved company.

A while later he felt strong enough to stand. At six feet six he was one to tower over most, always on the lanky side. But in recent months his ailment had emaciated him. He wore fringed buckskin, sun-faded and grime-blackened in places by dirt and sweat. In the Comanche fashion he wore scalps sewn to his tunic. They were all Indian scalps. A tanned wolfskin was stitched to the shirt at the shoulders. In bad weather he could lift the pelt up over his head like a hood, tying two strips under his chin, for he wore no headgear. A rawhide band encircled his head. His auburn hair was long, past his shoulders, and heavy with gray above the ears. His beard was thick and tangled. A Bowie knife and a Colt 1860 army revolver jutted from a beaded belt tied around his waist. He carried his extra pistol loads in a shoulder-slung pouch that also sported some handsome beadwork. Additional rounds for the Sharps 50/90 were carried in a *bandolero* draped across his chest.

Turning, he picked up his blanket and rifle and slipped deeper into the stand of oaks, his movements stiff. Old bones and old wounds were taking their toll. The coyote dog did not follow, not yet finished with its morning meal.

The oaks gave way to cypress, the thin soil to deep gravel. The creek bed was wide, littered with water-smoothed boulders and tangles of deadwood, while the stream itself was a narrow, shallow affair. Wolfhunter looked both ways and spotted the steeldust downstream, grazing on a patch of salt grass. The horse looked up at him, then went back to tearing up the countryside. Wolfhunter hissed, and the steeldust lifted its head again. Wolfhunter made a curt get-the-hell-over-here gesture. The steeldust snickered and slung its head.

Wolfhunter thought, "If a cayuse could make a face, ole Crowbait there would sure do her."

The horse was shaggy with vestiges of its winter coat, and in every other way not much for looks, but he hadn't kept it for its handsomeness. Crowbait could run like the wind. Even now the steeldust did not just canter over. It *galloped*, full-tilt, throwing its head, and stopping just shy of Wolfhunter in a spray of gravel. Crowbait had but one gait—full speed ahead.

Wolfhunter made to stroke the steeldust's muzzle, and the horse snapped at his hand. Wolfhunter grinned.

"It's just like you, you ignorant pile of bones," he said fondly. "Chewing on salt grass when you've got some fine bluestem sprouting up under them oaks. I swear, you got the brains of a jackass and the disposition to match."

The coyote dog was loping through the trees toward them, and Crowbait just whickered at Wolfhunter and contemplated the coyote dog with hostility.

"One big happy family," observed Wolfhunter.

He went to his centerfire saddle, draped over a nearby cypress knee. Crowbait followed him, standing by uncertainly while the man threw first the *bayeta* blanket and then the saddle onto its back. Wolfhunter didn't use bit and bridle, but rather a sisal rope, Comanche-fashion, looped over the steeldust's lower jaw with a lark's head knot. In younger and better days he hadn't used a saddle at all, choosing a hide pad instead. But he had recently come to require the assistance of a stirrup.

"Getting old is a bitch," Wolfhunter warned Crowbait. "I never aimed to live so long."

Crowbait looked away, apparently uninterested. The steeldust was used to Wolfhunter rattling on about things; the man liked to talk but rarely had the pleasure of human company.

Wolfhunter grunted a little climbing into the saddle, and as he situated himself, his thigh brushed the scalpbag tied to his saddle's bisquit. He kept the flies away from it with skunk musk. Essence of skunk did not smell pretty, but neither did scalps at a certain point, and not even flies could stomach polecat perfume. It didn't bother Wolfhunter, though. Most of the time he smelled pretty ripe himself.

The scalpbag reminded Wolfhunter of that Comanche girl again. He had done worse in his time. What amazed him was that he could commit such an atrocity without blinking an eye, knowing that he was not far short of meeting his Maker. Most men got to acting mighty pious when they felt Death gaining ground. But Wolfhunter wasn't most men. He was not that way at all. Just the opposite in fact. He wanted to commit as much sin as he was able in the days remaining to him.

"Hell," he told Crowbait cheerfully, "I ain't even gonna get a peek at those Pearly Gates. Ole Saint Pete won't waste his breath telling me to go to Hell. But don't fret none, you worm-eaten broom-tail. I'll be sure to take you along. I'll need a fast horse down there. God knows I'll have enough enemies waitin' on me. Why, I aim to dispatch a few more before I go. How's that suit you?"

Crowbait didn't bother to reply.

Wolfhunter tapped the steeldust's kidneys with his heels. The horse took off like a shot through the oak motte, exploding into the open and thundering toward Casa Piedra, head high and the wind in its teeth, scattering a flurry of grasshoppers out of the grass. The coyote dog loped along, well to one side.

Chapter Four

"*Rider coming!*"

Esmerelda Madrigal was in the kitchen, a long, brick-floored room at the northwest corner of Casa Piedra, kneading sourdough, when she heard the call of the lookout. She assumed that the rider was a Cyclone hand. Most of the cow crowd were out at the marking ground twenty miles north at Lodgepole Creek, road-branding the herd Señor Cale had contracted to provide the drover Snyder. One more set of boots under the table for breakfast. Well, no matter. Miguelito had brought more than enough eggs from his predawn raid of the chicken coop, and she had enough sourdough for a few more loaves of bread.

It was Esmerelda's responsibility to feed the bachelor hands when they were home. Lately, with all but a short handful out on the range, she had been having an easy time of it. Sam McKeller had always brought his men up to the big house at mealtime. The long table in the adjoining dining room could seat thirty in a pinch. It was a custom he had not abandoned even when Susanna had resided in Casa Piedra, and one that Cale, having grown up with it, felt comfortable carrying on. It was a job made easier with Katy's help. Unlike Susanna, Katy had insisted from the first on doing her fair share around the house.

"I'm not one of those la-dee-da ladies," Katy had told her once, back when Esmerelda had tried, fruitlessly, to keep the more menial tasks from her. "I was born on a farm in Indiana. I managed to survive the Oregon Trail. I helped my brother turn over a section of Dakota dirt. I doubt that it will break me to scrub a few floors around here."

At this very moment Katy was out in the smokehouse getting a slab of side-meat. Esmerelda smiled, wiping her dough-crusted hands on the apron protecting her brown gingham dress. The past year had seen the two women become good friends. Cale had done himself proud. If only, thought Esmerelda, her son Francisco would settle down and find as fine a woman!

She stepped out into the courtyard. The enclosure was as chill as an icehouse. In early spring it stayed that way until the sun was high enough to slant bright sunlight into it. Then it got as warm as toast. But this morning there would be no sun. Esmerelda didn't mind the cold. Katy had stoked the kitchen's big iron Windsor range at first light and now, as she scanned the roofline for the sentry, she wiped beads of perspiration from her upper lip.

Lo conoce usted?" she called out. "Do you know him?"

The head and upper torso of the lookout appeared. It was Lopez, and Esmerelda noticed that he had a firm grip on his rifle.

"*No, señora. No me gusta.* He rides like trouble."

Esmerelda was a stocky woman, with a jowly face, watermelon breasts, and an expansive derrière, but she could move like a hounded fox when she had to. In short order she was at one of the south-facing windows of the front room.

In her thirty-five years at Casa Piedra she had watched many strangers riding across that plain, white and red and brown. On occasion, especially in the early days, they had come in large numbers, with violence in mind. In those times Sam McKeller would order her and his wife and young Cale into the root cellar, accessible through a trap door in the kitchen floor, and connected to a timber-braced tunnel leading a hundred and eighty feet underground to a stall in the stables.

Now Esmerelda looked at the oncoming horseman and her first thought, when he was four hundred yards away, was that he looked vaguely familiar. At two hundred yards, seeing the long rust-colored hair flowing in the wind, she had a bad premonition. At a hundred yards she remembered fully. Twenty years closed in on her like a collapsed squeeze box, and she shuddered with the deathless horror of terrible memories.

The front door beside her opened, and she had a bad moment. True, her eyes told her that the man she feared most in all the world was still riding across the *loma*, but such was the presence of his evil that she immediately felt threatened from all sides.

Just then Katy entered the room.

Katy didn't look afraid, and that surprised Esmerelda. But why should Katy be afraid? She did not know this man as Esmerelda did. Esmerelda felt compelled suddenly to hide her beloved Katy in the root cellar. Katy was in danger. They were all in danger, but especially Katy. Katy was tall, attractive, brave, pure of heart. Evil always sought to destroy good. To bring good down to its level.

Katy brushed a stray tendril of mahogany-colored hair out of her eyes. They were blue eyes—wide, warm, and compassionate. And at the moment, filled with disappointment.

"I thought it might be Cale," she admitted.

"I wish," sighed Esmerelda.

Abner, one of the Cyclone hands, came clomping down the gallery and entered, buckling on his shellbelt. In his haste he had done half a job of tucking his trousers into his boots.

"Don't know who he is," wheezed Abner. He was no longer a spring chicken by a long shot, and the jog on horse-warped legs across from the bunkhouse had stolen his wind. "But he shore is bakin' that nag." Belatedly, he touched his hat brim, sheepish. "Oh, good mornin', Mrs. McKeller. 'Scuse me for bargin' in."

Katy smiled sweetly. "Good morning, Ab."

Esmerelda said, "I know him."

Katy gave her a quizzical look. She was sensitive to people, their unspoken thoughts. "Sounds like you wish you didn't."

"As we all may. It is Wolfhunter Geddes."

Abner blanched. Any sane man would be afraid of Wolfhunter. Wolfhunter needed no reason to kill. He killed because he had a knack for it, and everyone enjoyed that which they had a talent and taste for.

"Abner, go tell Lopez to sound the alarm," ordered Esmerelda.

"Yes, ma'am." Abner hastened to the courtyard.

Katy watched him go. "He's afraid. And so are you, Essie."

"You should be, too."

Katy looked out the window. Esmerelda studied her lovely profile, strong and beautiful and curious—and unafraid.

"Cale told me about him once. But only that his mother ran away with him. Surely that's not why you're afraid."

They heard the clang and clamor of the angle iron, for many years a permanent fixture on the rooftop. Once it had called men to grub from the Cyclone chuckwagon. Now it summoned them to arms from the lookout's post. Lopez kept striking it until the moment that found Wolfhunter checking the half-wild steeldust in front of Casa Piedra's gallery. The women, Katy in the lead, stepped out in time to hear the snicker of the sentry's lever-action repeater directly above them.

Wolfhunter paid Lopez no attention. He knew precisely where to put the bullet if the need arose. Instead, he glanced at Katy with appreciative curiosity, and then grinned at Esmerelda like a long-lost friend. Katy noticed that he sat forward in his saddle, shoulders bunched, like a man gut-shot.

"Damn, Essie! You ain't changed a whit."

Que quiere?" she demanded sternly. "What do you want?"

"Now, Essie," he scolded gently. "You can figure that out, can't you? But tell me. Who is this lovely young lady?"

Katy took a step closer. "I'm Katy McKeller, Mr. Geddes."

"I must say, you're even prettier than the last Mrs. McKeller I knew."

The tattoo of running feet announced the arrival of armed men at the southwest corner of Casa Piedra. There were three of them, all Tejano *vaqueros*, wearing sideguns and carrying rifles.

The coyote dog, standing well off to one side of Crowbait, curled its lips and put its ears back and looked at the men as if they were the second course of breakfast.

Esmerelda took a quick head count. These three, with Lopez and Abner, whom she heard at the window behind her, and one more cowboy, who probably had a bead on Wolfhunter from the bunkhouse, made six. Six against one were comfortable odds—except when the one was Wolfhunter.

Wolfhunter turned his deceptive grin on the trio at the west end of the gallery.

"*Como le va, muchachos? Es temprano.* Too early for grave-digging, don't you agree?"

They did not respond, more or less keeping one eye on the stranger and one eye on Esmerelda. True, Katy was the lady of the house, and they respected her, but she had been here only a year, and Esmerelda had been here longer than all of them put together. By tradition she gave the orders in the absence of the *patron* or the *caporal*. She would decide if it was too early for killing.

Gathering up her courage, Esmerelda left Katy's side and stepped off the gallery. Crowbait watched her approach with ill will, and was about to snap at her when Wolfhunter jerked him back with the sisal-rope and reins.

"This *mesteno* learned its manners from a diamondback," he apologized.

Unbidden, he swung down, and gave Crowbait a sound whack on the rump. The steeldust crow-hopped the kinks out of its back and ran off a ways before stopping to look back with resentment. With the buckskin-sheathed Big Fifty cradled in his arms, Wolfhunter turned to face Esmerelda.

"Essie, you're still a fine figure of a woman, I must say. Tell me, is that old *esposo* of yours still above snakes?"

"Joachim is dead," she replied stonily.

Wolfhunter nodded. "So is Sam, I hear. Guess that makes young Caleb the big augur in these parts now."

"If I were you, I would not be here when he returns."

"I have no bone to pick with him. My business is with Tom Samples."

Esmerelda threw a sidelong glance at the wary *vaqueros*, and judged that they were out of earshot, if the words remained soft-spoken. She had kept the secret far too long to let it loose carelessly upon the world.

"Tomas is no longer here. He has gone away."

Katy was not out of earshot, and she decided that this was the first time she had heard Esmerelda lie. She was wise enough, though, not to expose her.

"You're pulling my tail feathers, Essie," Wolfhunter admonished. "Not that I blame you. But I ain't here to make trouble. I wouldn't have come at all, 'cept that Susanna asked me to. It was her dying wish."

Esmerelda felt her heart twist. In spite of all Susanna's faults, Esmerelda had loved her. "She is…"

"*Muerto.* Last autumn, in Fort Smith. Just before she died she wrote me a letter. She'd learned I was in Taos. I hadn't heard from her, or seen her, for many a winter. She asked if I would come out and see that her boy was well. I thought I ought to. That I owed her that much. Besides, he's mine, too. *Como no*, I wasn't aimin' to tell him *that*. He won't know me, Essie. He was just a little smidgin when I took off down the Cimarron Cutoff for good and the New Mexico Territory. Not yet three summers old, if I remember right. And hell, in those three years he maybe set eyes on me four, five times at best. I was always on the prowl in No-Man's-Land, tracking papered men. Made a fair living at it. But you know me, Essie. I'm a two-legged tumbleweed. Besides that, I came back the last time to find Susanna hitched to that horse trader."

"Tomas does not need to know these things."

"I wasn't going to tell him. 'Cept the part about his mother. A person has got the right to know when his kin passes on."

"I can tell him that much," said Esmerelda tautly, her apprehension reaching new heights, for she feared Wolfhunter's response to her intractability.

But Wolfhunter surprised her. Instead of anger he seemed forlorn.

"I don't hold it against you, Essie, the way you feel about me. But he *is* my flesh and blood. And though I would never think to burden him with that, I do expect I've got a right to see him this once. See if maybe there ain't some little thing I can do for him. Never thought you'd deny any man that much. And you could say it's my *own* dying wish."

"You?" she queried, disbelieving. "You are too full of spite to die."

He grinned. "Yes, ma'am. I freely admit to being a curly wolf with rattler piss for blood. I have been shot twenty-seven times, that I know of, and so concluded some time back that no mortal man could do for me. As He never intended anyone to live forever, God Almighty saw fit to give me a dose of consumption. Seems the sawbones don't know much about it, except that it's gonna kill me deader'n last Sunday's sage hen. Best anybody could do was this ole *curandero*, who gave me a mess of black nightshade to ease the pain in my chest, and some tangy mustard for the coughing spells. But none of that cotton-wad therapy is gonna keep me above snakes too much longer."

Katy could stay out of it no longer, coming off the gallery to join them.

"You can't deny a father the right to see his son one time before he dies," she told Esmerelda. She looked at Wolfhunter. "No matter what he has done in his life."

"*Tiene razon,*" sighed Esmerelda. "You are right. But know this," she warned Wolfhunter. "Tomas was not yet eight years old when Susanna sent him to me. He traveled all the way from Arkansas with a Confederate ambulance train. There was war, and much trouble with irregulars and the Indian Nations. Susanna's *esposo,* the man whose name Tomas bears, had been killed. All this she told me in a letter Tomas brought with him. And I believe that there was more she did not care to tell me."

"I don't know how to sugarcoat it, Essie. I reckon she went to whorin'."

Her dark eyes flashed. "We do what we must to survive. She knew I would take care of Tomas, just as she knew that her world was no place for a boy. She had no one else to turn to."

"I can hardly believe ole Sam would take the younker in."

Her low-pitched voice was a fierce whisper. "He never knew. No one knows here except me. And now you, Katy. I never spoke of it to anyone, for the boy's sake. Señor Sam believed he was an orphan. That is what I told him. The war made many orphans. He allowed Tomas to stay. Tomas has always been a hard worker. He has made this *rancho* his home."

"You mean he don't know that Sam's woman was his mother? Hell, I never had no school-learning, but I can cipher two and two."

"Who knows what he has heard from others? Or what conclusions he has drawn? He does not speak of these things, even to me. But he does well enough. He does not need you, or anything you can give him. If you make trouble for him you will live long enough to regret it."

Wolfhunter was unperturbed by the threat. "I've got no regrets, and don't care to entertain one at this late date. And I ain't in no fit condition to make trouble. Way I feel now, ladies, I'd have to get better to die."

Esmerelda was skeptical. There was something so wicked about this man that she wondered if even death could extinguish it. He would always be dangerous, no matter how sick he was. Dangerous when he slept, perhaps even dangerous dead. And she put no faith in his smiles. They never touched his eyes; eyes that were cold green ice. She now remembered those smiles from twenty years ago. His return exhumed old ghosts. Those smiles had haunted her in the months after Susanna's leaving—those smiles and Sam's unspoken bitterness and young Cale's sorrow.

The thought of Wolfhunter Geddes setting foot in Casa Piedra again disturbed her. It was sacrilege, of a kind. But if she tried to send him away, would he go meekly? No, she knew he would not. He might turn away, but he would not *go* away. He would be nearby, lurking unseen, until he had done whatever damage he had come so far to do. He was not a man who would be so easily put off. And she couldn't trust the reasons he had given. Why had he really come? What evil did he have in mind?

For her part, Katy believed him. She looked at Wolfhunter and saw a sick, dying man who wanted only one brief look at his son. Abner and Esmerelda were deathly afraid of him, but in her opinion it was the legend they feared, not the man. There was no way of knowing what Essie had *heard* about Wolfhunter, but in the final analysis her only testimony against him was that Cale's mother had run off with him twenty years ago.

Most fascinating of all, this revelation meant that her husband and young Tom Samples were half brothers.

"You mustn't send him away, Essie," she said softly.

"*Esta bien,*" Esmerelda decided. Perhaps it was best to keep Wolfhunter in sight, no matter how repulsive he was to her. When one traveled through high grass and heard a snake, it was always a degree less frightening when it could be seen.

"That's mighty Confederate of you, Essie," said Wolfhunter gratefully.

"I will have someone see to your horse," said Katy.

"Now I'd strongly advise against it. Don't want nobody getting hurt on my account. Just leave him be, and the mongrel as well. They'll make do. So what time's breakfast? I ain't had much of an appetite for a spell, but seeing you, Essie, reminds me what a fine biscuit-roller you've always been. Poor Susanna couldn't boil water. I've heard men declare that their squaws were splendid cooks. So splendid they could make prairie flapjacks taste good. But I've never known that to be true. Hell, I might take a turn for the better, just eating your vittles."

"I hope not," she dared to say.

"Essie!" said Katy, shocked.

Esmerelda turned on her heel and went inside.

Katy looked at Wolfhunter. "You're welcome in Stone House, Mr. Geddes. But only on the condition that you wear a different shirt. I won't have scalps worn at the table."

"Yes, ma'am. I got a Sunday-go-to-meeting shirt in my war bag."

She nodded and followed Esmerelda.

Wolfhunter glanced at the *vaqueros*.

"Well, boys, what do you think? Got your belt buckles stuck to your backbones? I swear I heard a body puttin' it to the let's-eat bell as I rode up. What say we go shovel some chuck?"

They just stood there, silent, watching him.

With an indifferent shrug, Wolfhunter shouldered the Big Fifty and walked into Casa Piedra as if he owned the whole kit and caboodle.

Chapter Five

Mid-morning saw the wind really kick up in earnest. The smell of rain was strong as the treetops began to thrash. It could have been the noise and violence of the storm-tossed brush, or the proximity of the three men on horseback, that flushed a bunch of wild hogs out of a bois d'arc thicket. That got their horses dancing and snorting, and Tom Samples drew the Henry out of its saddle boot. He preferred a long gun, for he was no hand with a pistol. It took a better-than-average shot to hit one of those narrow-shanked razorbacks head on. Cale pulled back his greatcoat and laid his hand on the Colt Cavalry. He counted nine of the critters; three of the males had tusks. Javelinas were not common in these parts, but then, he thought, neither were Comanches, these days. It was just one of those years.

For a moment they had a standoff. Wild hogs had poor dispositions. They would charge a man without provocation, and it mattered little to them whether he was mounted or afoot. They ate cactus, especially prickly pear, and their bristles made fine hair brushes—and that was about all the good Cale could think to say on their behalf. The males were grunting and acting belligerent, taking their positions in front of the sows and the two shoats. One of the males would act as if he were charging, then trot back into position, and then burst forward again. Cale had seen Cheyenne Dog Soldiers do the same thing on the battlefield.

Then suddenly the rain came, a drenching downpour, bending tree limbs, smiting the earth with a crash that did not subside. Cale gasped at the cold onslaught, wiped his face with a gloved hand,

and looked to find the razorbacks gone, vanished into the brush. Tom put away his repeater, twisted in the saddle to untie the yellow slicker draped behind the cantle. In less than half a minute he was soaked to the skin, but he shrugged the slicker on anyway. Then they closed ranks and, with Frisco at point, moved single-file through the wet silver curtain of rain.

An hour later they came upon more trouble: a young cow bogged down in a muddy waterhole. The cow was a *sabina*—red-and-white-peppered—with a three-foot spread of headgear and an unfriendly eye. Most often the torment of heel flies drove cattle into such a predicament, but if the festering wounds were a true indication, this one had run afoul of a cougar. The damage done by savage claws had compelled the longhorn too deeply into the cool, soothing mud.

The deluge had degenerated into a drizzle, and the three men sat their horses a spell and took stock of the situation. The longhorn bellowed plaintively.

"That's cow talk," joked Frisco. "She wants to know if we intend to sit here like turtles on a log all day."

"Feel sorry for the critter," murmured Tom. "Some days you just can't help but wonder if it was worth your mother's pain."

Grunting skepticism, Cale swung down. "What say we snake him out so's you can pet the poor thing and make it better?"

Untying his Brazos lariat, he shook out a loop, stepped in close, and dabbed the rope neatly over the *sabina*'s horns. A cluck of his tongue brought Beau up, and he remounted, dallying the rope around the saddle horn. He gave the reins a straight-back pull. The savvy chestnut had been quick to learn the lessons a cow pony must know, and now back-stepped, maintaining a steady and relentless pull on the line. The red mire reluctantly gave up its prisoner and the struggling cow came free. The longhorn staggered on uncertain, mud-caked legs. Once freed, a bogged cow almost always got the urge to charge something, and this one proved to be no exception. Rolling its tail, the twisthorn lowered its head and made a sound that bode well for no one. But Frisco was ready, flanking the *sabina* and flicking his own lass-rope under the cow's belly. The cow rushed forward only a short distance before the loop closed on its back heels. The next instant found the longhorn stretched out on its right side, bawling at such rough treatment.

Tom dismounted and took a jar of liniment—carbolic acid and axle grease—out of his horse wallet. He smeared this smelly concoction on the claw marks. Blowflies laid eggs in open wounds, and the liniment prevented range worms.

Stepping back, Tom ran his eyes the length of the mud-splattered animal, making sure he had missed nothing. Then he jumped forward and brushed mud from a patch of hide below the thurl.

"Frisco," he called thickly. "You'd better have a look-see."

Securing the saddle-horn dally with a half hitch, Frisco got down off the dun mare and walked over.

It came as no surprise to Cale that Tom was carrying on as if he didn't exist. He too dismounted and stepped over, feet squishing in waterlogged boots. Frisco and Tom were studying the hip brand. It was the Diamond C mark of the Cyclone, all right, but…

"The hair," murmured Frisco. "It grows back."

Tom said, "This critter was cold-branded." He glared at Cale as if it were all Cale's fault.

"I can see that," retorted Cale crossly. When the opportunity arose Tom took pleasure in treating him like a greenhorn tyro.

Tom's eyes flashed anger at Cale's tone. Frisco interceded before the antagonism that jumped like foxfire between the two could escalate into full-fledged lightning.

"Those nightriders are plenty smart," mused the *caporal*, as though just talking to himself, looking at the cow and not the other men. "Too smart to carry running irons. They know that if they get caught with those they go before Judge Lynch."

"Why waste good rope?" growled Tom, slapping his hip where his sidegun lay beneath the slicker. "Judge Colt is quicker, and just as final."

Cale scanned the surrounding scrub and cactus patches with narrowed eyes. It wasn't so much that rustlers were making off with *his* cows, because for some reason he really didn't think of Cyclone cattle as belonging to him. No, he felt more like a caretaker. What chapped him was that rustling went against his strong sense of fair play. It was a quick and relatively easy way for worthless scum to make a profit off the honest endeavors of hardworking folk.

Frisco was right. They were dealing with a gang of hombres who knew a trick or two. These men were not going to take unnecessary chances. Worse, it was obviously their intention to make this a long-term operation. They weren't going to be satisfied with riding in one dark night to rustle a hundred or so head and take off for the Indian Territory and then call it quits. They had cold-branded this maverick months ago, placing wet burlap sacking between iron and hide to make a temporary mark. A Cyclone cowboy popping the brush for unbranded stock would then pass this one by. Eventually the cold brand would fade away and the moment would be ripe for this animal to be gathered and burned with the rustling crew's own brand. No one would be the wiser, and the nightriders stood a better chance of getting top dollar from reputable buyers who kept a sharp eye peeled for brand alteration. And less chance of getting crossways with honest range riders who could tell a "running iron" at a glance as a device forged specifically to alter an existing local brand.

Cale said, "Frisco, you've got an iron tied to your hull. We'll go ahead and hip-brand him. And he hasn't been earmarked, either. I'll see to the fire."

"Oh," said Tom, sarcastic. "You aim to build a fire out here in this mess."

"That's right." Cale was pleased at this opportunity to show Samples a thing or two. "This goes to show, I guess, that nobody's ever too smart to learn. You'll need to come over and take my rope."

As he walked back to Beau, Tom mounted his own horse and mosied over. Cale got aboard the chestnut and handed his lariat to Samples. The *sabina* felt the give in the line and took a shot at getting up, but Frisco's dun mare took up some slack on its own initiative, and as Tom dallied the lass-rope his cow pony immediately put the pressure back on. The cow, resigned to its fate, lay back down.

"Twenty minutes," Cale told them, and turned Beau around to backtrack.

Years of campaigning had instilled in Cale the habit of remembering every potential campsite or defensive position that nature offered along the trail he rode. Not a quarter mile back he had noticed a limestone bench on the side of a hogback ridge. The base had been hollowed out by runoff. A deluge long past had uprooted a Spanish oak and washed it over the bench. It had lodged in the rock hollow. The hollow faced away from the slant of today's rainstorm. As Cale had expected, the deadwood in the shelter of the hollow was quite dry. He reckoned it was the only thing in the entire county that was.

Taking the canvas tarp from around his saddle-tied bedroll, he gathered up several armloads of wood, wrapped it tightly in the canvas. As he groped deep under the bench to find the driest pieces, he noticed the mouth of a cave. It was large enough for a man to crawl through. Not that he had any intention of doing so. There were many caves in the hill country, and quite often they were the dwellings of animals that did not care to be interfered with.

Cale returned to the waterhole with the bundle of firewood across the saddle in front of him.

He had included four long pieces in his gather. They averaged about four feet in length. Two he stuck in the ground, upright, three feet apart. Borrowing Frisco's knife, he hacked a fork in the top of the uprights, then placed the other two pieces at a forty-five-degree angle, parallel, with one end braced in the forks. Across this frame he draped one of his bedroll blankets. It was quickly soaked and unlikely to catch, and he built the fire small but hot within this south-facing makeshift shelter. In minutes the fire was crackling and the blanket steaming, and Frisco hunched down facing the brunt of the easy rain to hold the business end of the branding iron in the flames.

Like all good cow ponies, the *caporal*'s dun mare didn't need a rider to carry out its duty. Alert to every move of the cow at the other end of the rope, the horse kept the line taut. Tom at first appeared content to sit in the saddle at the other end of the stretch-out. But as Cale worked on the latigo knot of his rig to loosen the cinches and give Beau a breather, Samples stepped down and came over, glowering at Cale across the dip of the saddle.

"Lot of trouble for one cow," remarked Tom.

"That's one cow less for them."

"We got to do something about these hideburners."

"I know that," said Cale brusquely, tugging sharply on the latigo to pull it through the rings.

"There's talk in the doghouse. Some of the boys have heard rumors from the men working other spreads. They're saying that Ocheltree and Blake and some of the other cattlemen want to hire stock detectives."

"The Association meets at Stone House day after tomorrow. I'll be sure to tell them what a mistake that would be."

"You don't seem too worried about all this," Tom accused, flinging an arm in the direction of the cold-branded longhorn.

Cale dragged a long breath through clenched teeth. It was a trial, remaining calm and reasonable in the face of Sample's bald-faced insolence. For the thousandth time he wondered what it was that kept Tom so hot under the collar. Yet he couldn't bring himself to do anything but bite back on occasion. He was reluctant to use his authority to solve the problem. Something about hoglegging Samples off the Cyclone payroll smacked of cowardice. Besides that, the Cyclone had been Tom's home since childhood. *Little wonder*, brooded Cale, *that he cares about it more than I do.*

"I've got a contract with Snyder to have two thousand head of prime beef ready in less than two weeks. These rustlers are the reason we're selling the herd to a professional outfit in the first place, rather than pushing them to railhead ourselves. Once Snyder takes delivery and his drovers take the herd, then we'll be free to deal with this gang."

"In two weeks we could lose hundreds of cattle. God knows how many they have cold-branded. The time's right for them to start gathering."

"You talk like you've got a bigger stake in this than thirty-a-month and found," badgered Cale.

"Maybe I do. I'll tell you one thing. None of the boys want to be looking over their shoulders for trigger-happy regulators. They've been known to mistake honest cowboys for cattle thieves, and they tend to shoot first and make apologies later."

"I said I'd stand against hiring stock detectives," said Cale.

"I've got a proposition of my own for the Association."

"Oh, you do? And what would that be?"

"One man from each ranch, working together to track these yahoos down. A floating outfit, of sorts. Volunteers, as long as they can cut sign and can shoot better than fair-to-middlin'."

"Something tells me you'd be the one to volunteer for the Cyclone."

"I'd be willing. Save you the cost of hiring so-called professionals."

"I've told you twice. I won't be a party to that."

"The others might. And you don't run the Association, like your father did."

"Just how old are you, Samples?"

"What difference does that make?" Tom shot back, defensive.

"Ever hunted men before?"

"I've done a lotta things."

"Ever killed a man?"

His manhood and abilities having now been questioned, Tom was at the end of his rope. Rainwater poured from the drooping brim of his hat, partially hiding his anger.

"Since you know so much, why don't you get out and find these men yourself, *Mister* McKeller? Or don't you care what happens to the Cyclone?"

"If I didn't, believe me, I wouldn't be here."

But Cale knew that it was a good question. He wondered, "Do I care enough to put my life on the line?" He was no coward; he had confronted enough Rebels and redmen to know that much. He had done so mostly out of pride for the service; he had been proud to do his duty. His problem now was in accepting the notion that he had a duty to Sam McKeller and the Cyclone.

Forever the peacemaker, Frisco looked around and raised his voice above the sound of the steady rainfall. "Hey, *caballeros*. Hot iron. Somebody come sit on this *ladino* while I burn some hide."

For a full half minute Cale and Tom just glared at one another. Then Samples snorted derision and turned away.

"You don't want to be a cattleman," he declared, disgusted. "You may not even have what it takes. So why don't you pack it in and sell out to somebody who gives a damn? We'd all probably be better off."

Cale let him go. There was nothing to say. He almost agreed with him.

Chapter Six

Lone Dog was afflicted by a deep melancholy.

Not long after he and the other five Comanche warriors went into midday hiding in a brush-thick pocket squeezed between two high granite outcroppings, he left the others and went off to be by himself. Leaving his pony and war lance in the care of He Finds Water, Lone Dog climbed to the brow of one of the outcrops, and from there to a rocky bench overlooking the River of Many Springs. There were several large boulders strewn across the bench. Wide veins of pink and white marble caught the amber rays of sun breaking here and there through the rain-emptied clouds. The wind carried that fresh scent of the earth renewed. Lone Dog sat cross-legged with his back to one of the boulders. It was his decision that he and the others would conceal themselves until the darkness of *to-oh-kar-no,* the night, came to cover their movements. He had thought it wise after their fight with the one Bow String had come to call Long Blue Coat. So it would be foolish of him to stand out in the open and give their position away.

"I hide like a thief," Lone Dog thought bitterly. "I am a fugitive in my own land." Once, he and his friend could have roamed these hills with impunity. Thirty years ago Lone Dog's father had sometimes gone even farther in the direction of the morning sun, to ford the broad turquoise river they called Talking Water and raid the Tonkawas, sometimes even the little settlements of the *tosi-tivo,* the white-skinned. Now the Tonkawas were no more, unless you counted the handful who scouted for the pony soldiers. Naturally, Lone Dog had nothing but contempt for Tonkawa army scouts.

The whites had spread like fire in dry grass. They had consumed the Tonkawa lands, and now they did the same to the land of the Comanche. From his vantage point Lone Dog could look north, where the river bent around a steep cedar-blanketed bluff. Beneath the pecans and willows and cottonwoods that lined the riverbank stood a small cabin. More *tosi-tivo*, come to claim another parcel of *Comancheria.*

Lone Dog's fine strong features tightened with anger, and his black eyes glittered with a fierce hatred. He was predisposed to call to his brothers and ride down upon those distant interlopers, to exact a terrible price for their thievery. But he thought better of it. Another of his *tah-mahs* might be slain. Where was the sense in it? The whites were as many as the blades of grass upon the Staked Plains. A warrior could expend all of his war arrows, and kill so many that he grew weary of killing, and still make no difference.

While the *tosi-tivo* grew more and more numerous, Lone Dog's people dwindled in number. Even Long Dog, only twenty winters old, could remember a time when there were so many young warriors eager to count coup that the leader of a raiding party could pick and choose those who would ride with him. These days it was no longer so. Forty years of warfare had taken a heavy toll.

The price paid was not only in young men who fell in battle. The whites fought without honor. Many times they had swept down on undefended camps, slaughtering women and children. Their goal was to exterminate the *Komantcia*, the people whom the Utes fearfully called Those Who Are Always Against Us. More deadly even than the guns of the whites were the diseases they had inflicted upon Lone Dog's people. Smallpox had taken his mother and younger brother. Now his sister was dead. Murdered by the tall scalphunter.

Thinking of family lost reminded him of Watchful Fox, the blood brother of his best friend, Bow String. Lone Dog felt responsible for that loss. He was the leader. The burden of failure was his alone to bear. Against his better judgment he had succumbed to the earnest pleas of Watchful Fox when the time came to ambush Long Blue Coat, in the daybreak now past. Although sixteen winters old, Watchful Fox had never before been on a war raid. His brother Bow

String was a warrior of much renown among the Penateka, heaping such honor upon the family by his exploits that the family had been able to shelter Watchful Fox without censure. Bow String had promised their mother, She Speaks Often, that he would bring Watchful Fox home safely. But Lone Dog had bestowed upon Watchful Fox the privilege of killing the lone rider and counting his first coup. Instead, Long Blue Coat had killed the youth.

Lone Dog, thinking of all this, sighed. He was to blame. He should have listened to his instincts and chosen someone more experienced in fighting. Better yet, he should have gone himself. His mistake had been in thinking that Long Blue Coat would be as easy to kill as the cowboy they had ambushed and slain two sleeps earlier. But Long Blue Coat's *puha*, his personal magic and power, had been too great for the untried Watchful Fox.

Long Dog thought, "Crooked Neck, why did you make us swear to forsake the use of guns?" The shaman had insisted that only traditional weapons could be used. The lance, the knife, the bow and arrow. They could not resort to the *ella cona*, the firearm of the white man. And they had made a solemn vow to abide by the medicine man's condition, leaving the revolver and repeating rifle of the first cowboy beside the lance-torn body, even though Eye That Kills had argued for their confiscation.

"We must have them if we expect to kill Wolfhunter," Eye That Kills had declared.

But Lone Dog had said no.

"It is madness!" raged Eye That Kills. "Wolfhunter's *ella cona* can kill at a distance of five arrows. Not one of us will get close enough with weapons such as Crooked Neck made us promise to use. Wolfhunter's *puha* is too great. He is more demon than human."

"You gave your word," Lone Dog reminded him curtly, provoked by Eye That Kill's insubordination. "As we all did. Everyone had a choice. You did not have to agree."

"Then I would have been left behind. The one who kills Wolfhunter will be honored above all others. And not just among the Penateka, but among all the bands of the *Komantcia*."

"If he dies we will all be honored. And if we do this with the weapons of our forefathers, Crooked Neck says it will be a great sign. It will bring new hope. It will say to all our brothers that everything is not lost, that Our Sure Enough Father has not deserted us, that we can yet turn back the *tosi-tivo*. We will do as Crooked Neck bade us do. And we will not break our vow. We leave the *ella conas*. *Suvate*. That is all."

Even before this confrontation Lone Dog had disliked and distrusted Eye That Kills. He was typical of so many warriors these days. His word meant nothing. He had no honor. Just because the whites fought without honor, that did not release a Comanche from the warrior's way. Eye That Kills, decided Lone Dog, would be better suited running with renegades.

So many of the old ways were being lost or corrupted. Pressed on all sides, the Comanche nation was shrinking, the traditional hunting grounds stolen. The great Southern Herd of the *potsana*, the buffalo, was no more. The white hidehunters had butchered them by the tens of thousands, leaving the high plains littered with the skinned carcasses rotting in the sun, enough meat to feed all the bands of the Comanche—and the Kiowa and Southern Cheyenne besides—for a hundred years and more.

Lone Dog sadly shook his head. The white hidehunters were much worse than the Mexican *ciboleros* before them. True, the *ciboleros* had killed the buffalo for the hides, but they had also taken the meat to sell in their villages. They had been much fewer in number, too, and so had done much less damage. And the *ciboleros* had feared the *Komantcia*, as had the Coahuiltecans before them, calling them The Snakes Who Come Back. White hidehunters feared nothing and respected nothing.

Lone Dog thought, "I wish I had lived when my father's father, or his before him, had lived." It would have been a good time to be alive, when the Comanche had been undisputed master of the southern plains, striking fear in the hearts of all his enemies. The future looked bleak.

He had admitted it to no one, but Lone Dog doubted that the death of Wolfhunter would make any difference at all. It was too late. Lone Dog was afraid that he had lost faith in omens and signs. Oh, he still sang his medicine song. He still spread the beaver oil on his body to repel bullets. He still carried his personal talisman—a large pink mussel pearl taken from the river the whites called the Concho. But he did not truly believe that killing Wolfhunter would result in great magic, that it would restore the shattered confidence of the Comanche people.

No, Lone Dog wanted Wolfhunter dead for a much more selfish reason. For Wolfhunter had scalped his sister. And sometime before, during, or after taking her hair, he had raped her.

Lone Dog was rescued from this bitter reverie by the whisper of a moccasin on stone. A heartbeat later he heard the plaintive *dee-ee dee-ee* of a killdeer plover. But Lone Dog knew that it was no bird that cried so, just as he knew that Bow String was not one to take a careless step. He was warning Lone Dog of his approach. They were all nervous. Not only because they were deep in country infested by *tosi-tivo*. But also because they all sensed that their long and perilous odyssey was nearing its end. Wolfhunter was not far away. So the others huddled in the brushy pocket, without even the comfort of a cedar-fragrant fire, sleeping lightly if they slept at all, rope bridles tied to their wrists. For if only half of what was told about Wolfhunter was fact, then they were all in very grave danger.

Lone Dog answered Bow String's call with a similar one, and Bow String emerged from the jumbled outcrop and loped across the bench to sit beside him.

"*Nei mataoya?*" asked Bow String, his voice pitched low.

"I am well." Lone Dog was deeply moved. His friend had sought him out and even asked after his welfare, despite the part he had played in the death of Watchful Fox. He wanted to tell Bow String how sorry he was. But he did not. Condolences of that kind were suitable for women, not warriors.

Bow String said, "I have brought *tara hyapa*."

Lone Dog took the pouch which Bow String offered. Though he had no appetite, he scooped some of the pemmican into his mouth, just to demonstrate his gratitude. It was dried beef pounded fine and mixed with buffalo fat, and so more palatable than *inapa*, plain jerky. In an agonizing throe of homesickness, Lone Dog found himself missing the meals his young wife, She Walks Softly, prepared for him when he was home. He had something of a sweet tooth, and missed most of all the paste of pounded plums she sometimes provided to enliven the flavor of her nut bread, and sweet mush made from buffalo marrow and crushed mesquite beans.

He thought of her, alone this night in their smoke-yellowed lodge so far away, and he could almost smell the scent of sage in her hair, almost feel the heat of her slender young body. For a moment the urge to mount his pony and turn toward home almost overwhelmed him. Then another mental image replaced the one of She Walks Softly: the naked, mutilated body of his sister. Even in death she cried out to him for vengeance. He was bound by his honor to avenge her by slaying Wolfhunter. And he was bound by his word to accomplish the task in the manner the shaman had specified.

Lone Dog glanced sidelong at Bow String, who was silently studying the distant cabin. He admired the way his good friend controlled his grief. Feeling Lone Dog's eyes, Bow String smiled faintly, pointing with his chin at the cabin across the river.

"Do you think he feels safe?"

Lone Dog knew what Bow String was thinking. That was so often the way with truly close friends, who did not need to speak all their thoughts to be understood. In his anguish Bow String wanted to strike out. Tonight the moon would be full and golden. Many whites believed that the Comanche preferred to raid by the light of such a moon. In fact the Comanche was a wholly practical raider, who would attack his enemies at dawn or dusk, in the middle of the day or the heart of night, whenever conditions were most favorable. What sport it would be, riding down to give them the surprise of their lives.

"Do we go on tonight?" asked Bow String.

Lone Dog nodded. The council had first nominated Bow String to lead the party, for he had counted more coup than any other volunteer, even Eye That Kills. But Bow String had deferred. The council had then passed over Eye That Kills, for he could not be trusted. So the mantle of leadership had come to rest on Lone Dog's shoulders. He had been grateful at the time to Bow String. Now, though, he wished his friend had accepted the responsibility.

"*Toquet*," said Bow String grimly. "That's good. I am ready for this to be finished."

"Are you homesick, *tah-mah?*"

Bow String was surprised by the question. Then his eyes clouded. "No. I am not going home."

"What does that mean?"

Bow String looked away. "I promised my mother I would see that no harm came to my brother." He could not speak the name of Watchful Fox ever again. "I broke that promise."

Lone Dog handed him the pouch of pemmican. He felt sick. "It is my fault. It is I who failed."

Bow String put a hand on Lone Dog's shoulder. "I am *e-haits-ma*, your close friend, *tah-mah*. And I tell you, it was not you who failed. My brother failed. And Two Hatchets failed, when he tried to catch up the horse of Long Blue Coat. And I failed to protect my brother, for I knew that to do so would break his pride. But you have led us well. You have kept us faithful to the orders of the council and Crooked Neck. And I believe that you will lead us to Wolfhunter. I only hope that it will be soon."

"It will be. Perhaps tomorrow."

"*Toquet*," said Bow String again. "When it is done then you and the others can go home."

"Home?" thought Lone Dog bitterly. "Our true home has been taken from us. We live now where the white man permits us to live, between the Red River and the Washita, with the Kiowa and Kiowa Apache. Instead of hunting buffalo, we must go to the agency and beg for beef. Old, diseased, and underfed cattle, and not enough of that to feed everyone."

The only thing that made it home, he decided, was the presence of She Walks Softly. He had been away from the reservation before, on other raids, but never had he put so many miles between himself and the woman he loved.

Belatedly, he realized what Bow String had implied. "What will you do?"

"What I must."

Lone Dog drew the cool, rain-scented air deep into his lungs. Once again he knew precisely what was on his friend's mind.

"The one you have called Long Blue Coat," he murmured.

Bow String nodded. A thought struck him, and he grabbed Lone Dog's arm in a steel grip.

"If I should die before my brother is avenged, will you kill Long Blue Coat, my good friend? Then my spirit, and my brother's, will rest easy."

"You have my word," Lone Dog said.

Chapter Seven

Whitetail Meadow was cut through by a happy little creek that trickled over limestone shelves, spring-fed a mile to the south and emptying into the Llano five miles north. Beaver had built a colony at the rim of the meadow, where a grove of pecans flourished, clogging the run and forming a marsh.

The line shack had been built at the western edge of the clearing and faced the ten-acre spread of grass, an occasional scrub oak, and tangles of wild mustang grape and beavertail cactus. Large horse cripplers lurked in the windmill and bluestem. The shack was a stout stone structure with a low-peaked cypress-shale roof and a picket arbor. It was backed up against a thicket of hackberry.

A handsome scene, and Cale took an instant liking to it: the type of quiet, lonesome place a line rider would be attracted to.

Off to one side was a cedar-post corral with a Goodnight gate, tack box, and water trough. No well was in evidence, so Cale assumed that water for man and horse was fetched from the creek. A line-backed *grullo* wearing the Cyclone brand stood within the corral.

The rain had stopped hours ago, and the low blanket of clouds had broken apart and drifted away, revealing a high scatter of cirrus. It was an hour until sunset. The bottoms of the high thin patches of cloud were painted orange and pink and purple. Occasionally a straggling rain cloud would hasten south, drifting like gunsmoke over a battlefield, and so close that it seemed a person might reach up and grab a handful. Golden bars of late sunlight slanted into the still-wet meadow, and the drops of rain captured by the grass glimmered like diamonds.

As the men splashed across the creek, bobwhite quail launched themselves into the air with an explosion of flapping wings that set the horses to prancing. The *grullo* came up to the corral fence and whickered, glad for some company, and Beau answered back.

Cale sensed that the line shack was unoccupied. Just as well. The problem of the rustlers and Tom's astute antagonism had filled his thoughts most of the day, and he had spared Billy Yellen precious little consideration.

The line shack was a one-room affair, with a hardpack floor, a small fireplace, and a single window draped with flour-sack curtains. The furnishings consisted of a split-log trestle table, a rickety bench, a three-legged stool, and a bunk sporting a cornhusk mattress and with a Mexican blanket rolled up at one end. The walls were adorned with an empty lateral gunrack and a whitetail's headgear near the door for hanging things on. There was a crate nailed up sideways to hold canned goods. Near the fireplace was a woodbox in need of filling. An ax stood in one corner.

Frisco helped himself to a tin of tomatoes and the bunk. He opened the airtight with his belduque, and the dexterity of a man who had opened thousands of cans in such a fashion. He drank the juice in one long draught, and wore a blissful expression when done.

Tom, unwilling to share such close confines with the likes of Cale McKeller, took one quick look inside and then went out to the corral. Cale prowled through the hooden, trying to get a read on the man who had resided there of late. A pouch of Winesap chewing tobacco, almost empty, and a bottle of "bobwire extract" in a similar condition shared the table with a bitch light, a tin can filled with grease and a rag wick. An old pair of boots stood beneath the bunk. In the makeshift cabinet he found canned peaches and sardines, a tin of crackers, jerky wrapped in a gunny sack, a bag of beans, a jar of molasses, a rusty Case knife, a bar of lye soap, a container of Bull's Sarsaparilla. A butternut-gray longcoat, ragged at the cuffs, hung on the antlers. This interested Cale. He had seen plenty of coats like that one in the war—worn by men bent on killing him.

"So this Yellen fought for the Confederacy."

"*No se*, for sure," replied Frisco, stretched out on the bunk with his hands behind his head. "I think he is too young for that. But it seems to me that he has an older brother. Maybe the brother was in the war. Maybe he gave the coat to Billy. Or maybe he just bought it as a memento, from some old warhorse in need of whiskey money."

Cale was staring at the *caporal* by this time. "I swear, Frisco. If words were dollars you'd be a rich man."

"I have work, and a home, and good *companeros*. I *am* rich."

"Must be a bitter pill for Yellen, being employed by an officer of the federal army. Ex-officer, I should say."

"Haven't had occasion to ask him."

Cale went to the open door, leaned against the frame. "What else do you know about him?"

"He is a loner. That's good for a line rider. I think his father used to earn a living collecting the bounty on wolf ears and coyote skins some of the smaller ranches used to give. Now he runs a small *cantina* in Llano. They say he tried farming, but was too lazy."

Samples charged around the corner of the line shack, his stride long and angry. His hat was in his hand and he was slapping it against his leg as he walked. He was muttering profanities. Clearly, his temper was at flood level. Cale tensed, ready for trouble, and wondering what he had done this time to antagonize the young hothead. Noticing Cale's long lean frame blocking the doorway, Tom pulled up just shy of collision.

"What now?" asked Cale.

"That horse in the corral been done wrong by."

Cale stepped out to see for himself, hearing Tom and Frisco coming along behind. He slipped through the fence and eased across the mud-slick hardpack, murmuring horse talk. The *grullo* made no trouble, and a quick inspection revealed that Tom's terse assessment had been on the money. The animal's sides were galled from a cinch-strap kept brutally tight. Its withers were fistulous; a bloody fluid seeped from the inflamed sores. Cale felt his own temper on the rise. This horse had been ridden hard, and that too often, and obviously neglected in its care.

There was little doubt in his mind that Billy Yellen was the culprit. Every Cyclone line rider was permitted to draw two or three mounts from the ranch remuda. In their work it could be a long walk to anywhere if they had but one horse to rely on and something happened to it. Cale decided then and there that whatever else Yellen may have done, he had bought himself off the payroll with his mistreatment of the *grullo*. Not that Cale put more weight in the wronging of a horse than in the wronging of a Llano chippie. But this was solid, firsthand evidence against Yellen. And it was enough, particularly in the eyes of a cavalryman.

He returned to the fence, where the others waited.

"You'll have to assign somebody else to this section," he told Frisco.

The *caporal* nodded. "Looks to me like Yellen ought to sell his saddle."

"He and I are gonna have a heart-to-heart, first," muttered Tom ominously.

"I'll take care of Yellen," said Cale tersely. "Why don't you see what you can do for that horse?"

"It's your ground," grumbled Samples, and he went to his horse to fetch lass-rope and ointment.

Cale turned back to Frisco. "Did you hire Yellen?"

"*Su padre.*"

"Need to be sure of the men who ride the line. You got to know they can be relied on to do their jobs without somebody on their backsides all the time."

"*Su padre* was the best judge of man, horse, and cow I have ever known."

"He fell short this time."

"So it would seem," said Frisco coldly, and went back inside the line shack.

Watching him go, Cale shook his head in wonderment. It never failed. Any remark he made that could possibly be construed as criticism of his father served to rub others wrong. Not even someone with Francisco Madrigal's generous nature would put up with it. That was the problem trying to fill the shoes of a man who was bigger than life, a legend in his own time. The kind of man other men would follow to hell and back, just for the privilege.

Returning to the door of the line shack, Cale glanced inside. Frisco was back on the bunk, hat over his eyes, a smoldering cornhusk cigarette jutting from his lips. Cale stepped back out, sat with his back to the rough stone of the line-shack wall. He watched the smoky gloom of dusk thickening in the meadow, but he was really looking into the past, to a happier time. In the army he had developed into the sort of officer whom men would gladly follow anywhere. The difference between then and now was plain enough. He had belonged to the army. He was out of place here. And the men he was supposed to be leading could see that.

The army had been his home. He had known it would be the first time he rode into Fort Chadbourne, at the age of sixteen. The garrison on the banks of Oak Creek had cut a deal with Sam McKeller for the supplying of beef. At Chadbourne, Cale had met a Lieutenant Elias Maxwell, a West Pointer. This friendly, well-educated career officer and the brash young *brasadero* had become fast friends. Before long Cale had decided that army life was for him. It was discipline and drudgery, but it seemed much more exciting than the ignoble toil of ranch work.

Two years later the Eighth Infantry had abandoned Chadbourne to the secessionists, and Maxwell had transferred back East. Cale had experienced a sense of loss more profound than that sparked in him when his mother ran off with the frontiersman, Wolfhunter Geddes.

When war broke out two years after that, many Texans, included Sam McKeller, felt that the clash-in-arms was none of their concern. Cale, influenced in part by Maxwell's strong pro-Union sentiments, enlisted in the Federal Army. It was, in a way, his own act of rebellion. Thanks to Maxwell's sponsorship and his own natural leadership ability, Cale soon earned a battlefield commission.

Twelve days shy of his twenty-fourth birthday, a battle-hardened Captain Cale McKeller had been present at Appomattox to witness Lee's surrender of the Army of Northern Virginia. For all intents and purposes the war was over, the Union preserved. But it was not over for Cale. Returning to Texas, he found bitter resentment from men he had once counted as friends. His hope was to make peace with his father. His mistake was to blindly trample Sam McKeller's fierce pride.

Sam McKeller had tried to stay out of the war, but he had sold beef to Confederate training camps. The Occupation government wanted his hide, the carpetbaggers his vast holdings. Sheridan was the military governor of the district, and Custer was in Texas at the time. Having served valorously with both, Cale had used his influence with both men to save the Cyclone.

Sam had never felt any real animosity toward the federal government or its army during the war, but when they tried to cut him down to size and take his land away from him, he learned to hate the uniform his son wore so proudly. And Sam could not abide other people fighting his fights, which Cale had done. Home for one turbulent year, Cale wrangled an assignment with the Seventh Cavalry, just prior to its transfer, under Custer, to Fort Ripley in Kansas. Cale had left the Cyclone for good, as far as he was concerned.

Blinking, Cale shook out of this retrospection and saw with some surprise that it was full night. Despite his best intentions, here he was, back on the Cyclone. When Sam McKeller fell off a bronc and broke his neck, the ranch had become Cale's. And for reasons he did not fully comprehend, Cale could not bring himself to relinquish the empire his father had fought and bled into existence.

Beau's whicker alerted him of a rider's approach.

Cale didn't move, searching the darkness of the meadow. Somewhere in the trees on the other side a horned owl spoke, five resonant hoots. Tom had long ago finished treating the *grullo*. He sat now on the tack box, whittling a stick. Now he dropped the stick into the pile of shavings at his feet, folded the clasp knife, and put it in a shirt pocket. The Henry repeater was propped against the corral fence, his lariat draped over the top of a post. Taking up both gun and rope, he moved with caution to the corner of the line shack. Ten feet away, Cale could not make out his features. It would be another hour at least before the full yellow moon lifted into the star-studded sky. Cale could, however, make out the silver length of the Henry's barrel.

"Reckon you're gonna need all that firepower?" he asked, barely above a whisper.

Tom said, "You never know how things are gonna turn out, now do you?"

"Remember. I'll handle this."

Tom's tone was sarcastic. "Time will tell," he replied.

The dark shape of a horseman separated from the blacker line of trees.

Cale had a sudden uncomfortable premonition that his troubles were only just beginning.

Chapter Eight

The newcomer was halfway across the clearing before he took note of the three mounts tethered over at the corral. He checked his horse roughly. The horse snorted, unappreciative of such hard treatment. It occurred to Cale that if this was Yellen, then Yellen might worry that they were rustlers or bandits, and do something that they would all regret.

"Frisco, you better fire up that bitch light in there," Cale said, keeping all the sharp edges off of his voice.

The *vaquero* had been thinking along those same lines, apparently, for immediately a match flared. In seconds, yellow light leaked through the open doorway to Cale's left. Frisco carried the bitch light out and put it on the ground, and then knelt down behind it so that his face was illuminated. His shadow swallowed up the line shack behind him, and plunged Cale into darkness again.

"Come on in, Billy," called the *caporal*. "It's me, Francisco."

Cale wasn't sure whether Frisco was just making an assumption or if he had better night vision than that old horned owl out there.

The rider urged his mount closer. At the edge of the pool of yellow light he checked rein again. But he didn't step down.

"Well," drawled Billy Yellen. "Ain't this one of those unexpected pleasures? What brings you all out this way?" He was peering at Cale in the shadow, trying to identify him.

"That's Cale McKeller, Billy," Frisco said.

Cale stood and stepped fully into the circle of light. He gave Yellen a long once-over, and saw a rangy, sharp-shouldered customer with straw-colored hair in dire need of trimming. The light wasn't right to divulge the color of his eyes but, whatever color they were, they glimmered like fool's gold. Yellen wore chaps over whipcord pants tucked into spur-hung boots, and a flannel shirt beneath a short *chaqueta* jacket particularly common along the Bloody Border. Instead of a bandanna he wore a black woolen muffler coiled around his neck. A rawhide quirt dangled from his left wrist. There was a .44 Dance revolver in his holster and a Colt sidehammer rifle in his saddle scabbard. It appeared to Cale's experienced eye that Yellen took better care of his firearms than he did his mounts.

"Well," said Billy again. He did not sound or look all that impressed. "I was wondering when I'd have the honor of meeting the old man's son. It's a real privilege, Mister McKeller."

His tone put the lie to his words, but Cale reminded himself that it was folly to expect much in the way of common courtesy from some line riders. As Frisco had remarked, the best of them were loners as a rule, who often went weeks without benefit of human company. Many preferred it that way. The line rider's job was important and required above all self-sufficiency. He held in the spread's stock and hazed neighbors' strays off home grass when such were come upon; kept an eye peeled for rustlers and feed-offs; hunted the wolves, coyotes, and eagles which threatened the well-being of calves; branded mavericks and reported on the condition of pasture and watering places in his section. All this, and more, a line rider performed unsupervised. Generally he was his own boss.

"We're not here to socialize, Billy," Cale said.

"That's fine by me. Been accused of a lotta things, but sociable ain't never been one of them."

"I'm here to tell you you're fired."

"Fired?" Billy glanced at Frisco with a crooked smile, as if he expected the foreman to break down and confess that this was all just a practical joke. "What the hell does he mean, fired?"

"He means what he says," said Frisco flatly. "You're hoglegged. You don't work for the Cyclone."

Cale made a sharp gesture meant for Frisco. "I'll handle this."

"He asked me," said Frisco.

Billy snorted. "Yeah, Francisco. Let the *patron* handle it. You got a reason, McKeller? Oh, I beg your pardon! Guess a man in your position don't need reasons. That's fine. I reckon I can figure what it is without you having to spell it out. Aiming to fire every Johnny Reb on the payroll?"

"You didn't fight in the war."

"The hell I didn't!" exploded Billy. "I rode with Bloody Bill Anderson."

Cale shook his head resolutely. He was sure he could tell a veteran when he saw one—even a veteran of an irregular outfit like Bloody Bill's partisan rangers, who had been little better than outlaws. And one thing was gospel certain: If Billy Yellen hadn't still been sucking his mother's teat when the war was raging, he hadn't been far removed from it. Billy tried to add years with that scraggly beard, but Cale wasn't fooled.

"That's not the reason, anyway," Cale said.

"You called me a liar."

Cale tensed as Billy's hand moved from its resting place on the saddle horn to a spot on his thigh, right close to the holstered handgun.

Tom Samples stepped out of the blackness at the corner of the hooden. The lariat was draped over one shoulder, the Henry in both hands and aimed from the hip.

"Didn't look like things were turning out so good," Samples remarked.

"Take it easy," snapped Cale. He stepped even closer to the mounted man, and Billy tore his gaze from the Henry to watch him warily.

"You went with one of the Llano crib girls," Cale said, "and then didn't pay her. The way I hear it, you used your fists on her when she objected. You were in town when you belonged out here on the job. I don't have the cash on hand, but you can stop in at the bank in Fredericksburg and draw your wages at your convenience. I'll write you a voucher. Minus what you owe that woman."

"Keep your damned money," growled Billy. "Use it to pay your own way, next time you sashay down to the cathouses. Or don't the whores charge a McKeller?"

"What I do is none of your business. What you do *is* mine. Men who work for me obey orders, do their job, and pay their debts."

"It's the cowboy's code," said Frisco reasonably. "You don't close your door to grubline riders, you don't take hold of a rider's reins, and you don't fail to pay a soiled dove for services rendered."

Billy glared at Frisco and then, with a derisive snort, looked away, as though Frisco and his lesson on range etiquette weren't worth paying any attention to.

"And since we're on the subject of manners," added Cale, "I don't particularly like having to look up at you while we're talking. So why don't you step down?"

"Why don't you go to hell? You just fired me, remember? Reckon you can talk all you want, but I ain't obliged to listen."

"This horse belong to you?"

"No. It belongs to you, McKeller. Like everything else around here. And you damn well know it."

"Yeah, I know it. And I know you've got a spade bit on him. No one uses a spade on a Cyclone horse." A spade bit had a sharp-edged plate which lay against the horse's tongue. Even the gentlest touch on the reins caused pain. "What's more, you came close to ruining that *grullo* over there. You've been doing a lot of hard riding, Yellen. Wonder how much of it was on the line."

"What are you saying?"

"I'm saying you'll leave that horse with me."

"Then what the hell am I supposed to do? Walk?"

"That's the size of it. Gather up your possibles and be on your way by first light. My advice is head due west. I don't want to catch you on Cyclone land. When you get across Dog Creek you won't be far from the San Saba road."

It was the worst possible humiliation to heap on any man, and by the look of pure mad-dog meanness Billy leveled at him, Cale thought for a moment that he had misjudged. Billy could slap leather and shoot him right between the eyes. The only deterrent was that he knew, along with everyone else present, that a second or two later Tom would blow him out of the saddle.

Cale had counted on Yellen being too smart to make such a play. But now it occurred to Cale that Billy might just be crazy enough. Standing there with his greatcoat flapping against his legs in the night wind, the lamplight throwing his shadow long out in front of him, Cale felt a cold down in his bone marrow.

"Your pa would have been man enough to come here and face me all by his lonesome," remarked Billy with contempt. "He didn't need any help when he rode roughshod over a body."

Cale's pride would not permit him to explain how he had fallen in with Frisco and Tom.

"Yellen, I'll say it just once more. Get off that horse and then get off this ranch."

"Mighty big words for a yellow Yankee sonuvabitch," Billy sneered, then spat at Cale.

Moving like greased lightning, Cale lashed out and caught hold of the horse's bridle. The horse, startled, jerked its head back and sidestepped. Billy's right hand moved, but it was out of Cale's sight. An instant later they all heard the deadly snicker of metal as Tom worked the Henry's action and brought stock to shoulder. Once again Billy thought better of gunplay.

"McKeller," he grated, "ain't you violating the cowboy's code?" His voice trembled with pent-up rage.

"Shut your mouth."

"Go to hell!"

Billy yanked savagely on the reins. The spade dug deep. The horse gave a shrill cry and went up on its hind legs. Cale released the bridle, knowing that if he held on it would only add to the animal's torment. The cry of the horse snapped something inside of him, something straining against the leash of patience and reason after months of frustration. Before Billy could turn the horse away Cale was lunging for him. Billy was cursing at the horse, but the horse was through cooperating and began to crow-hop. Billy had to forget about the Dance revolver and concentrate on staying aboard. Cale grabbed Billy's leg and belt, and was lifted off the ground as the horse humped stiff-legged into the air. Billy kicked with his foot still in the stirrup, catching Cale in the groin, and at the same time laid his quirt across Cale's shoulder. Cale hardly felt the rawhide through the greatcoat, but the kick sent waves of hot nausea straight through him. He lost his grip and fell, feeling like a complete and utter fool. Billy finally turned the horse and Cale rolled away from the flailing hooves, thinking that he had put on a fine show for Tom Samples.

For his part, Tom had decided that he couldn't shoot a man who hadn't drawn iron, and it looked now as though Yellen was bent on escape, not bloodshed. Of course, in this instance, escape amounted to horse theft. So Tom barked Frisco's name, and when Frisco looked, Tom threw him the Henry. Frisco caught it readily. Tom then shrugged the lariat off his shoulder, shook out the loop as he jogged forward, and had it flying just as Billy savagely gut-hooked his mount. The horse bolted into the darkness, but Yellen didn't go with it. The loop settled down around his shoulders, Tom dug in his heels and leaned back, and with a strangled shout Billy came off the backside of the horse and made a hard landing.

Billy, shaken by this unorthodox dismount, rolled over slowly, got up on his hands and knees, and looked down the length of hard-twist at Tom Samples. White-hot humiliation seared through him, and the killing craze blinded him to the foolhardiness of going for his gun. He grabbed for the .44 Dance—and found the holster empty. He swore again. When Cale had grabbed his bridle he had thumbed the hammer thong free, and his fall had shaken the gun loose. He cast about, saw the revolver a long reach to his right, and dove for it. Tom gave the rope a hard tug, and instead of going sideways toward the gun Billy nosedived forward.

Cale saw all this through a haze of pain. The idea of Samples finishing the fight he had picked chafed him so much that he got to his feet in spite of the sickening pain. A few stiff, shuffling steps brought him face-to-face with Tom, and he grabbed the rope with both hands.

"I'll fight my own fights," he rasped hoarsely.

Spitting dirt, Billy changed his tactics. Gathering himself, he charged up the rope. He would not abide being lassoed like some fool cow. Tom saw him coming, over Cale's shoulder, gave Cale an impudent smile, let go of the rope, and stepped away. Cale had only begun to turn when Billy hit him full-tilt, and a cry was squeezed out of his throat as Billy's shoulder struck him solidly in the kidney. His body jackknifed, but he twisted and slammed the length of his right arm across Billy's back. They both went down. Billy bounced up first and aimed a brutal kick at Cale's rib cage. The kick landed squarely, lifting Cale a foot off the ground.

Frisco moved to intervene at this point, looking forward to laying Billy Yellen's scalp open with the butt plate of the Henry, but Tom raised an arm as straight and rigid as a gate pole to detain the *vaquero.*

"He said *he* wanted to handle it," murmured Tom.

Frisco gave the cowboy a rough look, but realized that Tom was right, even if for the wrong reasons.

Shrugging out of the loop's embrace, Billy moved to stomp Cale's face. But Cale had gotten a stomach full of Billy's savage footwork. Fear and shame carried him across the line that separated a man who used his head in a knock-down-drag-out from one who goes in lashing out like a lunatic. He struck wildly at Billy's upraised leg with such blind force that Billy went down like a poleaxed steer. This time Cale got up first. Reaching down, he took Billy by belt and muffler, lifted him bodily, and drove him headfirst into the wall of the line shack like a human battering ram. Cale felt the impact himself, and felt Billy's body go slack.

He let go of Yellen and stepped back, dragging heel and stumbling. Billy collapsed into a crumpled heap, and Cale looked dumbly across at Tom and Frisco, but then Billy was on hands and knees once more, head lolling, bloody spittle leaking from his mouth.

The flame of anger washed right out of Cale as Billy, with great effort, lifted his head. Cale saw murder, deep and ugly as the pit of Hell, on Billy's face.

"Stay down," croaked Cale.

The advice seemed to spur Billy to do just the opposite. He got his legs under him and charged again. With a perfectly timed sidestep, Cale dodged Billy's headlong rush. As Yellen flew by, Cale brought his left up from way down low, connecting solidly with Billy's jaw. The punch lifted Billy off his feet and turned him halfway around in midair.

Again he went down. Again he got up.

Swaying precariously, he spat blood and a piece of tooth. He blinked rapidly at the funny lights in front of his eyes, trying to find his tormentor, but he wasn't even facing Cale anymore.

"Over here," Cale said.

Billy swung around so sharply that he almost lost what was left of his balance. "One day," he mumbled through the blood filling his mouth, "I'm gonna kill you, McKeller."

"You got grit," Cale said, commending him.

Billy went at him with a pigeon-toed shuffle. His arms, dangling at his sides, felt as if they had anvils lashed to them. Still, he managed to take a clumsy swing, grunting with the exertion. Cale stepped in and took the punch on the shoulder, planting a hard-driving fist into Billy's gut. All the air gushed out of Billy's lungs, preceded by a spray of blood. He doubled over. Cale straightened him out and finished it with a right cross. Billy went spinning away, his arms flung out, and then his legs corkscrewed and he went down for good.

Cale felt feeble of a sudden, and still qualmish from the kick to his crotch. He reeled to the wall, turned to put his back against it, and eased down into a sitting position, drawing his knees up. With dull eyes he watched Frisco hunker down alongside Billy. The *vaquero* looked over at him. "Not much of a cowhand, but *muy valiente*, eh, boss?"

"Yeah. Sure. Very brave. And don't call me boss."

Frisco ran his fingers through the matted hair on the top of Billy's skull. They came away sticky with blood. Seeing this gave Cale a solid shock. "Did I crack his head open, Frisco?"

"His pulse is strong. And there is only blood coming out. Nothing else. We will take him inside."

"Let sleeping dogs lie," Tom said. The last thing he was worried about was Billy's comfort.

Cale gave a deep sigh. He just didn't have it in him to get into another dispute, especially with Tom Samples.

Frisco turned a smile on Tom that carried mild reproof. "He too heavy for you, *hombre?* You just stand there and take it easy while I move him."

"Hell," growled Samples.

He stepped in and helped Frisco carry the unconscious man into the line shack. Blinking grit out of his eyes, Cale listened to a couple of bullfrogs down by the creek engaged in a singing contest. He could see the moon now, a huge yellow platter behind the trees on the other side of the meadow. He considered himself lucky. If things had gone just a hair different Billy Yellen might have done for him. He saw the Dance revolver lying in the mud, the lamp light gleaming off its barrel. He recalled Billy's pledge to kill him. The threat didn't worry him much. Such things were often said in the heat of a fight, and then usually set aside when tempers cooled.

Samples emerged from the line shack, circled Cale without a word, gathered up his lass-rope, and vanished into the night, making for the corral like a man with a mission. A moment later he was on his horse and riding out into the darkness.

"He goes to get the horse," explained Frisco from the doorway.

"Hell, that *could* wait until morning. It won't go far."

"He is restless," said the *caporal.* "He wanted to fight but you wouldn't let him. This gives him something to do. And the moon is up. He will find the *caballo.*"

"Well, we might as well night here. Leave at daybreak. We've got a long ride tomorrow." He faced the prospect without pleasure. He expected to be as stiff as a new pair of pants and as sore as mule-kicked dog come morning. Some days just trampled a man.

"I'll tell you one thing, Frisco," he added. "If Yellen comes around and wants to take issue with me again, I'm not in the mood. I'll put a hole in him."

Frisco went over to collect the .44 Dance, testing the feel of it in his hand, and weighing in his mind what Yellen might be capable of.

"Don't worry about Billy," he advised. "He will be no trouble."

Cale nodded, but somehow he felt it wasn't over yet.

CHAPTER NINE

"It's a crying shame," declared Wolfhunter Geddes, sitting in the dusty morning sunshine on the "opera seat" of the breaking pen. He was accompanied by Abner and the other *gringo* ranch hand, whose handle was Curt. The Cyclone men sat on either side of him, and gave him respectful elbow room.

Wolfhunter spoke thus just as the bronc they were watching "broke in two" and sent the wiry Mexican horsebreaker named Jesus flying through the air to land with teeth-jarring impact almost at their feet.

"Oh, you cain't hurt Jesus," said Abner. "He don't have no bones left in his body. They's every one broke already."

Jesus picked himself up, looking composed, and brushed himself off. The strawberry roan was still bucketing around the pen as though unaware that Jesus no longer clung to its spine. All it felt was the torment of the saddle and bridle, and it wasn't going to rest until these malevolent devices were gone.

"That cayuse," remarked Wolfhunter, "has got a bellyful of bedsprings."

Jesus looked at him. Beneath his dark, impassive *mestizo* features hostility rippled. Jesus and his little sister, fourteen-year-old Inez, lived with their father in the *ranchito*. The father was also a Cyclone *vaquero*, and was away at the marking ground up by the Lodgepole. Inez often helped Esmerelda and Señora McKeller in the *casa grande*, and as a result Jesus was permitted to eat with the "batch" hands in Casa Piedra's dining room. With her husband gone, Señora McKeller presided over the table. She and Esmerelda ate with the men, and Inez customarily served coffee kept hot on the Windsor stove.

Yesterday morning the one called Wolfhunter had also sat at table, and had cut his eyes all up and down Inez's trim, budding young figure, doing it so audaciously that Inez had become uncomfortably self-conscious and Jesus very angry. Wolfhunter had undressed her with his eyes. Katy McKeller, who could scout trouble, had sent Inez away on an errand that kept her out of the dining room for the duration of breakfast—much to the chagrin of Curt and Abner, who were unaccustomed to the inconvenience of having to get up and clomp off into the kitchen for refills. Both men sucked up a gallon of java every morning.

And last night Inez had become very frightened, for Wolfhunter was seen rimwalking the *ranchito* in the gray twilight. Inez had told her brother that Esmerelda had forbidden Wolfhunter to sleep under Casa Piedra's roof. That Wolfhunter had not taken offense. Inez had eavesdropped, and overheard his response.

"That's not very neighborly, Essie, but I don't hold it against you. Gotten to where I can hardly sleep if I ain't out in the wide open, under the stars. And more than ever lately. Four walls tend to close in on me. Reminds me of the pine box they might be nailing me into right soon, if I am so unfortunate as to die in a civilized place. Now, if I get my druthers, I'll breathe my last in the wilderness. Don't want no undertaker's cold hands on me. Nor do I care to leave my mortal remains in some damned bone orchard."

Inez had told her brother about this. And then, last night, Wolfhunter had prowled like a restless spirit, and Jesus had feared that Inez was his prey, and so he had taken up his old shotgun and, tamping down his fear, gone to stand in front of the *choza*. But Wolfhunter had disappeared.

This morning Inez had not gone to Casa Piedra to lend a hand. She had cowered, truly frightened, in the *choza*. Naturally, Jesus was not feeling friendly toward Wolfhunter Geddes.

Now Jesus looked at the two *gringo* cowboys perched on either side of the buckskin-clad legend.

"Well, are you *hombres* going to calf around all day?" he asked crossly.

Embarrassed, Curt took his *reata* from the post beside him, shook out the loop, and waited until the cavvy-broke roan twisted and hopped into range. A wrist flick sent the lasso snaking over the animal's head. Curt performed this catch-up so effortlessly that even Wolfhunter was impressed. The bronc immediately took off for the far side of the pen. Curt leaped from the top rail, ran forward, and wrapped the rope around the snubbing post. Abner got down, too, climbed the rope to the horse, and cheeked it, forcing its head back against its neck, dispensing with Curt's lass-rope and giving the roan a good ear twist at the same time. This subdued the bronc long enough for Jesus to set a foot into the left stirrup. Then Abner released his hold and jumped clear. The roan leaped into the sky, slamming Jesus into the crackerbox. Curt rolled up his rope and accompanied Abner back to the top rail and Wolfhunter.

"Jesus'll bust him," Abner predicted confidently. "That broomie ain't so wild. Just got a little uppity runnin' loose all winter. I rode him some last year. He's a clear-footed sonuvabitch. Jesus just needs to take him down a notch or two."

"I once seen a bronc throw a feller so far the poor bastard had to register to vote in the next county," said Curt, impassive. He flicked a brief glance at Wolfhunter. One did not look at such a man too long or too hard. "I bet you've busted a few wild 'uns in your time. I guess you done just about everything worth doing."

"I don't break horses," replied Wolfhunter casually. "I just ride them as is."

Abner looked anxiously over his shoulder. He didn't see Wolfhunter's shaggy steeldust anywhere. That was cause for relief. The horse looked plenty mean enough to sneak up behind a body and bite his head off. However, Abner could not rest easy altogether, as the coyote dog was sprawled in the dirt close by. The coyote dog felt Abner's scrutiny, opened one jaundiced eye, and stared back.

"They say you've killed a hunnerd Comanch'," Curt said, looking with curious wonder at the Indian-sheathed rifle propped against the fence. All Wolfhunter had to do to fetch it was reach back and down.

Wolfhunter nodded, watching the frenzy of action in the pen. "Yes, I was pretty busy that day."

"They say you scouted with Mackenzie, and that you was at the Battle of Adobe Walls."

"The second one. I was farther north when Kit Carson had his spot of trouble there in '64. But I did manage to make the fracas they put on there a few years back."

"I'd have liked to been there," said Curt. "If for nothin' else but to have seen Billy Dixon's shot."

Again Wolfhunter nodded. "Dixon had a dead eye that day, no question."

"I've heard that the shot was a mile long," Curt said in encouragement.

"Seven-eighths, as I recollect. We walked it off afterward. Those redskins had us boxed up behind what was left of Bent's fort pretty tight. Their problem was that we were all hidehunters, so we had plenty of shot and knew how to use it on moving targets. Quanah Parker himself was leadin' 'em. I'd seen him once before, when he walked out on the treaty being made in '67 at Medicine Lodge. He had with him some renegades from the Kiowa and Southern Cheyenne, along with his own Quohadi Comanch'. It was a Cheyenne buck that Billy killed. They were lined up on the ridge, yelling insults down at us. Some of them would dismount and piss in our direction. They figured they were safe out of range. Billy had a Sharps-Borschardt .45. That was about a year before they came out with the 50/90 Poison-Slinger like I carry now. But any Buffalo Sharps could shoot on Monday and kill on Tuesday. When Billy brought that loudmouth down, you better believe those copperbellies buttoned up their flies right quick."

"Why didn't you make the shot?" asked Curt. "You're the best shot in Texas, they say."

"I like working in close."

For some reason that remark made Curt feel restless. "So you hunted the shaggies some."

"I'll hunt anything when money's involved. Sure, I did a fair share of the damage done to the buffalo. Back then we'd get a dollar a hide. There was a big passel of us in that party in '74, and I'd say on the average we each brought down a hundred shaggies a day. But I knew it wouldn't last. Hell, I just come all the way across the Staked Plains and didn't see but two small bunches. Now, the first time I went out on the *llano,* this here herd come along and got 'twixt me and where I was aiming to go. So I made camp—along the Canadian it was—and waited for them to pass. I sat there a whole damn week. I believe it was then that I decided to do my part in cutting those herds down to size. I figured I'd never get anywhere in time if it wasn't done."

"Never could figure it out," said Abner, frowning. "Why they'd name a river in Texas for a country so far away. Must be a helluva long river to go all the way up to Canada."

"It ain't named for Canada, you fool," chided Curt. "It comes from a Spanish word meaning 'narrow valley.'"

"You ever been to Canada, Mr. Geddes?" asked Abner.

"No, I never could abide the cold for very long, and it must be cold up there all year round. Come winter I am obliged to find me a woman to keep my blankets warm."

They lapsed into momentary silence. Neither Curt nor Abner knew enough about women to carry on an intelligent conversation on the subject, although they wished that they did. They all watched Jesus for a while. The horsebreaker had stuck to the hurricane deck this go-round, and made some progress. The roan was prancing, but appeared to be half-persuaded that more cinch-binding was futile. Jesus was refreshing its memory on the subject of rein-pull.

Wolfhunter watched Jesus, too, but he was thinking about the bronc-buster's sister. Inez would make a fine blanket-warmer any time of year.

"Did you see any Comanch' out there this trip?" queried Abner. Comanches were on everyone's mind lately, after the ambushing of Dusty Blake's rider. Even though he was afraid of Wolfhunter, Abner felt much better protected from Indians with him around.

Wolfhunter thought about the Penateka who had tracked him down the Cap Rock and across the Callahan Divide. He had not once actually *seen* them—they were playing it pretty cagey—but he had felt them. Twice he had doubled back; twice he had laid up in ambush. But the Penatekas were too wily to follow in his footsteps. They traveled a parallel course, every other day or so quartering his trail, so that he never knew for sure where they were. One of them was always ranging ahead of the others, to keep closer track of him.

Once, he had backtracked, found their sign cutting across his, and trailed them for a spell. But a rainstorm had come down out of the north, a real fence-lifter, and he had lost the trail. There were seven, he knew that much. But not once did they try him on for size. Of course, he never gave them a genuine opportunity, and he could never lure them into bushwhack. They knew him and respected his prowess. Wolfhunter was duly flattered. They would shadow him until he took a careless step and gave them the advantage. Trouble was, after years of tracking, he'd forgotten how to be careless. He had places to go and people to see and so did not waste much time trying to fool or find them. They would come for him in their own good time. Wolfhunter just hoped that they would do so while he still lived. He hated to think he might miss out on a good fight.

"No," he told Abner. "I seen nary a one."

"Bet you saw plenty when you rode with Mackenzie," said Curt, fishing for another story. It was quite an event, talking to a living legend. Something that would liven up future campfire palavers. Curt anticipated with relish the envy and wonder on the faces of other men when he told them that he and Wolfhunter Geddes were pards, and that Wolfhunter had said this and that about something or other.

"Sure. Mostly women and children when we got to the Palo Duro. You'll hear the old bull sergeants crank it up something fierce, about standing toe-to-toe with a thousand bloodthirsty warriors. Fact is, only thing we killed a thousand of were the Comanche horses. We shot 'em down like buffalo. Some of the soldier boys didn't much care for the pony massacre, but Colonel Mackenzie was one tough, smart sonuvabitch. Which is why Sherman handpicked him to take care of the Comanche in the first place. Mackenzie knew that the best way to put a strong hurt on the Comanche was to kill their ponies. A Comanche on foot is nothing much to fret about. They make the finest cavalry in the world, but as infantry they aren't worth a bucket of shit."

Curt happened to look over his shoulder, and saw Esmerelda coming from Stone House, and he got as nervous as a big sinner at a prayer meeting. Essie was on the warpath about something, and Curt had a good idea what that something was.

"Abner—" he started, but Ab was already talking, and ignored Curt's attempt at preemption.

"Having hunted the Comanch', Mr. Geddes, I don't reckon these rustlers will be any problem for you."

"Rustlers?"

"Abner, we'd better—"

"Why sure. Ain't that why you're here? I got to tell you, once those hideburners get wind that you're out after them, I doubt there'll be one dishonest *hombre* left in the *brasada*."

Softly, and looking very interested, Wolfhunter said, "I didn't know you boys had a problem with nightriders."

"Uh, Abner, I think…"

Aware that he had made a false assumption, Abner was sheepish.

"I'm sorry as all get-out, Mr. Geddes. I just kinda figured, with you showing up the day before the Cattleman's Assocation meets…"

"What are you boys doing about it?" asked Wolfhunter.

Abner scowled. "What can we do? Mr. McKeller won't *let* us do nothing. Too much ranch work, he says. He's got dang near the whole crew marking a herd to sell. Ask me, we won't have a ranch to work if this keeps up." He squared his shoulders. "I reckon if we was given a chance we could show them owlhoots a thing or two. I wouldn't object to danglin' a few at the end of a rope."

"Abner, you're gonna be danglin' in a minute," snapped Curt, miffed at being ignored. He had slipped off the top rail and now stood inside the pen, fidgeting, kicking at clods of dried dung and with his hands shoved in his pockets.

Abner looked at him curiously. "You got a splinter in your behind, or what?"

Curt glowered back vindictively. "You're the one fixin' to be splintered."

At that moment Esmerelda arrived and gave Abner a hard shove. It caught him completely by surprise. He was the only one. Wolfhunter had heard her coming, but gave no sign. Abner's boot heel caught on a lower rail and he landed flat on his face. The coyote dog raised its head, drew back its lips, and snarled at Esmerelda.

Sitting alone on the fence, and without turning around, Wolfhunter said, "Shut up, ugly."

Stone-faced, Abner got up and brushed himself off. Esmerelda had her hands on her blocky hips, and her eyes were shooting daggers. Abner was happy to have the fence between them. But he wasn't happy with Curt, who was laughing silently. Abner threw his hat at Curt, hitting the other man in the face, whereupon Curt stopped laughing.

"So," snapped Esmerelda, "you two take the day off, eh? Maybe you want to take the rest of the year off."

"No, ma'am," mumbled Abner. "We was just waiting for Jesus there to finish with—"

"No excuses! Get back to work! *Rapido!*"

"Yes, ma'am."

They made for the holding pen to fetch Jesus another bronc. Abner had to come back and retrieve his hat. He refused to look up at Wolfhunter. To be knocked into the dirt by a woman was bad enough, but in front of a man like Wolfhunter Geddes it was downright humiliating. In spite of this, Abner knew better than to square off against Esmerelda Madrigal. A man would fare better tangling with a passel of Comanch'.

Esmerelda turned her wrath on Geddes. "You keep the men from their work."

Wolfhunter's grin was insincere. "Essie, I was just sittin' here enjoying this wonderful morning."

"*A si.* Even the lowliest grubline rider will do a day's work for a meal. Or are you too good for honest labor?"

"No, I ain't too good. Just too lazy."

Disgusted, Esmerelda turned to go. Wolfhunter swung his long legs around and eased his gaunt frame off the top rail. He leaned against the fence with his arms draped over it and watched her beeline for Casa Piedra.

"You know what the strongest part of this ol' body is?" he asked.

She faced him, and took a terrible chance. "*Sí.* The smell."

Wolfhunter's counterfeit grin did not falter. He shook his head, pointed the right forefinger at her, sighted down the length of his arm, and crooked the finger a few times, pantomiming the squeeze of a trigger. "How does young Tom feel about rustlers, Essie?"

Esmerelda almost swore aloud. Having lived her life around strong-talking cowboys, she had a healthy repertoire of colorful swear words, and her first inclination was to heap a string of them on Curt and Abner. She took a few steps back toward Wolfhunter, and stopped. Jesus was still riding around the breaking pen, using the reins on the pacified roan, and she didn't want anyone to hear them discussing Tom. But she didn't want to get *too* close to Wolfhunter, either.

"This *rancho* is his home," she said briskly. "He takes it personally when those *pelados* steal the cattle."

Wolfhunter nodded, looking as if he had reached a private decision. "*Bueno, hermosa.* Then maybe I *can* do a little work around the place."

Esmerelda shuddered to contemplate what that remark might hold in store for everyone.

"Why don't you leave us in peace?" she implored.

"Maybe I will," he murmured. "But I ain't seen my son yet. Why don't you tell me where he is?"

"I have sent for him."

"The rider that left at first light?"

She made no reply, turning her back on him once more and making for Casa Piedra across the hardpack.

"I sure hope they don't take all spring," he called after her. "I might get bored. Or I might just up and die on you."

Esmerelda just kept on walking.

"And, if I do die," called Wolfhunter, "will you bury me under that big oak next to ol' Sam, Essie? I talked to him about it last night. He don't give a damn. He said it'd be good to have someone to talk over old times with."

Esmerelda suppressed a shudder and hastened her step. "I will bury you," she thought. "I will bury you deep, and facedown, with pleasure."

She hurried through the side door into the dining room, shutting the heavy beamed door firmly behind her, and stepped over to peer out the window. Wolfhunter was still near the breaking pen, but now he was standing straight, looking intently off to the southeast, head held high. He stood poised in that manner for quite some time, like a whitetail buck testing the wind. The coyote dog at his feet was also looking in the same direction, sniffing the air. She thought, "Someone must be riding in." Her heart missed a beat as it occurred to her that it might just be Tom. Or Cale. Hurrying to the front room she looked out across the grass flat. She saw nothing but the distant line of oaks down by Encino Creek.

"What's the matter, Essie?"

Esmerelda almost jumped out of her skin.

Katy put a comforting hand on her arm. "Why are you so frightened of him, Essie? He's only a sick man. He can't be as bad as all that."

"He is worse than bad. He may try to kill you. Or Cale."

Katy was so astonished, so incredulous, that she laughed. "What on earth gives you that idea? Why would he ever want to do such a thing? You're not making sense, Essie."

"He does not need a reason to kill," said Esmerelda adamantly. "It is all he has ever done. It is all he knows. At first it was wolves, and the other animals that scare the stock. And then he killed the buffalo. Then the Indians. Then he took to killing wanted men. They say he never brought them back alive. He did not hunt them for the money, but for the pleasure of killing them, and he did not want to give up that pleasure to the hangman. Bounty was only an excuse to kill. But now he is dying, and he no longer has to worry about excuses."

"I can't believe he would want to take my husband's life."

"I hope I am wrong."

She stepped out onto the gallery and looked over at the breaking pen.

Wolfhunter and his coyote dog had vanished.

CHAPTER TEN

Lone Dog and Bow String lay belly-down behind a log in the oak motte a quarter mile from Casa Piedra. Their four brothers waited on the other side of the rocky creek with the horses.

"*Nadone!*" whispered Bow String fiercely. "Look! He is gone!"

Lone Dog said nothing. For only an instant his gaze had flicked to the big woman emerging from the house of yellow stone. But when he looked back, the tall-red-haired man in buckskins was gone. So was the dog.

"That was him," said Bow String.

"I know."

Unlike Bow String, who had seen Wolfhunter at the Medicine Lodge treaty talks, Lone Dog had never laid eyes on the man they had hunted for so long. His sister had been away from the camp, gathering wood for the fires, when Wolfhunter had come out of nowhere to take her to her death. The other girls had fled back to camp, and their description of the man had identified him to Crooked Neck and Bow String and a few others. And not once in the long days of tracking had Lone Dog seen anything but the black remains of Wolfhunter's fires, and bloody leavings where Wolfhunter had relieved himself, and the hoofprints of Wolfhunter's horse, which seemed capable of running from dawn to dusk without respite. Lone Dog had come to know those hoofprints so well that he could distinguish them in the well-trampled dust of the most heavily traveled road.

"Where did he go?" asked Bow String. Concern replaced elation, and he looked to his left and then to his right, peering into the brush.

Lone Dog scanned the dirty clutter of the ranch behind Casa Piedra. He saw a young Mexican woman putting wash out on a rope strung between two *chozas*. But he saw no sign of Wolfhunter.

"He looked directly at us." His own voice startled him. He had not meant to speak the thought that troubled his mind.

"How could he know we are here?" Bow String scoffed.

"He has strong medicine."

"Perhaps Eye That Kills was right. Perhaps we *should* have taken the guns of the man we killed. We might have struck him from here."

"I doubt it." Lone Dog was disappointed in his good friend. "Besides, Crooked Neck—"

"Crooked Neck!" Bow String grunted, and spat at a dragonfly that had landed on the log behind which they lay. "Good! *Mea-dro!* Let's go!" He acted as if he was going to stand up.

"What are you doing?" hissed Lone Dog. "Stay down!"

Bow String complied. He had not intended to stand up anyway, not really. If Wolfhunter lurked in the cover of those buildings, aiming his rifle at them, he would have no difficulty killing at this distance. But Bow String was agitated almost to recklessness. He was sick of the hunt and of the hiding.

"Let us ride in and finish the task we set out to do, *tah-mah*," he urged.

"No."

Bow String was ashamed of the way he was acting, but he couldn't help it. He was tired of living in a world that had lost all value. His brother was dead, his people were doomed. *Comancheria*, once free and beautiful, was soiled and tainted by the invasion of the *tosi-tivo*. Even while he admired Lone Dog for the leadership and supreme caution he had exhibited, Bow String was sick of skulking like a coyote.

"What are we to do, then?" he demanded. "Wolfhunter may stay in that camp until the snow comes again."

"We are too few and they are too many." Lone Dog was watching the lookout who paced the Stone House rooftop. "Even their women are good shots. I doubt that even one of us would get half-way there alive."

"We should have tried to kill him sooner, before he came to where there are so many other *tosi-tivo.*"

Lone Dog shook his head. "He was too careful. But now that he *is* among his kind, perhaps he will become careless."

"Then what do we do?" persisted Bow String, pessimistic.

An idea was coming to Lone Dog. It was evasive at first, as slippery as the offal of a fresh kill, and he fell silent until it was clear. It might be easier to slip up on Wolfhunter in the *ranchito* than it would be out in the brush. The stench of so many people and animals living so close together would fill Wolfhunter's nostrils. The sounds of the camp would deafen his ears. One warrior, with stealth and daring, cloaked in night, might manage to get close enough. And if that warrior failed...well, better that than all of them dying in a reckless daylight assault. The idea had much to recommend it. Lone Dog had seen the *acequia,* the manmade trench which left the creek a hundred paces north of their position. It crossed the grass-flat straight as an arrow to pierce the side of the *ranchito.* A warrior with the footsteps of a ghost might creep along the trench and into the enemy camp unseen, even with the night clear and the moon full. After all, a full moon made deeper shadows.

"We will go now," he told Bow String, with fresh resolve.

"*Hakai?*" Bow String could scarcely believe his ears. "What?"

"Not far. We must find a safer place to wait for *to-oh-kar-no.*"

"And when the night comes?"

"I will tell you later," was his curt reply.

Lone Dog belly-crawled deeper into the oak motte before rising into a crouch. He loped across the narrow creek, leaping like a deer from stone to stone. Bow String followed, pausing on the other side of the creek to warily scan the brush from whence they had come. He saw nothing. Still, he could not shake the feeling that they had exchanged roles with Wolfhunter, that they were now the hunted, he the hunter. Frowning, he joined the others.

Lone Dog had informed them of his decision to find a better hiding place. None of them liked the idea of retreat after so long a pursuit, but only Eye That Kills spoke out. As Lone Dog took a step toward his horse, Eye That Kills cut him off.

"You are telling us to turn back?" he hissed. "Are we Penateka warriors? Or coyotes that cower in the brush?"

Lone Dog resisted the urge to throw the insubordinate Eye That Kills to the ground and press his knife against the other's throat. "*Ob-be-mah-e-vah!*" he snarled. "Get out of my way!"

Considering his options, Eye That Kills removed himself.

They mounted up and followed Lone Dog single file, a silent and despondent procession, holding their hard-shod ponies to a walk. They carried their hide shields on their left arms, their red-painted lances in their right hands, their bows and arrow quivers shoulder-slung. Lone Dog kept to the trees, following the creek for two miles, up a draw between scrub-oak hills. The creek deepened and became more narrow, the banks rocky and steep, and finally Lone Dog led them up a granite shoulder strewn with boulders, small yellow flowers, and hedgehog cactus growing in the cracks and crevices. A diamondback, sunning itself on a flat rock, slithered into cover at their approach, then rattled its deadly warning as they passed. Another mile they went through the *brasada*, weaving around the oak and cedar thickets, the clumps of prickly pear, crossing meadows where paintbrush and bluebonnets testified to spring's rebirth.

Then, cresting a ridge, they drew up their horses and gazed down into a grass-covered basin, sheltered by shrubby hills and blessed with a rock pool nurtured, obviously, by an underground spring. Cattle grazed in this bottom, about thirty head. As soon as he saw them Lone Dog had another idea, and smiled across at Bow String.

"We will kill them," he said.

"Kill them? Why?"

"Why not?"

Bow String dubiously surveyed the small herd. He had come a long way to kill a man, and now Lone Dog spoke of slaughtering cattle!

"We dare not build a fire," said Bow String, "and personally I do not care much for raw meat. We have jerky, and a little *tara-hyapa*. What I wish we *did* have is *toopa*, some coffee. Besides, the meat of the white man's longhorn is tough. Not nearly as sweet as *potsana*."

"That is the point," said Lone Dog. "The great herds of the buffalo are no more because the whites slaughtered them. Why should we not slaughter their cattle in return? It will be great sport."

With it put to them in this way, the others saw merit in Lone Dog's scheme. They could appreciate the concept of an eye for an eye or, as in this case, a longhorn for a buffalo. And as he hoped, Lone Dog saw that the prospect lifted the spirits of the others.

As it turned out, Lone Dog was correct. Killing the cattle *was* great sport.

Bow String took Eye That Kills and Two Hatchets around to the high ground on the other side of the basin, while Lone Dog led He Finds Water and Black Tongue down to the edge of the brush. When Bow String was in place he fired an arrow into the cloudless sky.

The six Penateka burst into the open, guiding their war ponies with their knees. With shields and lances strapped to their backs, they had their bows of Osage orange unslung and the first arrows fitted. The cattle began to run. A calf immediately fell behind. Bewildered and bawling, it stood on trembling legs. The mother returned to take a protective stance alongside, legs spraddled and head lowered. An arrow pierced her dewlap, followed an instant later by another driven deep into her neck. She tottered sideways with a plaintive bellow, and fell, thrashing. The calf jumped away, only to fall dead from an arrow plunging through its girth.

The longhorns scattered as the howling Comanches swarmed among them. Some dove into the scrub bordering the basin. Others took several arrows before falling dead. Lone Dog suspected that this was due in part to the fact that they carried no hunting arrows with them. The points of hunting arrows were attached parallel to the bowstring in order to penetrate between an animal's ribs, while the points of war arrows were set at right angles to the bowstring, to better penetrate the human rib cage. Also, the point of a war arrow was loosely attached and tended to break off after impact. So it was not surprising that several arrows were required to kill a longhorn.

Lone Dog guided his fleet-footed pony right alongside a mouse-colored steer and sent an arrow between its withers at point-blank range, burying the shaft up to the fletch. The steer died running, and somersaulted. Lone Dog turned his pony to find another target, and saw a speckled-blue bull charging at him. Even as he loosed another arrow Lone Dog felt a surge of admiration for the longhorns. They had a fighting spirit. The arrow pierced one of the bull's eyes, penetrating the skull. The bull nosedived, forelegs collapsing, its body laying a deep furrow in the ground.

Two Hatchets received whoops of approbation from some of his brothers by closing with an agile chongo cow, leaning low to grab the animal's tail, and then flipping the longhorn hind over head. The cow struggled to its feet, stunned, only to be put down permanently by an arrow impaling its throat.

Great sport, yes, but over too quickly. Widely scattered, the six Penateka turned their horses this way and that, seeking more prey. Lone Dog counted nineteen cattle dead or dying. The rest had escaped into the thickest brush.

Lifting high his bow, Lone Dog uttered a drawn-out yapping cry. The others responded by rallying to him, and he impelled his horse into the chaparro.

Not wishing to drift too far from Stone House, Lone Dog led them north and then west, in this way making a wide quarter turn around the house. Eventually he found a suitable hideout, where a fast-moving stream cut deeply into the limestone, forming sheer twenty-foot banks. On the west was an overhang formed by a jutting lip of stone. To the south the stream plunged into a jumble of tall, cone-shaped boulders, through which a man could hardly pass on foot, much less on horseback. To the north was a high deadfall, an impenetrable tangle of dead trees which blocked the overhang from the view of anyone who happened to cross farther upstream.

Love grass grew on a pair of sandbars in the shallows near the overhang, within easy reach of the war ponies. It was a good camp, Lone Dog decided.

Black Tongue volunteered as lookout. Leaving his lance and shield, his bow and quiver on his back, the warrior waded across the purling creek and climbed the sheer rock face of the opposite bank with remarkable alacrity. He found a clump of cenizo at the rim and blended in so well that Lone Dog, look as hard as he might, could not see him.

The others spread their hide pads beneath the overhang and stretched out. There was very little pemmican left, but plenty of *inapa.* There were even some mesquite beans to go with the jerky, and the creek water was cold, clear, and refreshing. They spoke mostly of the cattle killing. It made them feel better about themselves. It was good to strike back at the hated *tosi-tivo,* even in some small way. Lone Dog was pleased that their morale was so improved.

But other thoughts troubled him, and he sat apart, on a flat rock, methodically tearing at a strip of jerky with strong teeth. He wasn't hungry, but a warrior ate when the opportunity to do so presented itself. He knew he would need the nourishment. In his mind's eye he traced the route, again and again—from the oak motte upcreek to the *acequia,* along the ditch into the *ranchito,* to slip like a shadow through the sleeping huts to the rear of the stone lodge. The rooftop sentry would pay the least attention to that approach.

No matter how many times he went over it, he could only get as far as the stone lodge. The image of Wolfhunter, standing in the far-off distance on the hardpack beside the breaking pen, would intrude upon his sober calculations like a bad dream infecting sleep. And the way Wolfhunter had vanished into thin air...

Lone Dog was gripped by a sudden and dreadful premonition of disaster.

Jumping to his feet, he looked sharply at the rim of the opposite embankment, where Black Tongue had concealed himself.

"*Tah-mah*, what is wrong?" asked Bow String, sitting ten paces away. Alarmed by Lone Dog's actions, he had reached out to grasp his lance.

Lone Dog shook his head mutely, then sat back down. Suddenly, he knew that Wolfhunter could not be killed and they would all die trying to do the impossible.

Chapter Eleven

The sun dancing across his eyelids woke Cale.

Blinking up at the bright blue sky, he knew he had overslept. Seventeen years of dawn reveille had built in him a strong habit of getting up in advance of the sun. In fact, sometimes he still heard the bugles. But not today. The sun had beat him to it. Low in the morning sky, behind the line of trees on the eastern edge of Whitetail Meadow, it threw long breeze-tossed shadows from the budding oak limbs.

Frisco had built a smokeless cedar fire in a circle of stones, and the *caporal* was squatting next to it, watching over the contents of a small, smoke-blackened skillet. Throwing aside his top blanket, Cale sat up—and winced.

"*Buenos dias*, boss. And a fine morning it is, too."

"Don't call me boss, dammit," croaked Cale.

Frisco nodded sympathetically. "I am also cranky before my first cup of coffee." Pointing with his chin, he indicated the coffeepot on the rimstones. "The java is hot, and breakfast will be ready *muy pronto*. Beans and blackstrap. Señor Yellen left his provisions behind, so I helped myself."

Cale squinted at the line shack. His head felt as if it were stuffed with cotton, but last evening's events came back to him in bits and pieces, and he put the fragments together and remembered. After the fight, with Billy laid out on the bunk in the hooden, they had spread their hot rolls out under the stars, over by the corral. They had agreed that it made good sense to stand watch in shifts. Samples, returning in short order with the wayward horse, had volunteered to take the bobtail shift. Frisco would relieve him for the graveyard turn, and Cale drew the cocktail stretch. Samples expected Yellen to make more trouble when he came to, and though Frisco and Cale were not of the same persuasion, they knew that careful was better than sorry. Besides, with nightriders and Comanches on the prowl, Billy wasn't all there was to look out for. With disgust, Cale realized that he had been passed over when the time for his watch had arrived.

"Yellen gone?" he said sourly, gingerly testing limbs and joints for sore spots. There were plenty.

"*Sí*. About an hour before first light. He said nothing. We left his saddle by the door, so he just took that and his guns and headed west. He was wearing that Rebel longcoat."

"I guess Tom's disappointed that he didn't start shooting."

"Billy would have been disappointed too. We took away all his ammunition."

Cale tried not to groan as he stretched his punished body to pull on his boots. "Could've been an extra box stashed away in there someplace."

Frisco shrugged, uncertain. "Maybe. Then I would have had to shoot him."

Cale smiled at the casual way the *vaquero* talked of shooting a man, then remembered something. The smile turned into a scowl. "Why the hell didn't you shake me out when time came for my watch?"

"I didn't feel like sleeping."

Cale looked around for Samples, and was relieved, at first, to find Tom absent. It was highly unlikely that Tom would have passed on an opportunity to make some smart comment about his late-rising. He then noticed that Samples's horse and rig were also missing. They had turned all the mounts into the corral and draped their tack on the top rail.

He got to his feet with some difficulty, went over to the fire, and experienced further discomfort in the simple act of sitting on his heels. Frisco had already exhumed the tin cup from his saddlebags. It was sitting on a stone alongside the coffeepot. On cold mornings it was always a good idea to heat the cup a bit, as well. That kept the coffee warm longer.

"*Como esta?*" asked Frisco.

"Just dandy," Cale lied crossly. "And I don't take to being coddled."

"You're the boss."

Cale glowered. "You just figure I'm in no condition for another go-round. You could be wrong."

It was sheer bravado. He doubted that he could whip a one-armed cripple in his present condition. His knuckles were scraped and stiff, and his ribs and backbone were sore. Cale decided that it was simply a case of getting old and brittle. Yesterday had been bad clean through, starting with Comanches and finishing with Billy Yellen. Things were bound to take a turn for the better today.

"I did it for myself," admitted Frisco. "I do not like the digging of graves, and I was afraid I would have to dig at least one if you were standing guard when Billy came out of that hooden."

Cale poured himself some coffee. Frisco had a knack for giving reasons for what he did that were scarcely arguable.

"Where's Tom off to?"

"Rode west at dawn. Said he was going to track Billy for a spell."

"Why would he go and do such a fool thing? Is he looking for trouble?"

"Well, you *said* you wanted Billy off the Cyclone. Tom is just going to make certain he does exactly that."

"What else *would* he do, for Pete's sake?"

"Well, he could head up the line to the next camp and steal a horse," proposed Frisco.

Cale shook his head. "I'd hang him."

"Don't worry about Tom. Billy won't even know he's being followed."

"Is that so? I recollect Tom was as quiet as a blind elephant race yesterday, coming up through the brush on my camp."

Frisco merely smiled, as if it were all a fine joke, and as he was apt to do, changed the subject.

"That was a pretty solid kick to the *cajones* Billy gave you. I was afraid you'd been goodnighted."

Again, Cale was forced to smile. Finding that sometimes bulls on long drives in hot weather suffered from a swelling of the testicles, an affliction that on occasion proved fatal, Charles Goodnight, if nothing else a practical and innovative man, had come up with a solution: cutting the sack, pushing the seeds up into the body, and then sewing the incision closed.

"Your wife would wonder," added the *caporal.*

Cale blushed furiously. Frisco was courting disaster, mentioning his private parts and Katy in the same breath.

"But then I thought, *no importa,*" Frisco carried on, blissfully ignoring Cale's growing discontent. "Even when a bull is goodnighted it can still breed."

Slack-jawed with shock, Cale stared at him.

"You've got a lot of gall talking that way!" he finally managed. "I ought to come over there and bust you right in the mouth."

"You are just like your father. You go around picking fights all the time."

"I'm not picking a fight!" shouted Cale, by now highly perturbed. "You are."

"I was only thinking."

"By God, I don't want to hear about it then," muttered Cale dangerously.

Frisco shrugged. Cale watched him closely, suspecting that a smile lurked beneath the *vaquero*'s suddenly solemn demeanor. But Frisco just stirred the beans and blackstrap and they lapsed into silence.

Cale sipped the coffee and felt the cobwebs in his head begin to clear. He listened to the sounds of the clear, brisk morning—the wind in the trees, the crackle of the fire, the bubble of the blackstrap, the raucous songfest of a nearby mockingbird, the caw of a distant crow. The subject of his wife made him suddenly restless.

"Tom had best get back soon. I should already be on the way back to Stone House. I don't plan to stall around camp all day."

Frisco didn't respond. He thought it would be interesting, if Tom Samples failed to return, whether Cale would search for him or turn his back and ride for home.

As it happened, Frisco was robbed of this opportunity to take Cale's measure. They were finishing up their helpings of the beans and blackstrap when Tom rode out of the brush. Samples hitched his horse to a corral pole and dug his tin cup out of his saddlebags. Coming to the fire, he aimed a defiant look in Cale's direction, expecting Cale to climb all over him for dogging Billy Yellen. Cale thought about it, but discarded the notion. The deed was done, and all he could accomplish by chastising Samples would be the harvesting of another bushel of hard feelings. So he kept his mouth shut. Surprised by Cale's silence, Tom hunkered down and poured himself a cup of coffee, gulped it.

"We got a little breakfast left over," Frisco offered.

Tom shook his head.

They sat in silence for a full minute. Frisco waited as long as he was able for one of the others to say something, but Tom looked preoccupied, as if he was giving a serious problem some strong study, and Cale looked as if the last thing he wanted to do was pass the time of day with Samples. Finally, shaking his head, Frisco surrendered to the irresistible pull of curiosity.

"*Madre de Dios, compadre! Decirme, por favor.*"

Tom looked puzzled. "Tell you what?"

"What happened out there?"

"Nothing happened. I followed his tracks a few miles across the boscage. Never saw him. Saw his saddle, though. He left it about a mile from here. Didn't bother trying to hide it. Just dropped it on the ground and kept walking." Tom shook his head. He wasn't going to cut Yellen any slack. "Ask me, a man who can't carry his saddle on his own back for a spell don't have much grit."

"He isn't in the best of health today, Tomas," said Frisco.

Tom shot a quick, funny look at Cale, as though Cale's getting the better of Yellen in last night's slugfest was cause for wonder.

"He made better time bareback," continued Samples, meaning that Yellen's stride had lengthened after the discard of the saddle. "He got into some rough country, and then I lost his sign in a dry creek bed. Never could find where he climbed out of it. I went down the creek about a mile, and then got up on top of a long ridge where I could get a good look all around. Then something strange happened."

He went silent again, pouring himself a second cup of coffee. This time he waited for the grounds to settle, staring down at the thick black brew. Frisco got thoroughly exasperated, though he could see that Tom wasn't intentionally holding out on him; whatever had happened was still bothering Samples.

"*Que?*" pressed the foreman.

Tom shrugged. "Sitting up on that rise I thought I heard some cows bawling. A bunch of 'em. I swear I did. Sounded like I was right on top of 'em, almost. But the wind was kicking up pretty strong, and I couldn't really tell which direction to go to get to them. I went all along both sides of that ridge and didn't see a thing. But I know I heard 'em."

"*Ladinos,*" guessed Frisco. "Those wild mossbacks know how to hide in the chapparal. You can go right by them and not see. I remember *mi padre* telling me that one day long ago he was riding through the brush with another *vaquero.* Suddenly a polecat bull burst out of a stand of agrito right next to them. This bull had horns that curved out low and forward. He gored the *vaquero's* horse clean through. One of the horns got stuck in that poor pony's rib cage, and the *vaquero's* leg was pinned between the horse and the bull's head. The horse and the bull and my father's *companero* all went down in a tangle. *Mi padre* had to cut the bull's throat. Only when the bull had bled to death could he work his friend's leg free."

"That sounds like a lot of bull to me," Cale said.

Frisco just grinned, and started collecting the dirty plates. He balanced these on top of the skillet and headed for the nearest creek.

"Watch out for *ladinos,*" warned Cale.

"*Siempre.* Always."

Cale emptied his cup into the fire. The sun had ascended above the tree line and was warm on his back. He was ready to travel. Past ready. It would take a day and a half to reach Stone House. If nothing delayed him he would arrive in time for the Assocation meeting. Not that he looked forward to it with any relish. But the meeting was a ritual he had inherited from his father, and he would not shirk his duty as host, although he had failed to establish much rapport with the other members. They were, after all, lifelong stockmen. They ate, slept, and breathed ranching. He could hardly say the same, and his lack of enthusiasm was apparent to the others, no question. And if what Tom had said was true, if the others *were* contemplating the employment of stock detectives, then he would not improve his standing with them by expressing opposition to the idea.

Mulling over the prospect of future trouble, Cale got up and started for the corral.

"Hey."

He turned to face Samples. It was a breach of range etiquette to walk away from a friendly campfire without making at least an idle comment, but he hadn't considered a fire shared with Tom as friendly. Still, it was typical of Samples to take offense to any little oversight. Cale braced himself for yet another argument.

But Tom said, "I'd like permission to stay on here for a spell."

"What?" Expecting something else entirely, Cale wanted to be sure he had heard right. He couldn't recall Tom ever asking his permission to do anything.

Tom nodded at the line shack. "I'll ride this section for a while, if it's all the same to you."

It made sense, Cale knew, especially with rustlers interloping on Cyclone range, to have every section manned. Otherwise it was akin to leaving the back door wide open. Someone had to do it, and it might as well be Tom. In spite of reason, though, Cale's first inclination was to say no. He managed to resist the temptation, knowing there was ill will at its source.

"All right," he said brusquely. "If that's what you want."

At least it would keep the two of them separated. He started for the corral again, took three steps, and then was struck by another thought, and spun around to face Tom once more.

"One thing," he added. "You'll stick to the job a line rider is supposed to do. You won't go traipsing off, a one-man posse, chasing hideburners all over creation and half of Texas. Savvy?"

"Sure," Tom snapped, resenting Cale's tone.

"I hope so. Because I just fired one man for wandering off the job. I can do that again if I have to."

Balling up his fists, Samples rose. "And if I stumble over one of these nightriders? What would you like me to do with the sonuvabitch, Mr. McKeller? Tip my hat and ride on?"

"Bring him to me."

Tom sneezed at that. "Bring him to you? And what will you do? Let him kick you in the balls?"

"I'll ask him some questions," grated Cale. "Then I'll turn him over to the law when I'm done asking. He'll stand before the circuit judge."

Utterly amazed, Tom shook his head. "You've been gone too long. You've forgotten how we do things in Texas. I said it before. There's only one judge for a rustler." He laid hand on the butt of his holstered sidegun. "Judge Colt."

"As long as you work for me you'll do things my way," Cale warned him.

Tom's lips thinned as he bit back on the words welling up in his throat, the words that would take him one step over the line.

Frisco, returning from the creek and his cleanup chores, was not surprised to find Cale and Tom at each other's throats again.

"You argue all the time, like brothers."

Affronted, Cale glared at the *caporal*.

"Grab your gear, Frisco," he snapped, "and let's ride."

CHAPTER TWELVE

When he arrived at the dry creek bed Billy Yellen was relieved, knowing then that he did not have much farther to go. That was good, because he felt like warmed-over hell. Turning south, he stumbled through the deep gravel. Before long he came to a shallow pool of rainwater, deposited by yesterday's gully-washer and trapped in a rocky depression. Kneeling, he cupped his hands and raised them to his lips, sucking thirstily at the water, and then gingerly laving his bruised face with his wet hands. His left eye was swollen shut from Cale McKeller's last punch. There was an unsightly purplish-blue goose egg on his jaw. When the surface of the pool had stilled he leaned over and checked his reflection. A guttural noise escaped him, half growl and half whine.

"Damn you to hell, McKeller," he sobbed.

The shame boiled inside him, and his eyes grew hot, and salt from tears of rage got into the raw abrasions where his cheek had grazed the line shack wall; half of the beard he was so proud of had been scraped off.

It was bad enough that McKeller had whipped him. But now he would have to face the boys. He wracked his brain, trying to think of a way to explain his injuries, and his being set afoot, and save face too. Maybe he could say that he had been thrown by his horse. But they would know better. And how could he account for the fact that he no longer rode the line for the Cyclone? It was through his section that the gang slipped onto Cyclone range and gathered up all the mavericks and cold-branded stock they could find.

Billy got up and started walking away, but he forgot his gun at the waterhole and had to go back and retrieve it. Pressing on, with his head throbbing and his feet hurting, he concluded that his getting fired would not set well with the gang. Running with hardcases was like running with a pack of wolves. If you wanted to be the big cheese you had to be tougher, meaner, and smarter than the rest. Hell, he hardly had sense enough to hold onto his weapons.

The creek bed ran up to a steep-sided ridge, its slopes thick with scrub cedar, and then curled around the base of the hogback. Billy trudged on around to the west side of the ridge. Here a broad curve of eroded bedrock formed a deep, low-slung grotto. The rock that formed the floor of the grotto was smooth, even treacherously slick in places; long ago abundant water had flowed here. Fifty feet from the creek bank, at the rear of the overhang, Billy found the entrance to the seepage cave. The mouth of the cave was tall enough and wide enough for three mounted men to pass stirrup-to-stirrup. Several coal-oil lanterns were stashed under a pair of steepled limestone slabs. He fished a sulfur match from the pocket of the gray longcoat he wore and lit one of the lanterns to carry with him into the cave.

He had proceeded but a few yards when he heard the scuff of boots on rock. The way sound ricocheted down here it was difficult to fix on the source, but a heartbeat later a man stepped from behind a flowstone and leveled an old butt-loading .52 Spencer carbine at him, not ten feet down-tunnel from Billy.

"Ease off, Sligo. It's me."

"Billy?" Lowering the Spencer, the man called Sligo stepped closer, giving Billy a long and curious study. "Damn, hoss, I didn't recognize you. What happened to your face? Looks like a herd of shaggies done stompeded over it."

Sligo was grinning. He was a short and stocky character, and he made up in pure meanness for what he lacked in stature. His pockmarked features were not improved by the shape of his nose, which looked as if someone had smashed it with an ax handle, flattening all of the cartilage, leaving only the nostrils. Sligo's nose resembled a pig's snout. He wore range clothes under a yellow duster.

"You're one to talk," snapped Billy, sensitive. "You got a face only a blind mother could love."

Sligo kept grinning. Billy couldn't remember ever seeing Sligo without that foolish simper. It made folks uneasy in his presence, giving them the notion that Sligo was capable of anything, no matter how atrociously coldblooded and inhuman. They were not wrong either. Sligo had ridden with Billy's brother Jake and Bloody Bill Anderson during the war. Jake had once told Billy that Sligo's favorite pastime when they raided a redleg town was smashing the faces of women and children with the butt of his pistol. Billy had never questioned the veracity of this. One look at Sligo and no one would doubt it.

"Now, I know I ain't much to look at," Sligo admitted cheerfully. "But I still get plenty of attention in them cathouses. Them whores don't care what you look like, only how quick on the trigger you are."

Billy grimaced. Whores were all Sligo would talk about if allowed free rein, so Billy cut him short. "Is Jake back yet?"

Sligo shook his head. "He's probably shacked up with one of them pretty little señoritas. You know how those bean-eater bitches are, hoss. Or mebbe you *don't* know. Well, I can tell you—"

"Some other time," said Billy curtly. "Who else is here?"

Sligo thumbed over his shoulder—there was nothing but a cold dark pit behind him, beyond the golden throw of lantern light.

"Hainey's workin' on that forty head we took in night before last. Cajun and Landon are back there too."

"I need a horse."

"Sure, Billy. What happened?" Sligo didn't stop grinning but his voice got more serious, and his small, close-set eyes glimmered. "We got law trouble?"

"No. I just need a horse is all."

"Well, go on back, then. The boys'll be glad to see you. You ain't got nobody on your trail, do you?"

"No. I wouldn't have come if I had."

"Oh, well." Sligo was disappointed. He was easily bored. He climbed back up behind the flowstone, which always reminded Billy of a giant buzzard's wing every time he saw it.

Leaving Sligo behind in the cold, damp dark, Billy pressed on down the tunnel. At least where Sligo stood guard weak blue threads of daylight leaked up under the overhang. Billy had not gone far before leaving even that behind. Soon there was nothing but pitch blackness coming and going. The natural tunnel was wide, in most places high enough to accommodate a man on horseback, and was steadily rising. Billy felt the strain of the gradual but constant ascent on the muscles of his thighs.

Soon, he was tired and sore, but he kept plodding along, paying attention to where he put his feet, for there was a great deal of cow and horse dung in the tunnel. Sometimes the floor was bare stone, but more often it was a layer of dried silt. And there were always piles of manure to avoid. Even as he watched the floor Billy tried to scout the roof of the tunnel up ahead for bats.

As boys he and brother Jake had ventured on many occasions into the cave, for it was the easiest access to the sinkhole. The sinkhole had been their childhood hideout, and in those days there had been plenty of bats. Hundreds, maybe even thousands. At dusk they would swarm out of the sinkhole like a black cloud exhaled from Hell. Billy despised bats. He shuddered violently just thinking about them.

The tunnel finally leveled off. Fifty yards farther on it made a hairpin turn. Here Billy saw signs of bats—dark stains on the ceiling where masses of them had dangled. But no bats themselves, thank God. Billy hoped that all the recent activity had scared them deeper into the tunnels that honeycombed the ridge, or better yet, driven them away altogether.

A bit farther on he came to the veins of crystal, like strips of rock candy, catching the lantern light. Seeing them for the first time as a boy, Billy had pried a chunk loose with his knife and taken it home, busting in on his pa's afternoon nap and carrying on about how rich they were all going to be. Jake, knowing better all along, had egged him on, and laughed fit to be tied when Rafe had cuffed Billy around for disturbing him, and then gone right back to sleep. The crystals were pretty—and worthless. Billy had been devastated.

Ever since then he had dreamed of striking it rich. It would be a splendid thing, to get rich so easily, to strike a mother lode of some sort without having to invest a miserable lifetime of sweat and toil.

Not far beyond the crystals Billy emerged from the tunnel into the big chamber. The chamber was about fifty feet high and twice as wide, roughly circular, with a hole way up in one corner, at the top of a steep slope of rubble, showing a patch of blue sky and letting in light. Billy extinguished the lantern and set it down. There were some big boulders scattered around. Up near the ceiling a cave swallow dipped and darted.

On their first visits Billy and his brother had discovered the vestiges of long-dead cookfires, flints and arrowheads, and shards of broken Indian pottery. Later, Jake and a band of Confederate deserters had hidden out here. A couple of them, Billy remembered, had tried making gunpowder out of bat guano. Only twelve then, in the waning days of the Cause, Billy had often come to visit his brother and his brother's compatriots. Perched on one of the big rocks, he had listened for hours on end to their war stories. Being in the company of those Rebel heroes made Billy feel like a man—and acutely resentful at life in general for having conspired to make him too young to go to war.

Of course there were some who did not call them "heroes" or even "soldiers." Jake and his friends did not wear uniforms, and they did not wage war according to the rules. Some folks called them partisan rangers, or irregulars, or guerrillas. Billy had asked his father what a guerrilla was.

"A big monkey," Rafe had replied. "In fact, I'd swear your mother was half-gorilla. Damned whore-dog."

That some people chose to refer to Jake and his fellow soldiers as big monkeys, and did so in a decidedly unfriendly fashion, had made Billy irate and defensive.

Standing there, remembering past events, Billy found his thoughts coming full circle, back to Cale McKeller, calling him a liar for claiming experience in the war. Billy hated McKeller most of all for seeing through his make-believe. Hated him more for that than for whipping him. Billy told everybody who didn't know better that he was a seasoned veteran. It made him feel like somebody, and he thought it made him *look* like somebody too. But McKeller had seen right through him. He imagined that McKeller was out there now, laughing it up, telling everybody who would listen what a bag of wind Billy Yellen was.

Billy licked his swollen lips.

"You're gonna pay, McKeller," he whispered.

To his right was a high natural arch, and beyond, the sun-brightened sinkhole. Twice the size of the cavern chamber, the sinkhole was a vast circular depression stamped forty feet deep into the ridge, wider at the bottom than at the top, with brush growing all along the rim, ferns and vines abundant in pockets on the layered lip, even an occasional cedar clinging to the rock with its sinewy roots. Plenty of dirt had been deposited by runoff onto the floor. When Billy had first discovered it, the bottom had been covered with grass and some brush. Now there was scarcely a blade of grass remaining. Just dust, drifting up under the hooves of the stolen cattle presently held there, dust that was caught and swirled by the peculiar downdrafts that ventilated the sinkhole. The pit had been overgrazed, to say the least.

Pausing under the arch, Billy spotted a string of horses tied to a stake rope up under the ledge. He saw Cajun on horseback, in the press of cattle. Cajun had just roped a yearling and was hauling the reluctant critter out of the herd. Or rather, Cajun's horse was doing the hauling, as the lasso was dallied around the saddle horn. The forty head were jammed up around the small pool that marked the dead-center of the sinkhole. The water in the pool was a luminous green at the rim, darkening to black at the center. Billy knew that the water was very cold year round, and that the pool was very deep.

Cajun had once lashed a rock the size of a horse head to his lariat and dropped it into the pool. The rock had not touched bottom. Cajun was always doing something strange like that, trying to figure things out in his head. He was a pretty smart character, and talked educated, using big words sometimes that stumped Billy.

Jake said Cajun had grown up in a family with money, on a plantation in the Louisiana delta country.

The yearling was bawling up a storm, and some of the other cattle were taking up the cry. The whole herd was restless, but they had nowhere to go. There were only two ways into and out of the sinkhole: the way Billy had come and another tunnel opening up on the other side. Both passages were blocked with Texas gates. In the archway where Billy stood, three strands of barbed wire were stretched between perpendicular wooden stakes; the end stakes were in turn wired to iron rods hammered upright into the stone floor.

Billy watched as Cajun drew the roped yearling out of the herd toward the branding fire. Hainey was holding the iron in the fire, and Landon was performing the bulldogging chores. The latter stepped up to the yearling, lifted it onto his knees with a heaving wrench, and then got out from under. The yearling landed on its side and then Landon hog-tied it with a piggin' string and sat on it while Hainey burned hide. The yearling bawled worse than ever. Billy smiled, even though it hurt his face to do so, as Hainey gave the cow a Bar Buckle tattoo.

"That's one less for you, McKeller," he crowed. "And one more for us."

It was Hainey who first saw Billy. He said something to the others. Landon freed Cajun's rope, untied the yearling's legs, and stepped back as the cow got up and indignantly trotted back into the herd. Landon gave it a swift kick in the hindquarters just for laughs, then waved at Billy. Cajun coiled his rope, Hainey laid the iron back in the fire, and all three of them started over, Cajun staying aboard his cutting horse. Billy went through the Texas gate and met them halfway.

"Lordamighty, Billy!" exclaimed Landon in his high-pitched way, turning his head sideways and looking out of the corners of his eyes. It was what he did when speaking to someone, making him appear shy and incredulous when he talked. "What happened to your face?"

"Forget it."

"Hey," Hainey gruffed. "If there's been some trouble we got a right to know."

Billy surrendered to the inevitable. Then, after hours of wracking his brain for a plausible story, he found one springing full-blown to his mind.

"Cale McKeller, Frisco Madrigal, and Tom Samples," he said. "That's what happened. They laid up for me at the line shack last night. Jumped me and pulled me off my horse. Then, while the others held me down, McKeller commenced to hammering on me."

"Lordamighty!" repeated Landon. "What didja do, Billy?"

"I got hammered, Landon. That's what I did. Course, when he was plumb tuckered out, I *did* manage to spit in Cale McKeller's Injun eyes."

Landon laughed. He was young, about Billy's age, and heavily muscled. He was gullible, easygoing, and uncomplaining. The others liked him around because he didn't mind doing the dirty, menial jobs. Billy had never seen him mad and didn't want to, for he had seen Landon bend horseshoes on a wager. Landon dressed like a sodbuster and wasn't much of a hand with a gun, but he could be trusted.

"Why'd they go and do a thing like that?" asked Hainey suspiciously.

"Hell. I went to town. Somebody saw me. McKeller got wind of it. But he didn't think it was enough just to fire me. They took my string and my cartridges and told me to walk out. So I did. They probably would've dangled me, otherwise."

"Damn!" swore Hainey, stomping his foot. "Ain't that just fine! You mean he fired you just because you went to town?"

"Yeah." They knew he snuck into town on occasion to report to his father. But they didn't need to know that it was his visiting a whore that had scotched things.

"You sure that's the only reason they done fired you?" Hainey pressed. "We got a right to know."

Billy got exasperated. Hainey was an old, potbellied maverick who forever carried on about his rights. He looked like a river pirate, and smelled like one, too. But he was one of the best rewrite men in Texas, and Rafe's old drinking buddy, or one of them, and so he believed himself to be a cut above the others. Even though this operation required no brand altering, Hainey still thought he was hot stuff. This, by itself, was enough to put him on Billy's bad side. Billy liked to think that he and his brother Jake were Rafe's lieutenants, but Hainey carried on as if he were second-in-command, and treated Billy like a snot-nosed kid.

"No," snapped Billy. "That ain't the only reason. There's another—because Cale McKeller is a goddamn bluebelly traitor."

Hainey snorted. "Whatever he is, we're in a pickle now. We used to could come and go as we pleased through your section. It won't be so easy to borrow Cyclone stock now. So what do we do? We got a right to know what we're gonna do, don't we?"

"Jake will be back soon," said Cajun, unconcerned. Bent forward in the saddle, his arms crossed on the apple, he looked very nonchalant. Like Sligo, he had fought with Billy's brother in the war, and depended on Jake for leadership.

"Don't know why Jake took off," Hainey muttered.

"Stop fretting," said Cajun. "We hit the other ranches and do all right without having an inside man." He was a slender character, with a long pale face set off by jet-black hair and long sideburns. There was a pencil-thin mustache above his wide, thin-lipped mouth. He had a gold tooth right up front. Billy had heard him say that the gold tooth would pay for the undertaker when they planted him six feet under. Billy knew little about him. There was not a trace of the French patois in his voice. He kept his fingernails clean and his range clothes brushed out.

"Well, I say we've been plain lucky," Hainey replied. "I say it's time we take what we got and hightail it for the Rio Bravo."

"We'll go when my pa says it's time," said Billy.

"Yeah, Billy's pa is the honcho of this outfit," said Landon uselessly.

Hainey glowered. "No shit, plowboy. We take all the risks, so we've got a right to know the plan."

"You and your rights." Cajun laughed softly. "You've got the right to hang, and that's about all."

"Quit bellyachin'," Billy advised the rewrite man. "We've done good so far, ain't we?"

"I'm still broke as a cowboy come Sunday morning," Hainey said.

"That'll change," Billy promised. "Cajun, how many have we got so far?"

"At least seven hundred."

"That's enough," said Hainey. "We're pushing our luck."

"Pa wants a thousand before we take them to Mexico," Billy reminded them.

It was a fine plan, in Billy's opinion. With the proceeds from a stagecoach holdup Jake, Sligo, and Cajun had pulled off last spring up near Sixshooter Junction, Rafe Yellen had bought forty sections over on the Frio, using the name Martin Short and registering the Bar Buckle brand in the county's brand book. All legal and aboveboard on the face of it. But the cattle now grazing those sections had been stolen in small bunches from the Cyclone and other ranches along the Llano. Billy had spent all late fall and early winter last year cold-branding Cyclone cattle, so there would be plenty of unmarked beef to brush-pop. Before long they would push the cattle down to Mexico, and to the *vaquero*-turned-bandit-turned-politician Juan "Red Beard" Cortinas. Red Beard made a handsome living off stolen Texas cattle. Rafe had sent Jake down some weeks earlier to arrange the deal with Cortinas. Jake, Sligo, and Cajun had all sold their guns to Cortinas during the Occupation years, when things were too hot for them in Texas.

"Seems to me like there's easier ways to make a dishonest dollar," Hainey lamented.

Cajun reached down and clapped the irascible brand artist between the shoulder blades.

"You'll feel different with the wages of sin heavy in your pockets. At ten dollars a head, your share will be almost fifteen hundred. Now, in my opinion, that's not bad for nine months' work. You'd have to take up robbing banks to do so well, and that is a lot more dangerous than this."

"Oh, you don't think rustling is hazardous?" Hainey chided. "I'm inclined to disagree. We're just lucky we ain't been caught yet."

"We play with fair odds," replied Cajun temperately. "Take a look at those cows over there. Once they've been marked, who's to say they don't belong to Martin Short? Who's to say we don't work for Martin Short?"

Hainey's tone dripped with sarcasm. "And what would honest cowboys like us be doing hiding out in the guts of this here backbone ridge, so far from the Frio and home range?"

Billy grew weary of the debate. "Look. I need a horse. And some cartridges."

Cajun nodded at the string of horses. As a precaution, they all wore the Bar Buckle brand. There were five in all, one each for Sligo, Hainey, and Landon, and two extras for packing or remount.

"Take that coyote dun," he suggested. "She can bite the breeze. But we don't have a spare hull."

"I'll make do." Billy had no intention of telling them that he planned to backtrack and retrieve his gear. He didn't want to admit that he had been too weak to carry his tack a few miles. Better to leave them with the idea that McKeller had not only put him afoot but also taken his rigging. "I'll fix up a hackamore if somebody has the rope."

"Where you goin' off to?" Hainey wanted to know. "Why don't you stay here and lend a hand?"

Billy glared out of his one good eye, waiting for Hainey to pitch in about his rights. "I'm gonna go pay a call on my pa, if it's all the same to you," he said.

"You goin' to town?" asked Landon dumbly.

"I reckon, as that is where Pa stays," replied Billy dryly.

"A real friend would spend a cartwheel on a bottle of whiskey and bring it back to his pards," Hainey remarked, suddenly deferential.

"Anything else?"

Hainey scratched his crotch, leered. "One of them soiled doves in Llano town, if you can bring her out here."

Cajun said, "When you get to Mexico you'll be able to afford a full-time whore."

"A lot can happen between then and now," growled the rewrite man.

CHAPTER THIRTEEN

"*E-haits-ma.*"

Lone Dog, lost in frowning thought, jumped.

"You look troubled, good friend," observed Bow String, sitting on his heels before him.

"I am only thinking." With a start Lone Dog became aware that the afternoon was fast waning. The shift of deepening shadows alerted him to this. Briefly the world lost its rich colors. The blue of the sky faded to silver. The limbs and the trunks of the deadfall were white as bones bleached by the sun. The rock that surrounded them was gray, the creek the color of iron ore, the lengthening shadows a charcoal shade. The men and horses stood out in sharp relief against this colorless backdrop.

"She Walks Softly?" asked Bow String.

Lone Dog flinched at the sound of his woman's name. "No," he said gruffly. "Tonight I return to the stone lodge."

Bow String was startled. "You go alone?"

Lone Dog nodded. "One, cloaked in *to-oh-kar-no*, may be able to get close enough." And he told his friend of the *acequia* route.

Bow String thought it over, then said, resolutely, "I will go."

"No. If I fail you must lead the others. Perhaps you should have done so all along."

"You have brought us farther than I could have. I only see things as they are. You see them as they might be. Back there, I saw only a small herd of cattle. You saw a way to encourage us and hurt the *tosi-tivo.*"

"It was a waste of arrows. Worse, it will tell the whites where we are. And we should not have tried to kill the one you call Long Blue Coat. We should not have killed the one before. I have made many mistakes."

Bow String exhaled sharply, confused, and feeling sorry for Lone Dog. "Let me go tonight," he pleaded.

"You only want the glory of killing Wolfhunter for yourself."

Lone Dog was joking, and they grinned at each other.

"No," said Bow String. "But if I fail, you will be alive to lead the others. Then there will still be a chance."

Lone Dog shook his head, unyielding in his resolve. It was his plan. He would go. Not for glory, but because in his heart he believed that they would all fail in this impossible task Crooked Neck, the shaman, had set for them. And he did not feel strong enough to carry the burden of sending his closest friend to almost certain death. He had sent Watchful Fox to *his* death; that mistake haunted him enough.

Something arched through the air above the creek, to splash in the shallows between the sandbars, down among the horses, which spooked and scattered.

Every warrior was on his feet in an instant. Lone Dog had no idea what the object was—it came so unexpectedly that he had not the time for a good look.

He and Bow String were closer than the rest—they reached the shallows first. The light was fading quickly and Bow String knelt for a closer look. Then he jumped backward with a cry, bumping into Lone Dog and knocking him off balance.

It was the severed head of Black Tongue.

Black Tongue's bulging eyes stared up through a veil of wet black hair. Dark ribbons of blood drifted away in the water from the neck stump.

Lone Dog tore his gaze from this grisly sight and looked up to see Wolfhunter standing on the rim of the stony embankment across the creek. With his Colt Model 1860 revolver in one hand and a bloody knife in the other, Wolfhunter was grinning down at them.

A second later flame spurt from the barrel of the Colt. Lone Dog leaped to one side, fell, rolled, and came up running for his weapons. The other Penateka were also scrambling. First weapons, then cover. But there was no cover from Wolfhunter's vantage point. Nauseated, Lone Dog knew that he had made yet another mistake. It would be his last, for Wolfhunter was going to kill them all, and laugh while he did it. Lone Dog knew fear as he had never known it. Wolfhunter was a demon. No normal man could have slipped up on Black Tongue and killed him without making a sound, and then, with such bloody delight, decapitated his victim. We are all dead men, thought Lone Dog, diving for his bow and quiver of arrows.

He heard three quick gunshots, followed by two more spaced apart, and then the hideous scream of a horse mortally wounded, followed by violent splashing. Snatching an arrow from the quiver, Lone Dog fit shaft to bowstring even as he spun, dropping to one knee to provide a smaller target.

What he saw stunned him.

Wolfhunter was killing their horses!

Four lay dead in the creek. A fifth was thrashing in its death throes. The last war pony was galloping upstream, past the dead-fall. Wolfhunter drew a bead; with his sixth shot he killed the sixth horse—like all the rest, a head shot.

Lone Dog was so proficient with bow and arrow, that he did not need to take aim. He knew immediately the angle, the distance, and where Wolfhunter was standing, and he let fly the arrow before visually fixing on the target. He had a second arrow notched before the first reached the rimrock.

But Wolfhunter had vanished. The arrow pierced only a gray drift of gunsmoke.

For a moment no one moved, crouched in the gravel of the creek bank, arrows or lances ready. No one spoke, either. They merely waited for their nemesis to reappear. Despite his fear, Lone Dog was infuriated by the slaughter of their war ponies. He knew that the others felt the same. To a Comanche brave, his war pony was more than just a beast of burden that could carry him from one place to another. It was his trusted friend, faithful companion. A warrior cared for and cherished it as much as he did his squaw.

Lone Dog had time to wonder if Wolfhunter had gone away. Part of him hoped so, and he reproached this part. Yet a man could not help but fear Wolfhunter. Lone Dog wished that he had a rifle in his hands rather than a bow and arrow. Eye That Kills had been right all along.

They heard the hammering beat of a galloping horse beyond the deadfall, and swung their weapons that way as a wild-eyed steeldust exploded into view, running down the creek, snorting as it leapt over the carcass of the last pony killed by Wolfhunter. Ironically, not one of the Penateka even contemplated killing the steeldust. Lone Dog, for one, knew this was Wolfhunter's horse. It carried an empty saddle on its back, and an empty saddle equaled an opportunity for escape.

A bloodcurdling cry broke their thoughts as Geddes reappeared on the opposite rim. Running full tilt, he launched himself over the edge. Distracted by the arrival of the steeldust, not one of the five warriors got an arrow in flight before Wolfhunter dropped feet-first into the middle of the creek. A geyser of water erupted. Several arrows flew harmlessly through it.

Eye That Kills lunged forward into the stream, racing across the sandbars, leaping over the carcass of a horse, his lance raised over his head, a savage war cry bursting from his lips. Wolfhunter rose from the water and closed swiftly. He emerged some distance from where he had plunged into the creek, and Eye That Kills collided with him, running into Wolfhunter's long knife and driving the lance downward too late. The warrior's momentum carried him up onto Wolfhunter's shoulder, for Wolfhunter had come in low. His knife smote Eye That Kills just below the sternum. The blade slipped in to the hilt and Wolfhunter bent his wrist to turn it upward, piercing heart and lung. Eye That Kills died almost instantly, vomiting blood all over Wolfhunter's back with his final convulsion. With a feral snarl Wolfhunter charged forward, the dead warrior's body a shield.

Two Hatchets sprang at the steeldust as it thundered by, dropping his bow and arrow to have both hands free. The horse jackknifed and snapped at him. Two Hatchets, avoiding the blunt teeth, stumbled and fell. The steeldust reared and came down with flailing hooves. Two Hatchets tried to scramble out of the way. A hoof caught him high in the back and the impact drove him into the ground.

Bow String rose from his crouch, drawing his namesake to his cheek and aiming at what little he could see of Wolfhunter behind the corpse of Eye That Kills. Hearing the clatter of loose shale and a low, menacing growl, Lone Dog turned to see a yellow beast spring from the lip of the overhang at Bow String. Lone Dog cried out a warning. Too late. The weight of the coyote dog bore Bow String down. He rolled, clawing for the knife in his belt sheath. The coyote dog sprang forward again. Bow String lifted his arms to fend off the attack, but not quickly enough. The coyote dog slipped through the warrior's defenses and closed its jaws around Bow String's throat. Blood spewed in every direction as fangs ripped open arteries. Bow String's body arched, slammed down, arched again. The beast's entire body shuddered as it worried at the neck until flesh and muscle tore away. The dog fell back, shreds of flesh dangling from its scarlet rictus. Then it struck again, this time at one of Bow String's flailing arms.

Shrieking like a madman, Lone Dog turned away from this horrible scene and threw himself at Wolfhunter. Discarding the bow, he drew his knife. With a mighty heave Wolfhunter shrugged the body of Eye That Kills into Lone Dog's onslaught. Lone Dog fell, twisted out from under the corpse, and sprang to his feet, lashing out with the knife. Wolfhunter parried with his own belduque. Steel rang against steel. Wolfhunter lunged and punched Lone Dog squarely in the face, knocking out teeth. Again Lone Dog fell, stunned by the blow, choking on his own blood. He could *feel* Wolfhunter closing in for the kill. In wild panic he rolled and thrust his knife upward.

Wolfhunter easily avoided Lone Dog's blind stroke. He caught the Penateka's knife arm at the wrist with his left hand and with the blade in his right cut Lone Dog's forearm to the bone. Lone Dog's knife fell from his useless hand, but he made no outcry. Wolfhunter twisted the arm just so, forcing Lone Dog over onto his belly. Pressing the warrior's shoulder down with one foot, Wolfhunter twisted the arm some more until it popped right out of its socket. Lone Dog's head snapped back, but still he made no sound.

"You're a proud one," Wolfhunter complimented him. "I believe I'll take your scalp, just to remember you by."

Twenty feet away, He Finds Water loosed an arrow that struck Wolfhunter in the back, just below the left collarbone. Had Wolfhunter not been in the process of bending down, the shaft would have pierced his heart. Wolfhunter stiffened, glanced down at the blood-smeared point jutting out of his shoulder. Releasing Lone Dog, he turned to face He Finds Water.

He Finds Water drew another arrow from his quiver and notched it—one swift and fluid motion, almost quicker than the eye—almost quicker than the smooth overhand throw Wolfhunter made.

When Wolfhunter reached him, He Finds Water had dropped his bow and fallen to his knees. He had both hands on the bone handle of the knife in his chest. Reaching down, Wolfhunter pried loose the warrior's grip, grasped the pommel himself, and lifted in one sharp motion. With a hoarse, rattling gasp, He Finds Water stood up. His face close to the Penateka's, Wolfhunter gathered up a handful of the Comanche's warshirt; holding He Finds Water upright in this way, he extracted the knife. A dark stain spread across the front of the warrior's shirt. His legs buckled, but Wolfhunter effortlessly kept him standing—long enough to drive the ten-inch blade of his knife straight up through the underside of He Finds Water's jaw. The point emerged through the warrior's right eye. He died instantly. But Wolfhunter would not let him drop. He twisted the knife a little. A river of blood poured out of the dead man's clamped-shut mouth and the pierced eyesocket, drenching Wolfhunter's arm to the elbow.

"You put the hurt on me, buck," scolded Wolfhunter, his tone stern but soft. "Still, I'm obliged that you sent the arrow clean through. It's a mite easier to get out when the point ain't lodged inside."

He was distracted from this one-way conversation by the sight of Two Hatchets scurrying on hands and knees in an attempt to escape Crowbait's relentless wrath. Wolfhunter jerked his knife free and shoved the carcass of He Finds Water away. Walking over, he sheathed his knife and picked up a convenient lance. A sharp gesture sent Crowbait away. Two Hatchets looked around to see this blood-splattered, creek-drenched killer coming for him. He got to his feet and forced himself to look into Wolfhunter's eyes with unflinching defiance. Wolfhunter, smiling pleasantly, nodded silent approval—before driving the lance clean through the Comanche's gut.

Drawing a long breath, Wolfhunter relaxed. He looked around. The coyote dog was standing over Bow String's remains, panting, waiting hopefully for the Penateka to spasm again. But Bow String was long past his death throes. Only when he saw Lone Dog stumbling like a drunkard toward the deadfall tangle did Wolfhunter remember the scalp he had pledged to take. He had forgotten all about Lone Dog.

"I'm getting senile," he lamented, and drew his Colt revolver. "At least," he mused, "I remembered to load this ol' thumb-buster before I took my swim."

He was bringing the gun up to bear when the coughing spell ambushed him, more violent than ever. Lungs burning, gasping for breath, the spasms sending pain washing through him, he got off one shot before falling to his hands and knees, and knew absolutely that the shot was wild.

A few minutes later the spell had passed. He sat up, and took some time to catch his breath, glancing with idle curiosity at the blood he had spit up on the gravel. The wounded Penateka was no longer in sight, having crawled deep into the deadfall. Wolfhunter sent a couple of shots clipping through the dense lace of limbs and branches, then stopped wasting his ammunition.

Some minutes more and he was on his feet. He walked unsteadily to where the coyote dog was pawing Bow String's outflung arm.

"You ain't had enough exercise?" asked Wolfhunter sarcastically. "Are you blind, or just ignorant? You didn't even see the one that got away, did you, you worthless mongrel bitch."

The dog just growled at him.

Shaking his head, Wolfhunter sat on a nearby rock and examined the arrow he was carrying in his shoulder. He broke off the point, but reaching over the left shoulder with his right hand, he soon discovered that he could not draw the shaft straight out backwards.

"Well," he muttered, disgusted. "This is damned inconvenient."

It was necessary to use the knife to saw away at the shaft where it entered his back. The cut made, it was simply a matter of drawing the rest of the arrow out from the front. Tossing the shaft away, he stood up and motioned for Crowbait to come.

As an afterthought he took four scalps; he could not find the severed head of the sentry. It must have washed on down the creek. Putting the scalps under his shirt, he picked up a lance and mounted the steeldust.

The sun had left the sky. The first stars glimmered weakly overhead. The uncertain twilight gathered thickly in the ravine as Wolfhunter rode away. The surefooted gray galloped right up the middle of the creek, past the deadfall. Wolfhunter didn't even glance that way. He didn't much care if the wounded Comanche lived or died.

Chapter Fourteen

In the gray twilight Billy Yellen rode into Llano. The town was backed up against a shallow stretch of the river with the same name. There was a scattering of small homes on the cactus-flat outskirts, but most of Llano was concentrated on both sides of a wide street scored with wagon-wheel ruts. The buildings were constructed for the most part of pickets and fieldstone, with a dash of sunwarped clapboard. Llano had more than its fair share of saloons, for the town's primary function was the serving of the area's ranch hands. The founding fathers had entertained great expectations for the future of their community. The Spanish had mined gold and silver in the vicinity. There were legends of lost mines concealing tremendous wealth. But Llano's mining ventures had produced more broken dreams than promising assays. And since the remote town was buried deep in rough country that was prime turf for hardcases, it soon acquired a notorious reputation.

It was Saturday sundown, still early, but already a smoky din presided in the watering holes. Yellow lamplight blazed in the windows, and loud voices spilled out through the doorways. Billy checked the coyote dun at a tie rail fronting an establishment called the White Elephant. Llano had been scarcely a year old when his father, forsaking a hardscrabble existence on the homestead, had moved in to set up shop. The White Elephant was by no means the best saloon in Llano, and Rafe Yellen did drink up a fair share of the merchandise, but it had survived for twenty years. Rafe Yellen had taken to peddling watered-down red-eye as a fish took to water.

"Only other thing I was ever any good at was huntin' wolves," Rafe had told his youngest boy on more than one occasion. "Runnin' a saloon fits me like a new pair of britches, and it's a damned sight easier than trackin' lobos. 'Sides, me and a few others like Bob Feagan and Wolfhunter Geddes done cleaned those critters out of these parts faster than a cowboy can lose money."

At first Billy had wondered why his father had chosen the White Elephant for a name. Rafe had never provided a satisfactory answer, but later Jake had informed his brother that one of Fort Worth's better known saloons was called the White Elephant. Rafe had patronized that place on his only trip to Fort Worth, and later borrowed the name. That hadn't surprised Billy. Yellens were forever borrowing things.

Very conscious of his damaged appearance, Billy sauntered through the batwings with an extra measure of swagger. He went to the corner of the plank bar and surveyed the long narrow room while he waited for the barkeep to notice him. The clientele consisted of three cowboys, one of Llano's two full-time town drunks, a confidence man with pomade-slick hair and a checked suit operating a shell game, and a dirty barefoot boy playing on a Jew's harp for tips.

Billy paid particular attention to the cowboys. He didn't know any of them, and none of the horses tied up out front had worn the Diamond C brand. Not that he expected to run into any Cyclone hands, since Cale McKeller had laid down the law about visits to town. But then he decided that it really didn't matter. He was no longer in McKeller's employ, and so answerable to no one.

Except his father. Billy scowled. Coming in to tell Rafe that he had been fired by McKeller was hard. Rafe was not famous for his understanding nature. But failure to do so promptly would lead to far worse consequences.

The barkeep wandered over, toweling a shotglass. His name was Burley Evans, a hirsute and heavyset character who had a talent for whiskey water-down and using his fists on rowdy cowboys. It was rumored that Burley was wanted for horse-stealing and murder in Kansas or Missouri, or both.

Burley looked at Billy's face and smirked.

"If you won that fight I'd hate to see the other feller," he said.

Billy glowered and drew himself up. "You got any real whiskey back there? Last time you gave me aged-in-the-gullet snakehead. It ate a hole in my stomach."

"Oh, we got the best whiskey in town. Ask anybody."

"Just fetch me a shot. If it's kerosene I'll douse you with it and strike a match."

"You didn't get *all* the stuffing knocked out of you, I see. Too bad." He left the clean shotglass on the bar and went to fetch a bottle.

Billy didn't give two hoots for Burley Evans. Like Hainey, Burley was one of Rafe's old drinking buddies, and Burley seemed to think he could treat Billy with the disrespect due a snot-nosed kid.

There were two rooms in the rear. One was Rafe Yellen's quarters. Out of the other now emerged another cowboy. His cheeks were flushed and he walked a little stiff-legged. He joined another range hand and they exchanged whispers, and then burst into bawdy laughter. When the girl came out of the room, though, they stopped laughing. She roamed the length of the saloon, parading her wares, in search of another man with money in his pocket and an itch that needed scratching.

Her name was Calico Anne. She was sixteen. Thanks to hard times and harder living she looked twice that age. Her dull yellow hair was mouse-brown at the roots, and she was plain, not at all pretty. No amount of rouge and powder could change that. And no bright-hued satin and silk could hide the fact that she was thin and poorly postured. There was a livid purple bruise around her left eye.

"Howdy, Billy," she said tentatively. "What happened to you?"

Billy resisted the urge to blacken her other eye.

"Leave me alone," he sulked.

The apron returned, splashed whiskey into the shotglass, and looked back and forth at Billy and Calico Anne, still smirking.

"You two have a lot in common," remarked Burley.

"Mind your own business," snapped Billy.

"Want I should tell your pa you've dropped in?"

"I'll tell him when I'm good and ready."

"Oh, excuse me, Mister Yellen." Burley went away, smirking even more.

"Billy, don't be mad at me," pleaded Calico Anne pitifully.

"I ain't mad," snarled Billy. "But on account of you I lost my job."

"I didn't tell nobody. But you made such a scene when you left out of here that Burley knew what had happened. He told your pa. I didn't."

Billy knocked the raw liquor back in two slings, hissed through clenched teeth at the whiskey's fire. "It don't matter now. Just let me alone or I'll do it again, and do a better job of it, too."

That hurt Calico Anne. For reasons she could hardly explain, she had a soft spot in her for Billy Yellen. A lot of men had been nicer to her, had treated her better. Billy's brother Jake for one, and even old Rafe himself. No, Billy was rough with her. She sensed that it made him feel more like a man. But she didn't mind. It didn't change the way she felt about him. She had never told on him. But last time he had marked her where she could not hide the evidence. Even that failed to persuade her to stay away from him.

"You're wearing the scarf I knitted for you, Billy. I'm glad."

"I wear it 'cause it's warm. Not 'cause you made it. And whoever heard of a whore doing such a thing, anyway?" Billy snorted. Secretly, though, he was fond of the black wool muffler. It was the only gift he had ever received.

"Come on, Billy. Let's go back to my room."

Billy's hands curled into fists on the bar. "I said leave me alone. Get the hell away from me, you slut."

She took a backward step. Billy brushed roughly by her, jostling her, and walked to the door that led to Rafe Yellen's room. He rapped on it with his knuckles.

Rafe Yellen opened the door. He was a big-bellied man with jowls and a white film over his left eye. His brown hair, streaked with silver, was thinning at the top and long at the back, straggling to his shoulders. He wore suspender trousers and no shirt, just the top of soiled longhandles sorely in need of mending. That was Rafe's way. Unconcerned with personal appearance, he wore his clothes until they fell off him.

"Hey, Pa," said Billy.

Rafe lashed out, snatching Billy up by the lapels of his gray longcoat and jerking him into the room. Spinning, he slammed Billy backwards on top of an old, battered desk. Holding Billy down with his left hand, Rafe reached for a nearly empty bottle of Baltimore Rye, grabbing it by the neck with his right hand. He smashed the bottle against the edge of the desk, then brought the jagged rim of the neck within an inch of Billy's eyes.

"I don't appreciate you markin' up Calico Anne, boy," growled Rafe.

"You used to do the same to Ma, dammit," said Billy, angered by his own fear. His father was a physically imposing man, with brutality and malice lurking just beneath the surface. "Now let me up, you sonuvabitch."

Rafe heard the snicker of a gun's hammer pulled back, and looked down between them. Billy hadn't drawn the Dance revolver, just twisted the holster so that the .44 was aimed at Rafe's groin.

Chuckling, Rafe put on an untrustworthy smile. "You wouldn't shoot your own pa, would you, Billy boy?"

"I'm no more likely to than you are to cut me open with that bottle."

Letting go of Billy, Rafe stepped back. He grinned at a man slouched in a chair over by the narrow bunk where Rafe slept off his daily drunk. "I declare, he's crazy mean, ain't he?"

"Runs in the blood," drawled the other.

Billy straightened and looked over at the seated man, surprised and pleased.

"Jake! You're back!"

"Quick, too," said Jake Yellen. "What happened to you, little brother?"

The question was a dose of cold water on Billy's delight at the return of the older brother he idolized. Jake was slim and compact. And like Billy, he had inherited their mother's yellow hair. He kept it close-cropped. A dragoon mustache draped his thick lips. His eyes were the small, clever eyes of a ferret. He carefully nurtured an I-don't-give-a-damn attitude, but a closer look revealed someone who kept his grudges in a hip pocket. He wore a black frock coat, leather vest, and trousers tucked into cavalry boots, and carried a Beal's Army Model .44, converted, on his hip.

"I had a run-in with Cale McKeller." Billy told them the same story he had given the boys at the sinkhole, a story of a courageous fight against impossible odds.

Red-faced, Rafe heard him out, then swore and hurled what was left of the bottle against the wall. It shattered, and in spite of being braced for more violence, Billy jumped.

"That damn well scotches things," growled Rafe savagely.

"It's not my fault," Billy protested. "You're the one told me to slip into town once a week, to tell you how things were going. McKeller just happened to find out I was here, is all. It had nothing to do with Calico Anne."

"The hell it didn't." Rafe slumped heavily into the chair behind the desk. Behind him was a window with a square of oilskin nailed over it. This kept the room dark and private. A lighted kerosene lamp on the desk corner illuminated the dingy room. Rafe took a cheroot from a tin cup, fired a lucifer with a blackened thumbnail, and lit up, looking morosely at his youngest. "It ain't hard to slip in and out of this town without being noticed. It was your big production with that whore that gave you away. Lucky for you I wasn't here at the time. I'd've beat hell out of you."

"What's done is done," Jake offered. "It don't much matter now."

Rafe glowered at him. "You just come back from tellin' Redbeard we'd have him a thousand head in a month's time. There are enough cold-branded cattle on the Cyclone west range to fill the bill. Only now it's gonna be a damned sight harder gettin' to them."

"Let's take what we got and call it quits," Jake suggested. "I bet we can rustle up a couple more hundred on the road to Mexico."

"Hainey don't like the idea of pushing the cattle all the way down to Mexico," Billy mentioned. "He thinks it would be safer and quicker just takin' 'em north to the Nations."

"Those damned agency men are crooks," complained Rafe. "They won't pay near as well as Cheno Cortinas. It's not that ol' Redbeard *needs* more cattle. He just hates Texans something fierce, and likes nothing better than taking their stock from them."

"Besides," said Jake, "we cut a deal with him."

"So? Pa always says deals are made to be broken."

"Not with Juan 'Cheno' Cortinas," Jake said, smiling.

"What's so special about him?"

Jake leaned forward in the chair, elbows on knees. "Well, I'll tell you, little brother. Cheno was born into a wealthy ranching family down Coahuila way. He grew up liking saloons more than saddles, though, and frequented the sour-mash mills in Brownsville. One day the city marshal began to abuse a drunken greaser who worked for the Cortinas family. Cheno shot and killed the badge-toter. Little later, he gathered up some tough hombres and captured Brownsville, lock, stock, and whiskey barrel. They killed a bunch of folks. The Rangers went after them, but Cheno and his men sent the Rangers back across the river with their tails good and tucked. All the Mexicans think he's some big hero for standing up against the gringos and protecting the poor peasants. Now he's the governor-general of Coahuila. He also runs the biggest spread down there. And every cow that carries his brand is stolen from Texas. Ol' Cheno wouldn't have it any other way. And he will not abide somebody welshing on a deal. I reckon if I went all the way up to the Absaroka I wouldn't feel safe, if we was to cross Cheno Cortinas."

"Fine," Billy said, shrugging, adopting Jake's apathetic attitude. "It makes me no never-mind. We'll go to Mexico."

"Damn right you will," Rafe barked. "And if Hainey don't like it, we'll just have to curl his toes, permanent."

"When do we go?"

"The sooner the better," Rafe replied. "There's talk that the Association may hire stock detectives. That's just a polite name for hired killer."

"What do we do once we deliver the cattle to Cortinas?" asked Billy.

"We'll stay at Redbeard's hacienda for a few months," answered Jake.

"Until I send for you," Rafe added. "Give me time to set up somewheres else. I been thinking about Goliad, or mebbe Refugio. Then we'll start all over again."

Billy took a deep breath. "Well, reckon I'll get back. Got to cross Cyclone land to get there, and I don't care to do it in broad daylight. McKeller or one of his men may shoot me from ambush next time and be done with it. You comin', Jake?"

Jake's smile was lazy and wanton. "You and the boys go on ahead and push that last bunch to the Frio. Wait for me at the Bar Buckle. I'll be along in a day or two. It's been a long ride from the border. All I had down there was tequila and those brown-eyed hot tamales. I got me a strong hankering for some American sour-mash and a white woman." He grinned at Rafe.

Rafe chuckled. "I hope that's all you got down there, boy. I don't want Annie to catch no furrin disease."

They laughed together, then. Their laughter, and Jake's intentions, bothered Billy. He didn't know why exactly. It had something to do with Calico Anne. He just wanted to get out of there, fast.

He left with their laughter ringing in his ears. And when Calico Anne came up and touched his arm as he crossed the saloon, he shook loose savagely and hurried on into the deepening night.

Chapter Fifteen

Lone Dog lay concealed in the deadfall for some time. He did not know how long, exactly, and he did not care. His was a world of pain. He could do nothing about his dislocated shoulder, but he'd cut one of the pieces of long fringe from his warshirt and used it as a tourniquet to staunch the flow of blood from his forearm wound.

All the while he wondered why he bothered. Several times he felt the hot wash of salty tears sting his eyes, brought on by failure, futility, and frustration. By comparison, the physical pain he endured was nothing.

The night prior to moonrise was very dark. He was suspended somewhere between heaven and earth in the thickly interwoven skeletons of trees. He could hear the creek rushing around him, but he knew not which way it rushed. He thought to reach down through the tangled branches, hoping to touch the water and feel the direction of the current, but he could not reach far enough.

The gentle and lulling sound of the creek reminded him of She Walks Softly. He thought that it must be because his happiest moments had been accompanied by that sound—all creeks sang the same gentle song. The happiest moments, of course, were when he lay in her warm embrace, knowing rare contentment. The Penateka usually pitched their camp along a watercourse; the camp itself would often stretch for more than a mile along one or both banks, and all the lodges would be raised quite close to the stream.

She Walks Softly. He had always loved her. For him there had been no other. Even before the Giveaway Dance conducted in his honor after his first success on the warpath—the celebration which marked the beginning of his adulthood, and before which no young man could hope to marry—Lone Dog and She Walks Softly had been lovers. She Walks Softly would often slip into his lodge, and countless times they had arranged clandestine meetings, for it was unacceptable for young unmarried couples to be seen too frequently in public together.

The day following his Giveaway Dance, Lone Dog had dispatched Bow String, his intermediary, to She Walks Softly's father, bearing Lone Dog's gift of five fine horses he himself had stolen. On the same day these horses were seen in the herd belonging to She Walks Softly's father. This signified permission to marry.

Rousing himself, Lone Dog realized that moonlight was filtering down through the thick latticework of limbs and branches above him. He looked up into the face of the Moon Mother, up through the bones of dead trees that almost blotted out the huge yellow orb.

Despondent, Lone Dog sighed. "Moon Mother," he whispered, "can you see her from there?"

He thought of all the miles between him and She Walks Softly, and sank deeper into despair. Closing his eyes, he saw her face with painful clarity. She was truly *naivi*, a good-looking young woman. Her eyes, accentuated with red and yellow lines above and below, were stoked with the fire of adoration when they gazed back at him. The red-orange triangle on each dimpled cheek, the smiling lips that never failed to greet him—he would never see that smile again. Of this he was convinced. All was lost. *He* was lost. The Comanche people were most surely lost. Crooked Neck was a senile old fool. What was all this prattle of great medicine? The ravings of an aging man lost in the revelry of proud and shining days long gone. Seven young warriors had left the camp of the Penateka seeking honor and glory. Six had found only death. What glory, Lone Dog wondered bitterly, did one find dying while carrying out a fool's errand?

Clumsily, Lone Dog worked his way free of the deadfall. He had crawled deep into it to escape death, with stark terror turning his blood into ice. Many times while extricating himself, his dislocated shoulder was jarred or prodded by protruding branches, and he would moan through clenched teeth, biting down on the agony, and squeeze his eyes shut against the queasy dance of lights.

Wolfhunter could be lying in wait for him, having feigned departure. But Lone Dog found himself unafraid. It seemed he had reached his limit for fear. And since he was certain that he would never see She Walks Softly again, he had even misplaced his passion for life.

Once clear of the deadfall, Lone Dog lay in the gravel, face down, exhausted. He thought he could hear the blood of his slain brothers trickling through the gravel. Lifting his head with a vast weariness, he looked at the dark, forever-still shapes strewn across the moon-washed rincon. Then he laid his head down and closed his eyes and remembered Wolfhunter's blood, too, had stained this gravel. He had glanced back through the deadfall after the first bullet had clipped through the brittle wood high above his head, and he had seen Wolfhunter fall and hack up blood. And he remembered seeing the old stains of blood at the cold camps of the man they had tracked so far across the *llano*.

Wolfhunter was just a man. And he was dying.

This realization carried with it a great irony.

"*E-haits-ma.*"

Lone Dog heard the voice of Bow String with startling clarity. He opened his eyes, but did not have the strength to raise his head.

"I'm sorry, my good friend," he mumbled, thick-tongued.

"*E-haits-ma.*"

Lone Dog found the strength, and looked up.

He could see Bow String standing there, ten paces away. Bow String's face was covered with blood from the scalping. His throat was a terrible open wound. His right arm had been savaged into pulp, exposing bone as white as the deadfall wood. His war shirt and leggins were soaked with blood.

Comanches had no fear of ghosts, and Lone Dog was not alarmed by the apparition, for apparition he knew it to be. There was no doubt in his mind that Bow String was dead.

"*Tah-mah*," murmured Lone Dog, somewhere between laughter and tears, "Wolfhunter is dying. We have been chasing a dead man."

"He scalped us," said Bow String. "Our souls are lost forever. *Kadih* cannot find us."

Lone Dog nodded. The Afterworld was, they said, much like this world, but without war and sorrow and hardship of any kind. Everyone was eternally young. There was game in abundance, and no enemies to be anxious about. The rivers ran pure and the plains were free. All who died went to this Afterworld—except those who were strangled, or died in the dark, or drowned, or were scalped.

"I am sorry," repeated Lone Dog, stricken with pity for Bow String's lost soul. There was nothing else he could think to say.

"What will you do?" asked Bow String sympathetically. In the darkness Lone Dog could not see the ghost's lips move, but the voice rang clearly in his mind.

Lone Dog pushed himself up with his one good arm and struggled to his feet. It hardly seemed proper, lying there feeling sorry for himself while Bow String's soul wandered lost between this world and the next.

"What would you have me do?"

"What do you *want* to do?"

"I am so far from home. I would see She Walks Softly once more."

"You have given your word. You would be without honor if you went back now."

"I know," Lone Dog sobbed wretchedly.

"You must kill Wolfhunter."

"What difference will it make?"

"You will see, when the time comes. Our Sure Enough Father has spared you for a reason. Go to the cave of our fathers. You will find Wolfhunter nearby."

Lone Dog opened his eyes. He lay face down in the gravel of the creek bank. But had he not been standing? He looked up sharply. Had he slept, and dreamed the visit by the ghost of Bow String? No spirit stood before him now.

Pushing up with his one good arm, he struggled to his feet. He stumbled like a newborn foal to the nearest body. It was that of Two Hatchets, run through with the lance. He could not bring himself to remove the lance, and went on until he found the weapons of Eye That Kills. He knew that they had once belonged to Eye That Kills by his mark, two blue lightning bolts, on the shafts of the dogwood arrows in the quiver and on the red-painted lance.

With but one good arm, Lone Dog knew there was no point in carrying a bow and arrows. He picked up the lance. The weapon could serve also as a staff for walking. Lone Dog ruefully glanced at the carcasses of the dead geldings in the stream, and contemplated with despair the long, dangerous miles that stretched before him. Even in undamaged condition he could not make good time on foot. But there was nothing else he could do—he could not ride the wind.

He had enough of his wits about him to seek out a pouch of *inapa*, for although he never expected to feel like eating again, he knew his body would need nourishment. And he found a horsehair rope—the one Two Hatchets had tried without success to put on the fighting horse of Long Blue Coat.

Gritting his teeth against the pain each step jolted through his shoulder, Lone Dog waded through the creek, past the deadfall, and out of the rincon death trap he was sorry to have survived. Then, turning back in the opposite direction, he let the stars he knew so well guide him south and west to the caverns where he had been taken as a young boy by his father. It had been a favorite Comanche meeting place for generations. Little used of late, for the whites had discovered it.

But there he would go. Many painful miles away, but he would make it. Perhaps he could sit there among the ashes of his ancestors' cookfires and dream himself into the past. Perhaps there he would comprehend the mystery of his survival, and be better prepared for one last chance at Wolfhunter. Honor, he thought, could be an unhappy burden. But he had given his word to his good friend.

He walked for what seemed a dozen forevers. The moon lazed across the sky. The night felt colder to him than it actually was.

Lone Dog knew well the *brasada*. There were countless ways it could injure or kill a man. And many ways that it could heal. A man struck by a rattlesnake could counteract the venom by stabbing his flesh around the bite with the point of the Spanish dagger. Tea made from boiling the bark of the huisache alleviated internal injuries. The gray-green bush called yarrow, or milfoil, when prepared in a certain way, was thought to cure many serious ailments.

What Lone Dog needed was easy to find. The prickly pear was in abundance. Countless times he had to detour around the impenetrable, man-tall stands of the spine-bristled cactus. Now he used his knife to remove one of the pads. Breaking off the inch-long spines, he sliced away the rubbery green skin to get to the moist and fibrous pulp inside. Into this he sprinkled a handful of dry dirt. Using the pommel of his knife, he pounded this into a paste, and applied the poultice to his wound.

He walked on, his legs and feet complaining about such unaccustomed labor. Comanche boys literally learned to ride before they could crawl. Often he stumbled over a stone or hedgehog cactus lurking in the clumps of grass, catching himself with the lance, afraid that if he fell down he would be too weary to get back up again. He frequently consulted the slowly revolving map of the stars to get his bearings, for it was impossible to travel anything remotely resembling a straight line through this country. Sometimes he would be lured down an apparent trail through broad fields of *chaparro prieto*, only to find a dead end and have to retrace his steps and seek a long way around.

Moonset darkened the endless night. Lone Dog came upon a little stream trickling through a rocky draw, and paused to drink and try, without enthusiasm, to consume a strip of jerky. His punished body clamored for sleep, but Lone Dog resolved to push on. Only a few moments to rest. Starlight was sufficient to travel by. His body stung with the pinprick pain of dozens of thorn punctures. Almost every plant in the *monte* was armed. Lone Dog had skinned many brush-country deer, and always the inner side of the hide would be thick with imbedded thorns lying horizontal. The same, he mused, might be found on the underside of the skin of a man who lived out his years in the *brasada*.

As he rested against a limestone ledge, his eyelids grew heavy, and Lone Dog fought a losing battle. Rationalizing defeat, he told himself, "I will rest my eyes for only a minute or two."

When he opened them again it was morning.

As soon as he stumbled out from under the stunted trees lining the creek he saw the buzzards, at least a dozen of them, circling low in the sky to the west-southwest. He forced himself onward. Within an hour he was crouched in the brush that grew thickly on the slopes that enclosed the bottomland where he and his brothers had slaughtered the longhorns only a day before.

Thick clouds of flies swarmed around the stiff carcasses. There were as many buzzards on the ground, feeding, as there were aloft. The scene depressed Lone Dog, because it had taken him so long just to backtrack this far. The caverns were at least a good day's ride from here. In his condition it would take three sleeps to get there on foot. He wished for a horse to steal.

Five minutes later a white man appeared on the far side of the grassy basin, riding a roan.

Chapter Sixteen

Cale McKeller had been pushing the chestnut since an hour before daybreak, and pushing hard, but when Casa Piedra hove into view across a half mile of gently sloping grass, he touched Beau with his gut-hooks once more, and the horse surged ahead, stretching out its long-legged stride. They left Frisco and Lopez behind, for the *vaqueros* had melted every bit of tallow out of their ponies just keeping up this far. The chestnut's neck, haunches, and muscle-rippling shoulders were covered with froth, and Cale could feel the massive lungs heaving beneath his legs as Beau attacked the distance. Cale had a strong rush of pride and strong affection for the chestnut. This horse would burn the breeze for as long as Cale required it to do so. It would run until its heart ruptured.

Esmerelda emerged into the shade of the gallery as Beau thundered across the hardpack. She took a step back, as it looked for a moment as if Cale's intention was to ride the chestnut right through the front doors and into the house. But Cale checked at the last possible moment and the chestnut locked leg and sat back. A cloud of yellow dust rose up behind, then was borne forward to envelop horse and rider, and out of this dusty veil Cale came at a running dismount.

"Where's Katy?" he rasped. "*Katy!*"

"*Señor* Cale ..."

But he was already past her and making for the doors as Katy came out. He swept her up in his arms, and she gasped at the sudden embrace. Cale carried her off her feet and swung her all the way around, laughing like a fool with sheer relief.

"Cale!" she wheeze, her own startled laughter rimmed with pain. "Cale, darling, you're … you're squeezing the life out of me!"

Released from long and nerve-wracking hours of apprehension, he felt suddenly drained of strength. Exhausted, he set her down and fell back against the wall. Breathing hard, he grinned at her.

"Thank God you're all right," he heaved fervently.

"Of course I'm all right. Why wouldn't I be?"

Cale nodded at the two approaching riders.

"I got to the marking ground sundown yesterday. Lopez was waiting. He'd expected to find Tom there. But Tom was with Frisco, looking for me. The rain had carried away their sign, so he couldn't follow, and none of the boys knew where Frisco and Tom had gone off to. So he just waited. And when he told me Wolfhunter was here …" Cale shook his head. There was no way he could adequately describe the irrational fear that had gripped him when told the news that Wolfhunter Geddes was at Casa Piedra. "I don't know, Katy. He took my mother away last time. Somehow I was afraid I'd come back and find that he had taken you away, too. I was afraid I'd never see you again. I know that sounds crazy."

She started to laugh his fears away, to make light of them, but then glimpsed a vestige of the wild panic glinting in his eyes, and she went to him, curled her arms around his neck, and pressed her body to his, feeling the rapid hammering of his heart.

"Wild horses couldn't drag me away from you, mister," she breathed into his ear. "Much less one sick old man."

Again he wrapped her up in his arms, this time with more gentleness. He was intoxicated by the warmth of her breath on his neck and the sweet scent of her mahogany-brown hair.

Suddenly he heard the heavy fall of boots from inside and swung her away from the door with his left hand, his right hand falling to the butt of the Colt Cavalry on his hip, thumbing the thong off the hammer. It was reflex, and he was no quick-drawn artist, but he made a creditable showing. The gun was drawn and cocked before he identified the man stepping out of Casa Piedra as Dusty Blake, owner of the adjacent Rocking Chair ranch.

Dusty Blake had reflexes too. He jerked backward, fetching up sharply against the door frame, hands leaping away from his sides. Blake was a square-built man, with sandy hair and beard and a florid complexion that went a few shades less florid as he looked down the six-inch barrel of Cale's revolver.

"Jesus Henry Christ!" yelped Blake.

Abashed, Cale relaxed, and leathered the Colt. He heard the beat of hooves behind him as Frisco and Lopez arrived on their mounts.

"I apologize, Dusty. I thought you were somebody else."

"Sure glad I wasn't," gusted Blake, mollified. "I was trying to recall doing something to you that required repayment in lead."

"You're about the only one I can call friend outside the Cyclone." Of all the members of the Association, Blake was the only one who displayed more than average civility to Cale.

Blake shoved his hands into the pockets of a brown broadcloth suit coat that still carried traces of a long trail. He wore a white straw planter's hat and Kelly spurs on benchmade boots.

"Well, if that's your rendition of friendly, I'll remember to come heeled next time." He squinted past Cale at the *vaqueros*. "Howdy, boys."

"*Como esta, Señor Blake?*" asked Frisco, climbing stiffly off his horse. "Hello, Mamma."

Blake turned back to Cale. "You figured I was Wolfhunter Geddes, perhaps? I hope you don't go killing him before I get to meet him. It's none of my business, true enough, and you can tell me so if you think I'm out of line on this, but are you dead set on gunning him because he took off with your mother twenty years ago? That's a heap of water under the bridge."

Cale reflected on his feelings. "I reckon some things die hard, Dusty. I know I shouldn't hold against any man what happened so long ago. Hell, it might not have been all his fault, or even half. My mother went of her own free will. But one fact remains. He was a guest in this house and my mother was a married woman. And even if she'd latched onto him like a cocklebur on a coyote, he shouldn't have taken her away."

Blake nodded. "Some men are stronger-willed than others when it comes to women. And, like I said, it's none of my never-mind. But right or wrong, out here cow-stealing may be a transgression that will get a man killed—wife-stealing isn't. I suppose that may be a sad commentary on frontier ethics."

Cale looked at Katy. "Where is he?"

"He left yesterday, before noon. Didn't say where he was going, or when he'd be back."

Cale grimaced. The fact that Wolfhunter had come back at all put a sour taste in his mouth. "Essie, Lopez said you told him to warn me. Warn me of what?"

"Where is Tomas?" Esmerelda asked, a frantic edge to her tone.

"Whitetail Meadow," replied Frisco, glancing at Cale. "It's a long story."

Esmerelda appeared alarmed. "He is alone?"

"*Sí.* But why do you ask? Is something wrong?"

Esmerelda looked at Katy.

"What's going on that I don't know about and ought to?" demanded Cale.

Solemn, Katy said, "Cale, we need to talk."

Dusty Blake knew when to make an exit. "*Amigo,*" he said to Cale, "I am here before the others for two very simple reasons. One, because I live right across the river and have less miles to travel than the rest. Two, because since my missus passed away I have been deprived of the woman's touch, so to speak, and it pleases me to have an excuse to pass the time of day with two lovely ladies like Katy and Essie. But since there is family business needing some attention here, I'm gonna stray. The two of my men I came with turned our ponies out in your corral and then raised dust hightailing it on into that pueblo out back. I suspect they are strutting a tight circle around those young señoritas, all robin-breasted, so it's high time I go ride herd on them."

"Thanks, Dusty."

They watched him walk the length of the gallery to disappear around the side of the house.

Cale wasted no time asking Katy and Essie the question foremost on his mind. "Why did Wolfhunter come back here?"

Katy looked at Esmerelda. The secret of Tom Samples's past belonged to Essie. It was not her place to make it public. But Esmerelda got a tight-lipped look that Frisco was quick to recognize.

"Mother, you are hiding something," said Frisco. "Tell us."

Suddenly Esmerelda looked on the verge of tears. "Señor Cale," she said, barely above a whisper, "he brought word that your mother is dead."

"I'm sorry, darling," said Katy.

Cale shook his head. "It's all right."

"There is more," said Esmerelda stiffly. "He came to see Tomas. That is why I sent Lopez to the Lodgepole, looking for Tomas. And to warn you."

"What does Tom have to do with Wolfhunter Geddes, Essie?"

She had to struggle to get it out, this secret she had so faithfully kept all these years. "Wolfhunter is Tomas's father."

"What?" Cale was sure he had misunderstood.

"It's true," said Katy. "And Susanna was his mother. Tom is your half brother, Cale."

It was a warm and sun-bright day, freshened by an easy breeze that made music in the tops of the courtyard's Spanish oaks, and cotton-puff clouds drifted lazily across the amethyst sky. So they carried the long dining room table out into the courtyard and, a few hours after Cale's return, the six members of the Llano Cattlemen's Association were seated around it.

Besides Cale and Dusty Blake, the Association roster included Josiah Ocheltree of the Lazy J, Drew Eddings of the EX, Mitch Blevins of the Jackfork, and Ben Mackey of the Two Sixes. Every one of their creased, sun-dark faces carried the tough, hardened reflection of a resolute, ambitious, hard-working, and hard-driving *hombre del campo*. For Cale they were strong reminders of his own father. They were ruthlessly dedicated to their trade, and accustomed to dealing out quick and certain violence upon anyone or anything that threatened their livelihood.

For years the Association had met every other month or so at either the Cyclone or Blake's Rocking Chair, the two spreads most centrally located. In the beginning the town of Llano had been the meeting site, until it became apparent that walls had ears. The Association was its own law—made it and lived by it. Its business was better conducted behind closed doors.

It took Ocheltree and Mackey a day and a half to get to the meetings, and Eddings the best part of two days. Usually they would bring along one cowboy, just to talk to. But with the Comanches on the rampage they had doubled the size of the escorts. They were brave men, but not fools. Most of the hands were out in the gallery, tale-swapping, with Inez serving refreshments.

The ranchers had been well fed, first and foremost. Business was more ably handled on full stomachs, and all of them were sincere in their declarations that the trip was worth every mile just for a meal prepared by Essie and Katy. These two cleared away the table, brought out the bourbon, brandy, sour mash, and tequila, and then made themselves scarce. The Association was a men's club, frontier-style.

"I reckon we all know our most pressing problem," boomed Ocheltree, reaching for a bottle of Tennessee sour mash and pouring himself a generous dollop. He was a big man, with a voice that could drown out a shotgun's full-choke blast. "I hear there is a man name of L.C. Bickers, used to be one of Parker's marshals. He can be reached in Waco. Has a crew of handpicked fellers who know no equal when it comes to reading sign and making smoke. They don't come cheap, but they guarantee results."

"I vote for giving it a try," growled Drew Eddings. He was an unsmiling, puritanical character, hard on himself and all others. Thin as a rail, he had a lantern-jawed face and big, burning eyes. "I wouldn't be surprised if we've lost a thousand head among us to these infernal thieves. One thing is certain: They're crafty sinners who know the lay of the land. They've danced circles around my outriders."

"We used to pay a bounty on wolves," said Mackey. "I still shell out hard money to any of my men that bag a coyote. What's the difference here?"

"Difference is," replied Dusty, "we're talking about hiring professional manhunters to gun down men, not animals."

"That's a distinction that could be argued," said Ocheltree.

"A distinction that the law still makes," Blake persisted calmly.

Ocheltree snorted. "John Law doesn't make the rules around here."

"What about the Rangers?" asked Blake. "I'd pick any Texas Ranger against L.C. Bickers and his shooters. You can't find tougher, better men than the likes of June Peak, John Jones, or J.C. Lonaker."

"Rangers!" barked Ocheltree. "Try to get some, Dusty. They're all down south fighting the Salt War, or west of the Cap Rock trying to make the Panhandle safe for Goodnight and the others. There are too few Rangers and too many problems. Besides, the Rangers sort of expect a man, if he's any kind of man at all, to try and take care of his own problem. Only when it gets too big to handle will they step in and set things aright. Far as I'm concerned"—and he directed a meaningful glance in Cale's direction—"we haven't made a real effort yet to clean these scoundrels out. The long and short of it is that it's up to us."

Cale was hardly listening. He was trying to put into perspective the incredible news that Tom Samples was his half brother.

"We haven't heard from you on this yet, Cale," remarked Blake.

Cale snapped to, and saw that the others were looking down the table at him. Only Dusty's eyes held even a glimmer of friendship. As keenly as ever, he felt like an outsider.

"I won't have men like Bickers and his outfit roaming the Cyclone," he said flatly.

"Well, ain't that fine!" snapped Ocheltree, balling up his fists on the tabletop. "I guess you'd just as soon give these damned nightriders all the cows they can carry away."

"You'll be putting the lives of your own men at risk," Cale argued. "They'll be jumping at shadows, watching their backs. Sooner or later somebody who doesn't deserve it will get killed. Why don't you ask your hands what they think of the notion?"

"What they think doesn't matter," declared Eddings.

"That's right," agreed Ocheltree. "If they don't like it they can draw their pay and haul off."

"It's not just our men," Cale continued. "There are more than a few hardscrabble homesteaders out there. They struggle to stay alive day in and day out. I don't begrudge them a steer or two when they have to do something desperate just to feed their families."

"Those damned plow-chasers are fair game if they take one of my cows," muttered Mackey.

Cale shook his head. "That's real generous of you, Ben."

"I got to look out for my own."

"You don't even know how many hundreds of head wear the Double Six. And you'd kill a man for butchering one old twisthorn so he can feed his hungry kids."

Ocheltree threw his arms up in exasperation. "What is all this talk about feed-offs, anyhow? We're dealing with an organized gang of rustlers, for Christ's sake."

"We're talking about hiring killers and giving them free rein," Cale corrected. "Men like Bickers will bring anybody in over the saddle and nobody will argue the difference. You all know it happens. You'll have to take their word for it that the dead man was a rustler, and you'll have to pay the bounty. Or call them liars." He shook his head again. "I won't be a part of it."

"I'm not surprised," Ocheltree railed. "You don't give a good goddamn for your father's ranch, do you?"

"It's my ranch now," Cale replied with dangerous repose. "You go ahead and call in your hired guns. But if one of 'em sets foot on the Cyclone I'll cut him down."

They stared at him, disbelieving what he had just said.

Into this lull came the lookout's cry.

"Rider coming!"

Cale could look down the length of the table, across the courtyard and through the front room, for the courtyard doors and the front doors were open. He saw a couple of cowboys cross the gallery, peering out across the long grass.

"Wonder who that could be?" asked Blake.

"Lord, I pray those heathen Comanche haven't hit one of our places," Eddings murmured.

The sound of a hard-coming horse reached them. Katy and Esmerelda appeared from the kitchen door to Cale's right. He kept his attention focused on the portion of gallery and hardpack he could see. Then, a drift of dust, and a gravel voice he did not recognize, but which filled him with a curious foreboding all the same.

"Howdy, boys. Don't try friendlyin' up to that dog, now, 'less you've got a hand to spare."

A tall, lean figure, buckskin-clad, filled the front doorway and crossed the front room. Cale stood up as Wolfhunter Geddes strode into the bright light of the courtyard.

"Gentlemen, I'm glad I made it in time," said Wolfhunter.

He was carrying a red-painted Comanche lance, and Cale noticed fresh scalps tied to it with rawhide strips—and then Wolfhunter was lifting the lance and pulling back to throw, and Katy cried out a warning. But Cale didn't flinch as Wolfhunter hurled the lance. Its iron point *thumped!* into the trunk of the Spanish oak a few feet to Cale's left. Blake leaped to his feet, overturning his chair. Ocheltree swore.

"I happened to be in this neck of the woods," Wolfhunter continued cheerfully, "and learned you good folks had a couple of problems. I took care of one yesterday. You don't have to worry about those Comanche bucks any longer."

"Who the hell are you, anyway?" barked Ocheltree.

"I have a hunch this must be Wolfhunter Geddes," said Blake, with a sidelong glance at Cale.

"I declare," breathed Mackey, awed.

"That's me," Wolfhunter said. "And I've come to tell you gentlemen that I can do the same for those rustlers as I did for them Comanches."

Chapter Seventeen

In need of ninety-proof nerve medicine, Ocheltree poured himself another glass of sour-mash with almost steady hands. As he poured, he shot a quick look at Cale, who still stood, stone-faced, at the end of the table opposite Wolfhunter. Ocheltree, like all the others present, knew all about Wolfhunter Geddes and Susanna McKeller. And, again like the others, Ocheltree had been a true and longtime friend of Sam McKeller's. Susanna had been Sam's wife, Cherokee or no, and this man had stolen her away, so he had no right to expect any outpouring of good-fellowship from Sam's friends. Ocheltree would not show such disrespect for the memory of Sam McKeller.

"That was quite an entrance, Mr. Geddes," he said coolly. "I reckon we all have heard of your many exploits over the years. But I'd like to hear it from you—why you think you can single-handedly rid us of these vermin. A job that, apparently, a hundred cowboys can't begin to do."

"Oh, your men are good at what they do," said Wolfhunter generously. "But that's working stock, not hunting men. Most cowboys I've come across couldn't hit the broadside of a Quaker barn with a short gun, and only this side better than that with a rifle."

"They say you can shoot the neck hairs off a sage hen at a hundred *pasos* with that long torn of yourn," said Mackey.

"Don't need to spend the cartridges. Sage hens just keel over dead when they see me coming. Point is, I'm good at what I do. And my reputation is worth something. Word gets out I'm working for you men, and some of those yahoos will light a shuck."

"You can't very well go to the newspaper and advertise," said Eddings. "This kind of business has to be kept under the hat. We can't be openly associated with it." Eddings was jealous of his standing as a pillar of the community.

"No need to make a public declaration," said Wolfhunter, smiling. "I'll just mosey into Llano and say a few careful words over a bottle of nose paint. The news will spread abroad."

The ranchers exchanged glances. Cale kept his eyes locked on Wolfhunter. As the Association members tried to judge each others' feelings on the matter, Wolfhunter grinned at Cale.

"You must be Caleb. I've heard a lot about you. You have a fine-looking woman there."

Cale realized that Katy had slipped up beside him. Now she put her arm through his, leaned her shoulder into him.

"How much do you want, Mr. Geddes?" asked Ocheltree.

"How bad do you want to be rid of the rustlers?"

"A hundred dollars a head sound fair?"

"A hundred dollars an ear sounds even more fair."

Again Ocheltree scanned the faces of his colleagues. He saw no resistance, and nodded. "Done."

"I'll expect cash on delivery. Which one of you will act as paymaster?"

"I will," Ocheltree volunteered.

Blake looked at Cale. "Gentlemen, we've left out one of our members."

"You know where I stand," said Cale, his voice hollow. "Now that you've struck your deal, Geddes, I'd advise you to waste no time getting the hell and gone off my property."

With that he left the courtyard, Katy by his side.

His second morning alone at the Whitetail Meadow line shack, Tom Samples saddled his horse as the black of night faded into the gray that presaged dawn. He had spent one whole day abiding by Cale McKeller's rules, and that was enough. Now he was going to ride sign—to look for any indication that a bunch of cattle had been removed from the Cyclone range through his section. He had already made up his mind what he would do if he found any such clue. He would follow it until one of three things happened: He lost the trail, he came up on the rustlers, or hell froze over.

Tugging the cinch strap tight and then knotting the latigo over the front rigging ring, Tom heard his stomach growl like a hostile cat, and when he was through screwing the hull down on the back of his sorrel, he tightened his belt a notch. He had been spoiled by the breakfasts that Essie and Katy served the batch hands at Casa Piedra, and that the old Mexicano camp cook stirred up at the marking ground. He could almost smell the overland trout that was sizzling over the cookfire forty miles away by Lodgepole Creek, and could damn near taste the hen fruit little Miguelito took from the chicken coop back of Stone House every morning. He had been forced by circumstances to settle for an airtight of peaches from the line shack's cupboard. It had scarcely dented his appetite.

Fetching his Henry from its lean against the hooden's front wall, Tom stepped up into the saddle. Yesterday he had cleaned the rifle and made certain that the front-loading magazine tube carried fifteen rimfire shells. He housed the repeater in the saddle boot and, taking up the reins, headed due south.

He did not have high expectations. Tom had learned to keep his hopes on short rein, and did so in all things. It was better that way—a man cut down on disappointment. He decided to ride a straight line all day, taking it slow, night out on the range, then make a wide loop to the north and east tomorrow, returning round-about to Whitetail Meadow. Even if he failed to find any sign of rus-tling, it was better than loafing around the line shack. He had spent yesterday treating the horses Billy Yellen had abused, cutting some firewood—after sharpening the axe—hauling water, cleaning out the hooden. That was all there was to do, except sit and contem-plate on life's injustices. Tom didn't care for idleness, or pondering. He was already too well-acquainted with injustice.

As he rode through the scrub hills, Tom thought about Cale. He couldn't help but resent McKeller. Oh, he didn't blame Cale for the antagonism that just naturally seemed to crop up between them. No, he himself was to blame for that. It just irked Tom that Cale was so unenthusiastic about the prosperity of the Cyclone, that he carried on like it was such a burden running the ranch. At the same time Cale acted like he knew everything there was to know about ranching and refused to take anyone's advice. Worse, Cale had forgotten the way cow people dealt with the problem of rustling. It didn't matter if the thieves took ten head or a hundred. There was a principle involved. When a bunch of yahoos started stealing a spread's livestock, then the men who worked that spread dropped everything and busted butt until the rustlers were caught. You didn't wait until it was convenient. You took care of the problem *muy pronto*. And when the nightriders were caught, you didn't *talk* to them, for Chrissakes! You made an example of them for future would-be rustlers to think on.

Walking the sorrel around a big thicket of *quebradora*, Tom shook his head. Why was it that God gave the people who didn't deserve it all the best things in life?

Well, he couldn't change that. But he could show everybody who cared to see that *he* knew how to deal with the *hombres* who had the gall to steal from a ranch that should've been, at least partly, his. Best of all, he would show Cale.

So deeply was he lost in thought, Tom didn't realize at first that the sorrel was no longer moving. They had just emerged from a brake of stunted cedar, into a narrow draw running east and west. The sorrel was snuffling at the sparse grass. Looking down, Tom saw that a considerable number of cows had passed through the draw all at once, and not too long ago.

"Well, I'll be," he said softly, laughing. "Good thing one of us was paying attention."

He stepped down, ground-hitching the horse, and strolled around to take a closer look at the sign. He made several educated guesses. There were about forty head in the bunch, pushed by three men on horseback. Of the forty head, more than half were heifers, five were bulls, the rest steers. A steer's front hooves were sharp. A bull's were distinctly blunted, while all four of a heifer's hooves were quite sharp.

This time his job had been made easy because the bunch had been pushed through the draw not long after the rainstorm of two mornings ago. The wet ground had dried to hold the imprints clearly.

Tom stood there, looking west up the draw, thinking it through. Three men were driving forty head, and if they had continued due west for a mile or two, they would have pushed those cows right off the Cyclone. Most troublesome of all, they had done the deed in broad daylight only a few miles from the line shack at Whitetail Meadow.

Mounting up, Tom turned the sorrel west and followed the trail.

In less than an hour he came to a dry creek bed embraced by deep cutbanks. He could see where the cattle had been pushed down the bank, but there was no sign of their climbing out on the other side. A closer inspection revealed hoof scars on the larger rocks in the creek bed. The creek meandered roughly north-south, and the scars were north of the entry point. A little farther on Tom found cattle dung. It was two days old. He looked north up the creek bed and saw the hogback ridge, knew immediately that it was to that ridge that he had followed Billy yesterday morning. And he remembered hearing the sounds of bunched cattle, and yet being unable to locate the source.

His blood began to race. No question, he was close to the rustlers' hideout. Dangerously close. He knew that it would be reckless to ride straight up the creek. If the rustlers were still there, and had any smarts at all, they would post a lookout of some kind. So Tom turned the sorrel into the brush and swung a wide loop, climbing to the top of the hogback some distance from the creek. He pulled the Henry from its scabbard and rode with the repeater laid across the fork of his saddle.

The top of the ridge was thick in places with large stands of devil's head, and coma and wait-a-minute were in abundance. There were few trees up here, a scattering of wind-sculpted cedar and pale green mesquite. Plenty of rocks. At one point Tom crossed a granite basin, and checked the sorrel sharply as he heard the hollow sound the horse's hooves made as they struck the rock. An idea teased at the back of his mind.

The ridge could be hollowed out. There could be caves down below him. And if they were large enough … what a perfect place to temporarily hold stolen cattle!

But he didn't hear any cattle, this time. He didn't hear much of anything. The morning was still, the earth dozing under the warm hand of the sun. Off in the distance some crows were raising a ruckus. Closer, locusts were ticking in the brush. But no cattle.

A little farther on, the sorrel snorted and began fiddle-footing. Tom calmed the horse, and his gaze followed the point of the sorrel's ears to a dense patch of catclaw. The horse was a veteran of the *brasada*, too, and could point like a setter. Something, or someone, was concealed in that stand.

Tom swung down, bringing the rifle with him. Casting about, he saw an imprint in a little patch of dust caught in a pocket of rock. He stepped closer, bending down, reins in his left hand. Animal tracks, similar to a deer's, but half as large, and fresh-made.

Razorback.

With a shrill whinny the sorrel jerked back violently and Tom, tightening his grip on the leathers, was pulled off balance and bowled over backward. He tried to catch himself with his right hand and keep hold of the Henry at the same time, and managed to scrape the skin off his knuckles as they caught between rock and the rifle's receiver. The sorrel tried to rear, wanting to get free and run, and stretched Tom out in the process. Cursing, Tom felt the reins slipping through his fingers. He let go of the Henry then, and grabbed the reins with his right hand, pulling the wild-eyed horse down. Only then did he hear the short, rapid grunting of another animal, and looked around to glimpse the javelina charging out of the cat claw.

He let go of the reins. The sorrel promptly bolted. Tom dove for the Henry. The razorback started after the horse, and then changed directions and came for Samples. Reaching for the Henry,

Tom grabbed hold of the barrel and swung the rifle as hard as he could—just in time. The stock caught the razorback squarely on the side of the head. The javelina went over sideways. With a strangled cry of fear and rage, Samples brought the point of the stock down as hard as he could on the animal's skull. The grunting turned into a sharp-pitched squealing. Again Tom struck for all he was worth. The razorback stilled, blood leaking from head and jaws.

Getting up, Tom stood for a moment on shaky legs, jacked a shell into the breech, and looked around. The sorrel was gone. Accustomed to the vantage point of horseback, Tom felt hemmed in and blinded by the thick brush. He swore again, under his breath. He knew that the horse probably wasn't far—he just couldn't see the damned hayburner. Something went thrashing through the catclaw. More razorbacks. Tom backed away, reminding himself over and over again: don't shoot unless you have to. Remember, there could be desperados in the vicinity.

Catching his heel in the crack between two sun-whacked sheets of granite, he almost fell. Enough of this backstepping, he decided. Turning, he climbed a tent-blister, and from this modest vantage point saw the sorrel on the other side of man-tall prickly pear. He worked his way around the stand of cactus, clambering over a stack of corestones.

The sorrel was skittish, and Tom approach slowly, with soft-spoken horse-talk. Reaching the sorrel, he gathered up the dragging reins, booted the Henry, and set foot into stirrup. He was swinging his leg over when another javelina shot out of the stand of prickly pear and launched itself at horse and rider, grunting up a storm. The sorrel kicked like an Arizona nightingale and the saddle came up sharply to meet Tom, and it was all he could do to stay with it. He felt as if somebody had laid a two-by-four into his breadbasket. The sorrel's kick just grazed the razorback, and then the horse went to highbinding like an unbroken mustang. The hog swerved into the shelter of the nopal. The sorrel took off in the opposite direction. For one desperate moment Tom had no control over the animal. Catclaw reached out and whacked him across the head and chest. He pulled hard on the leathers, and the sorrel's head came back. The horse slowed.

That was a mistake.

They crashed through the brush and then the earth just seemed to open up in front of them. Tom saw the hole too late. He let up on the reins and put his spurs to the animal, and the sorrel made a game try, but the hole was a good twelve feet in diameter. They were going too fast to stop or swerve and too slow to make the leap. The sorrel touched stone on the opposite lip with its forelegs, but missed it with the hind legs, and the world turned upside down. The back of the horse just dropped out from under him and Tom began to fall.

He hit the shale slope on his belly, and rock came up to smack him in the face, but didn't knock him out. The full weight of the screaming horse landed on him. Sharp pain lanced through his leg. Tom tried to suck in air, but he couldn't. It felt as if his lungs had collapsed. The weight of the sorrel rolled away, and then he was rolling downward. When he stopped, more rocks came pouring down on top of him, augmenting his pain. Suddenly, he was surrounded by darkness.

Tom spat copper-tasting blood. He opened his eyes, and more blood impaired his vision. Through the roaring in his ears he heard a familiar sound. A hammer locked back. He snapped his eyes open again, blinking away the blood, and saw the barrel of the short gun first, then the face behind it.

The face belonged to Billy Yellen.

"Hello, Tom," said Billy.

Tom flinched at the report of a gun. But it wasn't Billy's gun. No, he was still alive. He tried to swallow, and couldn't. His heart was galloping like a runaway horse.

"I had to kill the mare," someone said.

Tom saw Billy nod.

"This is great," lamented someone else. "This is just larrupin' wonderful! Now we're gonna have to kill this sonuvabitch. On top of being cattle thieves we'll be murderers into the bargain!"

Looking into Tom's eyes, Billy said, "They can only hang you once."

Chapter Eighteen

Katy couldn't find her husband. She checked every room in Casa Piedra and then went out onto the gallery. Frisco was there, leaning against an upright, sprinkling tobacco out of a drawstring muslin sack into a *hoja*, then rolling the *hoja* tightly just so. The Cyclone *caporal* was only keeping his hands busy. He had a fresh horse saddled and tied to a post just a few strides away. It was clear that Frisco expected to do some riding in short order.

"Have you seen Cale, Frisco?"

"*Sí, señora.*" Frisco nodded in a southwesterly direction.

She looked that way, saw Beau standing in the afternoon shade of Two Mile Oak. So Cale was paying a visit to his father's grave. She wanted to go to him, and wondered if she should. Frisco, watching her closely without seeming to, understood her indecision.

"Take my horse, señora," he offered.

Katy smiled at him. Frisco wouldn't just out-and-out give unsolicited advice to her, but the offer of the horse was a subtle suggestion. Obviously Frisco sensed, as she did, that something big was in the offing, something that would affect all their lives.

Accepting his offer, Katy climbed into the saddle. She was wearing pants, and so did not have to concern herself with modesty and decorum when forking the horse like a man. And her legs were long—the stirrups needed no adjusting to accommodate her.

She was about to turn the horse when Frisco shrugged away from the upright and stepped out onto the hardpack, squinting up at her.

"Señora."

"Yes, Frisco?"

The *caporal* debated, wondering how far he should butt into someone else's business. Then he said, "Señora, I wish only to say that Señor Cale is a very lucky man."

Katy knew what he was getting at, and was flattered by the compliment. "Thank you, Frisco."

"You should know, he feels bad when he leaves you. You are his only happiness now."

"It didn't used to be that way," replied Katy. "Used to be the army first. The cavalry was his mistress. It took him away from me for such long periods of time. Terrible times. On each occasion that he left the post I had to wonder if it was the last time I would see him. Coming here was the best thing that could have happened for me. I've come to see how selfish I was."

"It is not my business," Frisco said in apology. "But maybe you should tell him this. He can see that you are happy here."

Katy nodded, bestowed a grateful smile upon the *caporal,* and turned the horse, touched heels to it, and set off at a high lope toward Two Mile Oak.

Watching her go, Frisco couldn't help but feel a little envious of Cale. The boss was one lucky man.

It was a shade under a quarter mile across open ground to Two Mile Oak from Casa Piedra. Close enough to walk. But on the frontier no one but a certified fool would stray so far afield on foot if they didn't have to. It took Katy only a handful of minutes, but in that brief span she thought of turning back a dozen times. She had never intruded into Cale's privacy before.

Cale was standing alongside Beau, an arm hooked around the saddle horn, leaning into the chestnut, when Katy rode up. He straightened and walked around the picket-enclosed gravesite as she dismounted. She put her arms about him, laid her head against the wide span of his chest. Resting his chin on top of her head, he looked up the long slope of grass at Casa Piedra.

"I guess the others are long gone," he sighed. "I wasn't much of a host, I'm afraid."

"You stood up for what you thought was right. You always give me reason to be proud of you, darling. Too many men would have given in to the will of the Association, as the price of acceptance. Dusty admires you. He told me so, before he left."

"Dusty's a good man. They all are, I guess. And I don't know that I'm right and they're wrong."

"What's right for one isn't always right for another."

She lifted her head, and he looked deep into her eyes, trying to divine her thoughts.

"I've been a poor husband of late, Katy," he said morosely.

"You've never been that."

"Yes, I have." He looked at the granite headstone with its simple inscription: SAMUEL LEWIS MCKELLER 1815–1876. "And a poor son."

Taking him by the arms, she shook him gently.

"You'd better straighten up, Caleb McKeller," she scolded. "You seem to be under the impression that your father built this ranch just for you, and that you're obligated to take it over."

"That's the way I saw it."

"I never had the privilege of knowing Sam McKeller," she said sternly. "But I've heard enough about him to get a pretty good handle on what kind of man he was. You may hate me for what I'm about to say, but I'm going to say it anyway."

"I could never hate you, Katy," he said softly.

"Remember you said that." She laughed, a twinkle in her eye. Then she turned serious again. "Cale, your father built this ranch for himself, as much as for you. You mustn't forget that. And he was as decent a man as one who had to survive on the frontier could afford to be. But you don't owe him, darling. You don't owe him anything. He did what he wanted to, and you must do the same. That's what he would want."

Cale was silent for a while, looking at the headstone. Finally, he said, "You know, at first I resented my father—resented him for devoting every waking moment of his day to the Cyclone. Resented the fact that he could not even spare the time to go after Geddes and my mother. He carried on like her leaving didn't bother him, when it tore me up inside. But I've come to see things different. He was hurt, all right. He was cut to the quick when she ran off with another man. It was just his way of handling the grief. We all have different ways. And he didn't go after her because he loved her that much—enough to let her go on and do whatever made her happy. He wanted her to be happy, most of all. Even if it was at his expense."

"He'd want you to be happy, too."

"You know, I came to realize that it was the ranch I blamed. It was the Cyclone. That's why I left, why I found a new home."

"You should go back to the army, Cale."

"But what about you? The army gave me everything, Katy. But it gave nothing to you."

"I don't need anything from the army. I have everything I want being your wife."

He pulled her close again. "I reckon it was a mistake coming back here, wasn't it?"

"Oh, no. It wasn't a mistake. It was a blessing. I thank God every day for it. If we hadn't come back you'd probably be dead, Cale. You'd have gone off to die with Autie and the others. It was no mistake, your resigning from the Seventh. But it might be one if you didn't go back to it. Back home."

"What about the Cyclone?" Then he laughed at himself. "Listen to me. Why am I so all-fired concerned about this ranch, anyway?"

"Because you loved your father. And you know how much he loved the Cyclone. But there are people here who call it home. Who love it as much as Sam McKeller ever did. Leave it in their hands, Cale. They'll take good care of her, as well as Sam ever did."

"You mean people like Tom Samples."

"Your voice holds a sharp edge when you speak his name."

"We haven't been what you might call sociable to one another."

Katy nodded. "I've been thinking about that. It always seemed to me like Tom had a chip on his shoulder. And I think I know why, now. I think he's known all along that you're his half brother. He couldn't have lived here for as long as he has and not found out that his mother had been Sam McKeller's wife."

"Why didn't he just speak out?"

"Pride, I suspect. He's not Sam's blood. He has no rightful claim to the Cyclone."

"I don't know. Maybe he has as much right to it as I do. I'm beginning to think that it's not enough just to inherit something. I mean, a man inherits a horse, that doesn't give him the right to mistreat it. So maybe the fact that Tom loves this land so much gives him as good a claim on it as I have."

Katy smiled at him. "You are wise beyond your years, mister."

Cale grunted his skepticism.

"But one thing is bothering me," Katy confessed, her smile fading.

"Wolfhunter Geddes."

"Yes. Essie thinks he might try to harm you or Tom. I can't imagine why he would, but…well, Essie is so seldom wrong about people."

"Don't worry. I won't let anything happen to either one of us. You see, Tom—he's my ticket out of here."

Men were shouting up at Stone House. Cale could see them gathering in front of the gallery, and then he heard the old angle iron being laid into. He couldn't make out any words, but a half minute later a man was running away from Casa Piedra, heading for the line of trees that marked Encino Creek. He could tell that the runner was Frisco, but he couldn't figure out what was happening. Not until, looking toward the creek, he saw a man stumbling in the tall grass. The man fell, got up, fell again. At this distance Cale couldn't identify him.

"Go back to the house, Katy," he said.

Running to Beau, he swung aboard without benefit of stirrup and tapped the chestnut with his knees. Beau took off at a lope, and when he felt the brush of Cale's spurs, stretched out into a gallop.

Halfway, Cale knew the man was Abner. Abner had stopped walking; he stood there with an arm outstretched, as if he was reaching out to Cale, and then he fell. This time he didn't get up. Cale hit the ground running. Beau thundered on by the fallen man, slowed, and cantered back. Cale turned Abner over, made a quick check for wounds. The only evident injuries were an ugly gash across Ab's forehead and a purplish welt on his cheek close beneath the right eye. There was blood on the old cowboy's face, but it looked worse than it really was. He was suffering more from sheer exhaustion than the head wound.

Cale cradled Ab's head in his arm. Abner opened his eyes, focused on Cale's face, and licked his parched lips.

"Mr. McKeller … cattle … dead … Comanch' …"

"Rest easy, Ab."

Cale looked up, watched Frisco close the gap, and when Frisco was close enough to hear him, shouted, "Get my canteen!"

Frisco went to Beau, fetched the canteen, and sat on his heels, breathing hard, while Cale trickled a small dose of water into Abner's mouth. That revived Ab enough for him to sit up without assistance.

"The lookout saw a passel of buzzards off to the east this morning," said Abner. "Did they tell you, Mr. McKeller?"

"No, Ab. Nobody told me. Lot of things have been going on around here today."

"I rode out for a look-see. Found about twenty head, slaughtered. I'd say two, three miles from here."

"Slaughtered?"

Abner nodded. "Comanch'. Had arrows stickin' out of 'em all which a-way. Then I heard something movin' around in the brush. The Injun sign was a day old. I figured them for long gone. I guess I thought it was a cow in the brush, wounded maybe. But it weren't no cow. It was a damned Comanch' buck, that's what it was. Had a rope tied to that brush and was off to one side, pullin' on the rope." Abner shook his head. "Call me a blunderin' old idiot if you've a mind to. You won't catch me arguing the fact. I rode right in there like sheep tagging a Judas goat. And this heathen jumps out and lays a lance across my face. Knocked me into next week. When I came to he was gone. So was my horse. That damned buck stole my horse." He looked at Frisco querulously. "Do you believe that? Took my goldurned horse!"

"And left your scalp," commented Frisco.

Abner lifted his battered, sweat-stained hat off his thinning hair. "Mine ain't worth lifting."

"He didn't kill you, at least," said Cale.

"I guess I ain't even worth killing," Ab lamented.

"Be grateful for small favors," Frisco advised.

"I got here as fast as I was able, Mr. McKeller. Ran as far as I could. My feet are so swole up I'll have to cut these here boots off."

"Take Beau on up to the house. Let Essie see to that head."

"I'd feel awful bad, riding in on your horse and you havin' to walk."

"Well, we can't carry you, Ab."

"No, sir. And I don't reckon I could take another step." He sighed dejectedly, anticipating the ribbing he would suffer around future campfires. He'd had his horse stolen right out from under him, and he hadn't even been able to walk all the way in on his own. It was a black day.

"Go on and take Beau in," urged Cale. "No one can blame you. And you'd do better not to take chances with a head injury. I'll make it an order if I have to."

"Yes, sir," said Abner morosely.

They helped him to his feet. As he hauled himself into the saddle, Cale turned to Frisco. "You ready for a lick of hard riding?"

"Beats running," said Frisco. "When do we go?"

"*A hora mismo, amigo.*"

"I've been waiting."

"Yeah. I know you have."

"Do we go after the Comanche horse-stealer?"

Cale made a throwaway gesture. "We'll leave that to others. Send Jesus to the Lodgepole. Tell him to bring back a dozen men and get to tracking that buck. There could be more where he came from, and I don't want to leave Stone House undefended."

"Take men from the road-branding?"

Cale glared at him. "Isn't that what I just finished saying?"

"But what of our contract with Señor Snyder?"

Cale thought, "History does repeat itself." When his mother had taken off with Wolfhunter Geddes twenty years ago, Sam had been too busy getting a herd ready for a push up the Shawnee Trail. Sam had put the ranch before the people. Cale figured it was time he stopped doing the same.

"We'll still make the delivery date. And even if we don't—some things are more important. We can't have Indians running around killing our cows and attacking our men. If Snyder doesn't like it we'll push the herd north ourselves."

"You and I—we ride for Whitetail Meadow, maybe?"

"You're so godawful smart, Frisco. Since you know so much, why don't you tell me in advance what I'm gonna do, instead of always standing around with that know-it-all smile on your face, waiting for me to figure it out for myself. It would save everybody a heap of time."

"Whatever you say, boss."

"You can't call me that anymore, because you're a part owner of the Cyclone as of now."

"What?" For the first time, it pleased Cale to see, he had caught Frisco completely off guard.

"You heard me. I'd say the Madrigals have as much blood and sweat and tears invested in the Cyclone as the McKellers."

"Part owner," murmured Frisco, looking around him as if he was seeing this familiar ground in a totally new light.

"That's right. You, me, and Tom. Of course, you and Tom will have to run things. Me, I'm going back to doing what I do best."

Chapter Nineteen

"I say we might as well kill him and be done with it."

Ever since Samples had fallen through the sinkhole, literally into their laps, Hainey had been acting as if it was just a matter of time before they'd all be dancing at the end of a rope. He poked morosely at a cookfire the gang sat around in the large cavern, away from the dust and noise and smell of the stolen cattle penned in the big sinkhole. Samples lay pretty much where he had fallen, at the bottom of the debris slope across the way, out of earshot.

Sligo was sitting cross-legged on a flat boulder. He kept looking across at Samples like a buzzard perched on a tree limb, watching and waiting for life to depart a wounded animal. It was getting dark in the cavern. The day was old and clouds had begun to gather, promising rain come night. Cajun had put a lighted lantern over near their prisoner. Not that Tom was likely to slip away in the darkness, for he had broken a leg in the fall. But there was no telling what a man might try if the situation was desperate enough.

"I'll blow his lamp out," Sligo volunteered. "It won't bother me none."

Billy glanced sidelong at Sligo. Billy had never killed a man before. He'd wanted to, on occasion. Most recently when Cale McKeller had whupped him. But he had never gone the full distance. He suspected that when the time came he would kill with a bullet. The way Sligo preferred was too close and messy.

"So what d'ya say, Billy?" Sligo pressed. "Want I should kill him?"

Billy didn't fancy being pressured. "He dies when I say, not before."

"Hell's bells," Hainey barked, disgruntled. "Get it over with. We sure cain't take him with us. And you said we was to move these cows on for the Frio come morning. What else can we do? We cain't just leave him here. He knows who we are now."

"You don't have to tell me," Billy snapped crossly. "I'm here. I know what's going on."

Sligo straightened out his legs as if he was about to stand up. "I'll go ahead. Then we'll be done with it."

Billy jumped to his feet. "Pa and Jake put me in charge, Sligo."

Sligo looked at Cajun, and Cajun merely shrugged.

"It's a tough call, Billy," said Cajun, sympathetic. He knew why Billy was so indecisive. Rafe Yellen would not like it, having his operation muddied up with a killing. And there was no telling how the volatile older Yellen would react to whatever Billy decided to do.

"Well, I wish Jake was here," Hainey grunted. "He'd know what to do."

Angered, Billy stalked away from the fire. He went over to where Samples lay among the rocks at the foot of the debris slope and sat on his heels six feet away from the *brasadero*. Tom heard him, lifted his chin off his chest, and opened pain-rimmed eyes.

"How you doin'?" asked Billy.

"You care?" Tom croaked. "I always knew you were low-down enough to steal cattle."

"Cows belong to the man who's got them. It's always been that way in this country. All the rich ranchers got started by stealin' cattle. How do you figure Sam McKeller put his first herd together?"

"Those were wild cattle, Billy."

"So he just put his mark on them and that made them his. Which is what we're doing."

"Sure, Billy," said Tom, disgusted and weary. He tried to shift his position slightly, and winced.

Billy looked at Tom's left leg. He couldn't help but feel some admiration for Samples. None of them had wanted to bother setting Tom's leg, so somehow Tom had managed to do it himself.

Wedging his ankle between two large rocks, Samples had heaved his whole body straight back and then twisted in an attempt to pop the lower leg bone into place. It had taken him a few tries. He'd been yanking and turning like a coyote in a steel trap. But not once had he cried out.

Afterward Tom had asked for a splint, but no one had come up with anything. Samples was the one who had suggested the Henry, still in the boot tied to the saddle on the dead sorrel mare. Hainey had expressed a strong interest in confiscating the rifle for himself, but Cajun had told him there was time enough for that later, and fetched the repeater, taking the precaution of emptying the magazine. Billy had checked Tom's pockets. They had already taken his Colt short gun and shellbelt. Tom had strapped the Henry to the outside of his left leg, shoving the barrel inside his boot and using his own belt and the latigo strap Cajun had cut from his saddle. All the while Hainey had complained that they were going to too much trouble on account of a man who was going to die anyway.

"The boys want to kill you, Samples."

"So what's stopping them?"

"I am."

Tom glowered at him. "I hope you don't expect too much by way of thanks," he said.

"You're a tough customer, aren't you? I ain't forgettin' you put a rope on me."

"I'd give a lot to be the one who puts a rope around your neck."

"You talk like you expect to see the sunrise."

"No," said Tom tautly. "I don't expect that at all."

Billy peered up through the sinkhole. He couldn't see a single patch of blue sky. Nothing but gray and white thunderclouds building, painted with dabs of old rose, compliments of the plummeting sun.

"It'll come a rain before long. Likely wash away your sign. Doubt anyone would ever find you, were they to even miss you and start to trackin'."

"Look," grunted Tom, aggravated. "If you want to pass the time of day, find somebody else. I'm not interested in anything you've got to say."

Billy stood up slowly. "You ain't no better than I am, you sonuvabitch. So don't go trying to act like you are."

Yellen strolled back to the fire. Cajun was stirring up a skillet of beans. He was the one who, by common consent, usually did the cooking, for he carried little bags of spices that livened up the plainest fare. Even Arizona strawberries.

"Shore wish you'd thought enough of us to bring a bottle of tongue oil back from Llano town," lamented Hainey. "It stays a mite cold and damp in these here caves."

Billy didn't say anything. He sat with his back to a boulder and looked moodily across the cavern at the lamplit figure of Tom Samples. He couldn't shake the feeling that somehow Tom *was* a better man than he, and that annoyed him.

"So what was you and that cowboy talkin' about?" asked Hainey. "We got a right to know. We're all in this together."

"The voice of democracy," murmured Cajun, smiling.

Billy stood up. He was feeling too restless to sit still for very long. All of a sudden he didn't like being around these men anymore. Years ago he had delighted in sitting on these very stones and listening to the likes of Jake and Sligo and Cajun stretching the breeze, thinking of them as heroes, men he could look up to and hope to emulate. Now he wanted no more to do with them.

"I'm about half tired of you and your rights, you old fart," snapped Billy. He shrugged out of the gray longcoat his brother had given him and let it fall to the ground. Hooking his boot under it, he kicked it straight at Hainey.

"Hey!" hollered the brand artist, throwing the coat aside. "You better respect your elders, you young shit, or I'll cook your goose three ways to Sunday!"

"Come on then," urged Billy, barely above a whisper. "I'm sick of your bellyaching. You think you can run this haywire outfit? Well, you'll have to put me under first."

Hainey looked at the steady hand inches away from the .44 Dance at Billy's side, then lifted his eyes to Billy's. What he saw there took all the anger out of him, and started him to thinking about survival. A glance at Cajun and Sligo informed him that these two weren't going to buy in. They weren't his friends; they were here on account of Jake, and Billy was Jake's brother. He and Landon were the real outsiders.

"Hell," he grumbled, averting his gaze. "You ain't worth a bullet, Yellen. Leastways, not before supper."

Billy snorted and walked away. He went to the barbed-wire Texas gate strung across the high natural arch and looked out at the stolen cattle, all wearing the Bar Buckle brand now. A thunderclap rolled across the sky, shaking the stone beneath his feet. And then the rain came.

Chapter Twenty

The thunder woke Rafe Yellen from his drunken siesta. He was sitting behind the desk in the White Elephant's back room that served as his office and living quarters. His head was resting on the desk, his arms dangling, his knuckles brushing the floor. Straightening, he saw that the dingy room with its dirty floor and raw-board walls was dark. The rain was beating on the oilskin cover of the window behind him.

He listened hopefully a moment for any sound issuing from the saloon proper. Nothing. Quiet as a damned church. A storm was bad for business, as it would dissuade some range riders from leaving the dry amenities of the bunkhouse for a ride to town. And then too, Rafe remembered, it was Sunday. Day of thanks and prayer. Rafe smirked. All he had was a high-grade headache and an empty stomach. It was time to stumble next door to the Chinaman's hash house. Rafe reminded himself to say grace before he dug into that slant-eye's bait: "Good bread, good meat, good God let's eat." Of course, calling the Chinaman's vittles "good" was out-and-out bald-faced storytelling.

Rafe stood up, fixed his suspenders, and groped through the darkness for the door connecting the room to the rest of the saloon. He opened the door—and then Burley Evans came hurtling into him, with such force that Rafe had the wind knocked out of him. Feet tangling, Rafe went down and Burley fell on top of him. Rafe fetched the back of his skull a good lick on the floor, which really got his dander up good and high. He commenced to cudgeling Burley with his fists, cussing a blue streak, kicking Burley off him, and leaping to his feet with an agility that surprised him. Still swearing like a mule skinner, Rafe laid a solid kick into Burley's side, but Burley lay face down, as lively as a bag of cavalry oats.

"That's the Rafe Yellen I remember," came a familiar voice. "Kickin' a man when he's down."

Rafe looked up to see Wolfhunter in the doorway. Standing in front of Wolfhunter was Calico Anne. Annie was barefoot, wearing only soiled pantalettes and a frayed camisole, its cheap lace yellowed and tattered. The camisole was only half-buttoned, but there was nothing there that Rafe hadn't already seen plenty of. He devoted all his attention to the long knife that Wolfhunter held against her belly. One quick slice and Calico Anne would be trying to keep her guts from falling out on the floor.

"Wolfhunter Geddes," Rafe breathed raggedly. "I'll be damned."

"No doubt about that, *amigo.*"

Rafe looked down at Burley, sprawled at his feet, and then it dawned on him. He used his foot to roll Evans over. Burley's arm flopped like a dead fish, flung out. Rafe saw the deep gash across Burley's throat, then looked at the blood on the front of his own soiled longjohn tops. He ran his hand across his face. It came away smeared with more blood. Burley's blood. He had been wrestling with a corpse.

"You're still doin' what you do best, I see, you long bastard," he told Wolfhunter. Then a very sobering thought struck him, and he fixed his one good eye anxiously upon the girl. She had been with Jake in the room next door. And she looked plenty scared. Pale, too, with that shocked, glazed expression often seen on the faces of people who had witnessed a horrible thing.

"God in heaven," croaked Rafe, suddenly sick with a bad premonition. "Where's my boy?"

"Oh. Was he yours?" asked Wolfhunter.

"Sweet Jesus." Rafe felt his knees go loose, and he slacked back to sit down hard on the edge of the desk.

"Jake's dead," said Calico Anne, her voice shaky and high-pitched. "I was asleep. I heard something, and woke up to … to see

Jake's blood come spurtin' across my eyes. He was lyin' there beside me, with the blood just shootin' out of his neck…and this awful rattle…" She sobbed, her frail body shuddering violently.

"Light the lamp, darlin'," said Wolfhunter, and shoved her forward.

She fetched up against the desk. Catching herself, she overturned the bottle of rye whiskey Rafe had polished off that afternoon. The dead soldier fell off the desk, rolled across the floor. Rafe felt it bump against his heel. As Calico Anne tried to steady up enough to light the kerosene lamp, Rafe lifted his head to look at Wolfhunter. There was no wrath in that look, only plaintive puzzlement, and resignation.

"Why'd you go and kill my boy, Geddes?"

Wolfhunter shrugged. "Why not?"

Stepping into the office, he kicked the door shut. "By the way," he said, "I closed you down. Hung the sign. Didn't want you to fret that somebody might come in and pilfer your merchandise, what with your bar-dog out of circulation."

Calico Anne had found some matches on the desk and lit the lamp wick, but she had a time getting the chimney back in place. When finally she accomplished this, no mean feat with a violent case of the shakes, she backed into a corner of the little room, as far away from Wolfhunter as she could get, and looking every bit as if she wished she could melt right through the wall.

"What do you want?" asked Rafe. "Why'd you come in here, killin' Burley and my eldest?"

"Your barkeep was a wanted man, up Missouri way, Rafe. Now don't tell me you didn't have an inkling. At least he had a fatal resemblance to a face I seen once or twice on a handbill. You know I never forget a face. And as for your boy, well, I might've had second thoughts had I known the particulars of his parentage at the time."

"I doubt it."

"So do I. He was a Yellen. And I reckon anybody who's a Yellen is wanted for something someplace."

Rafe nodded. "You'd kill a body on an off chance."

"Nobody's innocent," declared Wolfhunter. "You sure ain't. That's an ironclad fact."

"You're still manhunting?"

"I learned a valuable lesson early in life, hoss. You gotta work with the law. That's something you never figured out for yourself. Right now I'm employed by a bunch of fine upstanding gentlemen what call themselves a Cattleman's Association. These gentlemen seem to be the law around here. And they are having some trouble with cow thieves. When I heard that, I knew right where to come. If there was skulduggery in these parts, it was a cinch that Rafe Yellen would have his hand in."

Moving like a tired old man, Rafe pushed himself away from the desk, and tried to keep his good eye on Wolfhunter rather than the knife Wolfhunter was holding, the knife that carried the mingled blood of Burley Evans and Jake Yellen and, Rafe suspected, would soon carry his own.

"If you aim to do for me, you crazy bastard, you'd best get on with it."

"Go sit down," advised Wolfhunter. "Before you fall down."

Rafe shuffled around the desk and slacked heavily into his chair. He wasn't going to argue with a chance, if Wolfhunter wanted to give him one. And that was, apparently, exactly what Wolfhunter was planning to do, for he said, "I reckon you got a gun in that desk, partner. Whenever you're of a mind to, you go on ahead and try for it. We go back a long ways, you and me. Shared many a camp together. Fought the Comanch' back-to-back a time or two. I guess I owe you a fair chance."

Drawing a deep and ragged breath, Rafe put his hands on the desk top. "How much they payin' you?"

"Two hundred apiece. But I ain't really doing it for the money."

"No,' sighed Rafe, "I didn't think so. You're doing it because it gives you an excuse to kill. You're bad medicine clean through, Geddes."

Wolfhunter went over to collect the extra chair, placed it at the corner of the desk, and eased his long frame into it. He was close enough to reach out and touch Rafe. He drove the long knife blade first into the desk top, a swift and savage downward thrust that made Rafe jump. Calico Anne jumped too. Over in the corner shadows, she cut her eye at the door, for now Wolfhunter no longer blocked her path to it. Wolfhunter folded his arms, smiling as if they were all old friends having a casual talk.

"Go ahead, darlin'. You might make it."

"You might as well try it," muttered Rafe flatly. "He's gonna kill you anyway, sooner or later. In this case it might be better if it's sooner."

But Calico Anne couldn't make her legs work. "Don't kill me, mister," she whined. "Please don't go killin' me. I ain't done nothin'."

Rafe barked a harsh laugh. "Guilt and innocence don't mean nothing to this man."

"Why, you're getting downright wise in your old age. I'll bet you can tell me where your boys are hiding out."

Rafe stared at him, incredulous. "You think I'd tell you? You oughta know me better."

Wolfhunter nodded, and seemed pleased. "Oh, I do, I reckon. Just thought I'd ask. Never hurts. Besides, time's been known to change people. But it's good to know that some things never change."

"I'll tell you!" cried Calico Anne, seeing an opportunity and seizing it. "I know where they are. I'll tell you if…if you promise not to kill me."

Rafe's head swiveled sharply. "Shuddup, bitch. She don't know nothin', Geddes."

"Yes I do!" gasped Annie. "Billy told me once. He was all likkered up. I don't think he remembered afterwards, but he told me about the caves—"

"Shuddup, you god—!" Rafe was coming up fast out of his chair, but Wolfhunter was faster, slamming him back down.

"That ain't no way to speak to a lady," Wolfhunter admonished, looming over Rafe, their faces close. "I thought you were better brought up."

"Go to hell," spat Rafe. "Cut my throat like you did Burley's and my son's, and then get the hell off my property."

Wolfhunter sat down. He looked at the window, the flesh-colored square of oilskin letting in the last soft light of the dying day.

"The rain's let up," he commented. "You see that big drop there, Rafe?"

Rafe looked. A wind-thrown drop of water was working its way down the outside of the oilskin, cutting a wide swath through a sheen of moisture. The drop would inch down the oilskin, stop, then plummet another inch or two, and stop again.

"Like I said," murmured Wolfhunter. "I owe you a fair chance, for old times' sake. When that drop gets to the bottom of the window, I'm going to kill you, Rafe. Now, you can try for the gun in your desk, or my knife, anytime you want. Or you can spend what time you have left making your peace with your Maker."

"He and I got nothin' to say to one another."

Wolfhunter chuckled at that. "You and I will make things plenty hot for Ol' Scratch down there, I reckon."

Rafe made no reply. Slanted back in his chair, arms folded, Wolfhunter watched Rafe give the drop of water his undivided attention. At the same time Rafe's one good eye seemed to glaze over, as if he wasn't really seeing that drop on the oilskin at all, but rather the parade of misdeeds that had marked all his misspent years. The room got deathly quiet. Calico Anne, huddled half clad and pitiful in the corner, moved not an inch. She scarcely seemed to breathe.

"What are you thinking about, hoss?" asked Wolfhunter, idly curious.

"All the things I've done, and ain't had a chance to do."

"You may come out of this alive."

A gust of wind fluted through the alley behind the White Elephant and shook the oilskin in passing. The drop of rain made a run down the sheet. Rafe stopped breathing. But the drop slowed to a stop a couple of inches from the bottom.

"No," said Rafe. "I won't."

"Sorry I did for your boy, Rafe. I know what it's like to be a father."

"I have another. I guess it won't do no good to ask you to spare him, will it?"

"Like I said before, it don't hurt to ask."

Rafe watched the raindrop begin to move. "No," he said, again, lips thinned. "I won't beg."

"You're a proud man, Rafe. I knew you wouldn't go down without a fight."

"You're right about that."

Rafe lunged for the knife imbedded in the desk.

He got his hand on it. He pulled it free. And then Wolfhunter, rising, closed his hand over Rafe's, and twisted Rafe's wrist with the other. Rafe grunted as the bones in his wrist snapped like brittle twigs. He gasped as Wolfhunter drove the knife into his belly. Rafe's body went rigid as the cold steel rippled through his innards. Wolfhunter, his face very close to Rafe's, inhaled deeply the other man's dying exhalation.

"Watch for me, partner," whispered Wolfhunter. "I'll be along right soon."

Then he turned the knife upward, piercing Rafe Yellen's heart.

Chapter Twenty-One

Not far from the site of the cattle slaughter and his subsequent ambush of the cowboy, Lone Dog decided that he had endured the discomfort of the saddle quite long enough. Sliding off the horse in the concealment of a cedar brake, he secured the reins to a tree and studied the instrument of torture, grasping the means by which the double-girthed hull was secured to the back of the roan. It wasn't hard to figure out, but it *was* hard to undo with only one good hand. Lone Dog draped the offside fender and stirrup over the seat and began working on the latigo knot embracing the front rigging ring. The horse refused to cooperate. Bashful in the presence of this stranger, the cow pony would not stand still, intensely aggravating Lone Dog. It even managed to put its left foreleg down on Lone Dog's foot. That steelshod hoof had nine hundred pounds behind it as it came down on the Penateka's instep. Trying to get out from under, Lone Dog lost his balance and fell, and fresh pain from his arm negated the pain in his foot. Lone Dog was so tired and so infuriated that he entertained the notion of killing the roan then and there. But only for a single, irrational moment.

He decided to cut the saddle off. But he had neglected to bring a knife out of the arroyo death trap. Searching Abner's saddlebags, he found a Russell Barlow folding knife. He used this to cut the mohair cinching. In short order saddle and blanket lay on the ground. Lone Dog returned the blanket to the back of the horse, then loosely looped Abner's lariat several times around the roan's barrel, just back of the forelegs. He tied it off, using his teeth and one good hand to pull the knot taut.

Lone Dog rested a moment, loosening the tourniquet. Then, rummaging through the saddlebags, he found two stale biscuits and some jerked beef. But he carried a pouch of *inapa* tied to his belt of braided horsehair, and so did not burden himself with more food. He did, however, confiscate the Barlow and, almost as an afterthought, drew the long gun from its saddle scabbard.

Sitting on a rock with the rifle across his knees, Lone Dog ran his hand over it. He had fired an *ella cona* before, the old breechloader his father had bought from the *Comancheros* for the price of three stolen horses. Ammunition had always been in short supply, and Lone Dog had never had the opportunity to indulge in the long hours of practice required to achieve accuracy with a firearm.

For quite some time Lone Dog sat there looking at the rifle. He had given his solemn vow to forsake the use of the *ella cona* on this expedition. But the old shaman had been wrong, and Eye That Kills right. Of this Lone Dog was firmly convinced. One thing was certain: he had to try to kill Wolfhunter. This for the lost souls of his *tah-mahs*, whom Wolfhunter had scalped. As long as those scalps were in Wolfhunter's possession, Lone Dog's brothers would have no peace in the afterlife. In that harsh light reality gives off, Lone Dog knew that he stood no chance at all against Wolfhunter without this rifle. But to use it would mean breaking his promise, given upon his honor as a warrior of the Penateka Comanche.

Lone Dog sighed, thoroughly depressed. Life was unfair. Sometimes it offered only unacceptable alternatives.

Remembering the trouble he had experienced the first time, trying to mount the roan on the right side, the Indian way, Lone Dog went around to the animal's left. He slipped the rifle under the rope and across the withers, then jabbed his lance point-first into the stony earth. Gathering the reins, he used the lower part of the rope as a stirrup to assist him in mounting. Settling wearily on the coarse blanket, he nodded satisfaction. Much better without that saddle. He slipped his knees under the rope, retrieved the lance, and kicked the horse into motion.

Making note of the way thunderclouds were closing ranks as the day progressed, Lone Dog anticipated the rain—and thought no more about it. Rain, heat, cold, pain, hunger—these tribulations would no longer affect him. He felt nothing but a twinge of heartache at his thoughts of She Walks Softly. And a twinge of wonder as he tried to rationalize his failure to kill the cowboy he had ambushed that morning, and whose horse he now rode to personal destiny.

He had counted coup, that was certain. His warrior brothers, had they been alive to witness it, would have heaped congratulations upon him for the feat. Only Eye That Kills, probably, would have reproved him for not taking the white man's life. But there was greater honor in striking or touching a live enemy than in killing him from a safe distance.

The ritual of counting coup was really an excuse. Lone Dog had spared Abner because by now he was strong in his belief that there was no point in killing white men anymore, just because they were white men. They were too many. It was a lost cause. The *tosi-tivo* could not be turned back. The Comanche people were doomed. Even the death of Wolfhunter would not make the slightest difference in the final outcome.

Nonetheless, Lone Dog was committed to attempting to take Wolfhunter's life. Not for Crooked Neck. Not to inspire the Comanche people. And not altogether for his brothers. He would do it for himself. He had made many mistakes. Mistakes that had cost the lives of his fellow warriors. And Wolfhunter had murdered his sister. Maybe killing Wolfhunter would, in some small way, be atonement for his making so many mistakes. And it would certainly avenge his sister.

The rain came, cold and drenching, but Lone Dog did not feel it. He rode tall through the wet silver curtain, on a relentless course for the caves of his fathers.

Wolfhunter, too, was making for the caves. Even taking a roundabout route from Llano he had fewer miles to cover than the lone Penateka. And while Lone Dog had to cross open country, Wolfhunter relied on two roads, the one west out of Llano and, later, the one south from San Saba. The night was pitch-black and stormy, and he knew better time would be made on the roads.

At first Calico Anne dared to hope that their use of the roads would improve her chances of rescue. It was unlikely, though, that anyone would be abroad on such an inclement night. Fierce gusts of wind thrashed the trees, and sudden showers drenched them. And as the night and her fatigue wore on she gradually relinquished her grip on that tattered shred of hope. What if someone did happen by? Wolfhunter would simply cut her throat before she could finish her cry for help, and then proceed to kill the would-be rescuer. She doubted that one man, or even two men together, would stand a chance against the killer whose horse she shared.

She rode the hard-galloping steeldust in front of Wolfhunter, wedged between the horn of the saddle they shared and the body of the man she feared. She could feel the buckskin-sheathed rifle between them. Her wrists were tied to the saddle horn with a long strip of whang-leather. Her ankles were lashed together with another strip beneath the steeldust's barrel. She loathed the feel of Wolfhunter's body pressed against hers. In her mind's eye was the vivid image of Wolfhunter's face as he drove the knife deep into Rafe Yellen. She could not escape the memory.

When they started west on the road out of Llano she'd begun to wonder what Wolfhunter was up to. Billy *had* told her about the caves, in a careless moment of drunken bragging, and had even described the location in such detail that she, no native to this region, had come away with a fair idea as to how to reach them. But the west road out of Llano was not the most direct route. Her imagination took flight. Perhaps Wolfhunter was taking her all the way to the Cap Rock and beyond, onto the Staked Plains. Maybe he intended to trade her to the Comanches, or the *Comancheros*. She had heard plenty of horror stories about the fate of white female captives. Well, men were men, red or white. What distressed her most was that, assuming this was Wolfhunter's intent, she would never see Billy again.

They rode on through a night as black as the heart of hell. She could scarcely see ten feet in front of her. But the steeldust galloped on through the muck as though it possessed the night vision of a cat. What would happen, she wondered, if the horse were to stumble and fall? Bound as she was, she would probably be seriously injured, if not killed outright.

Before long her camisole and pantalettes were soaked by the rain. Wolfhunter had not allowed her to get dressed, or even to get shoes on her feet. It was pure meanness—and maybe something else. "You look fetchin' just the way you are, darlin'," he had told her, and his eyes on her frail body had made her uneasy. Calico Anne prayed that he would not try to cover her. A whole passel of Comanche bucks would be better than *that.*

A mile shy of the hamlet of San Saba they left the road and delved into the brush. Now Wolfhunter restrained the steeldust, holding the horse to a walk. Thorn-laden branches reached out to tear at Annie's flesh and rend her scant clothing. In no time she lost all sense of direction. She was so tired. So drained. Several times she all but slipped into unconsciousness. Once she caught herself crying, whimpering like a little lost child. And once, to her surprise, she found herself in the middle of muttering the Lord's Prayer. She thought she had long ago forgotten all her childhood prayers.

His lips brushing her ear, and in a voice that made her shudder, Wolfhunter said, "God ain't ridin' with us this night, child."

At one point he began to cough, his body convulsing, and she felt a warm spray of something on her bare neck and shoulder. He checked the steeldust and almost fell out of the saddle. She could barely see him on his knees beside the horse, and it sounded as if he were hacking up his tortured lungs, bit by bloody bit. Annie thought about trying to escape on the horse, but he still had the reins, and besides, she was convinced that she could not escape this man, any more than she could escape Death itself, when it came for her.

After a time the coughing and spitting subsided, and then she felt him untying the ankle bindings, then the thong that lashed her hands to the saddle horn. He drew her from the saddle, none too gently, and she tried to stand, but her legs were numb. He let her fall to the wet and rocky ground. Exhausted, she lay there, shivering. She heard a snuffling sound, felt a cold, wet something on her arm, and shrank away with a stifled cry. The coyote dog crouched and growled, startled by her sudden movement. It was the first she'd seen of the dog.

"Go ahead and run if you want," Wolfhunter rasped hoarsely. "Dog don't mind an early breakfast."

He sounded put out by the violent coughing spell. She could discern his darker shape sitting or kneeling on the ground in front of her. It was barely drizzling now, and she dared to move slowly and finger wet tendrils of hair from her eyes.

"Y'know," he continued, "Injuns and animals don't much cotton to moving through wet brush. It leaves your scent everywhere strong when you do."

"You're going to kill me, aren't you." It was a statement, delivered flatly and without hope.

"Now that would be tellin'."

"Where are you taking me?"

"To the last of the Yellens, if I guess right."

It dawned on her then. "You know the way."

"Missy, I know every foot of this country. There are lots of caves, but only one that would suit a gang of *cabrons* led by a crafty bravo like Rafe Yellen. It's got at least two ways in and out, and a body'd never find it 'less he knew right where to look. The Comanch' used it, long time ago. I nighted there once or twice myself, back when I hunted lobos. I'm obliged for your offer to lead me there, all the same."

Calico Anne sorted through her feelings. She was ashamed that in her fear she had offered to betray Billy just to save her own life.

"I changed my mind anyway," she said, with a trace of defiance that amazed and pleased her.

"You have spirit, after all. That's good. I like women with a little fire in their blood."

"Stay away from me, you bastard."

He laughed softly and stood up. Annie's heart leaped into her throat. But he only reached down to lift her roughly to her feet.

"Time to move on. I've got more good work to do."

She was tied as before. Minutes later they came to a road. Calico Anne was so turned around that she had no idea which road it was. But if Wolfhunter knew the caves, then it was probably the road south out of San Saba. The road that passed within a couple of miles of the hideout where Billy and the others were holed up.

Cale and Frisco made good time until nightfall, and then the storm struck, and they found a limestone ledge on a hillside that offered some degree of shelter. Reins tied to their wrists, they huddled under the ledge, and Frisco donned his slicker, and Cale draped the canvas tarp that normally encased his blankets over his head and shoulders, for the ledge was narrow and the rain slanted in.

Frisco managed to find a dry match, struck it with a fingernail, and fired a cornhusk cigarette. He offered one to Cale, but Cale shook his head, moodily watching the rain. Frisco could sense Cale's impatience.

"Tom will be all right," said Frisco. "He can take care of himself."

Cale grunted skepticism. "Not against Wolfhunter Geddes. I don't care who you are. A hundred dead men, at least, could testify to that."

Frisco was silent a moment. The storm-lashed night was so dark that Cale could see the glowing orange tip of Frisco's quirly, and that was about all. He was hoping that the storm would pass before moonset—he wanted to put more miles behind them tonight. If they stayed here until morning it would be late tomorrow before they arrived at Whitetail Meadow. And late tomorrow would be too late. Of this Cale was convinced, for reasons he could not explain.

"I'd say that Geddes plans to kill you," Frisco decided. "*Mi madre* says that in the old days he and your father were rivals in many things. She says that Sam McKeller was the one man Wolfhunter seemed to be afraid of. Maybe if *su padre* were alive today he would be the one Wolfhunter is after. But, since he isn't, it is you. And maybe Wolfhunter thinks that killing you would be helping Tom."

"That's a hatful of maybes, Frisco."

"Wolfhunter thinks like an Indian. The warrior believes that when he kills an enemy, the courage and strength of the dead man become his. So it follows that the stronger and braver the enemy, the more power the warrior acquires by killing him. The stronger his *puha*, his personal medicine."

"Well, one thing is for damned sure, with no maybes attached. If it comes down to it, Frisco, you'd better be ready, willing, and able to kill Wolfhunter. Don't waste time thinking about it. Do for him as you would a mad dog. Otherwise, you might not live to regret it."

"I will do what I must. But I tell you what I think. I think he would rather see you in that Big Fifty's leaf sight than me, Cale."

Cale said, "At least you've stopped calling me boss."

Frisco laughed.

Chapter Twenty-Two

As the first gray threads of daylight slipped in through the sink-holes, Tom Samples woke from a fitful sleep. He was amazed that he had slept at all, considering the predicament he was in. His leg was badly swollen and hurt like the dickens.

Billy Yellen sat on a rock, elbows on knees, the .44 Dance dangling loose-held in his right hand, a rawhide quirt dangling from his left wrist.

"How you feelin'?" asked Billy.

"I can tell already that this won't be one of my better days. Least I'm alive. That kinda surprises me."

"Well, there are good surprises and then there are bad surprises."

Tom's throat was so dry it hurt. "Think I could get a drink around here?"

Billy smiled faintly. "You may get a bigger drink than you want. Hainey over there wants to tie a big rock to your leg and drop you in that pool out yonder. It's plenty deep. They'd not likely find your body. That's what's been bothering the others. They figure they've got to blow your lamp out, but they don't hanker for a murder charge chasing after them. Hainey's way don't leave no evidence."

Tom was scared clean through, but he did his level best not to show it. "Put a bullet through my head first, Billy."

Billy didn't say anything. He looked across the cavern. Tom followed his gaze. The others were breaking camp, gathering up their possibles. There was a crackling fire going, with the smell of strong coffee rising from the blackened pot set close to the flames. As they watched, the slim, black-haired man who managed, somehow, to look well-heeled despite the well-worn condition of his dusty range clothes started toward them.

"We're about ready, Billy," he said, looking at Tom.

Billy stood up. "Ya'll go on without me, Cajun."

Cajun studied Billy's grim-set demeanor. He didn't look surprised by this development. But then, thought Billy, Cajun was plenty smart. And sort of coolly impartial to everything that happened, good or bad. He just accepted it and went on about his business.

"Dealing yourself out, Billy?"

Billy nodded, strung as tight as brand-new bobwire.

"I can't say that I blame you. You've still got a choice. The rest of us … well, we're too far gone. You've been trying all along to fill the wrong boots, if you ask me. I did the same thing. I had a good life, but I threw it all away. Fell in with the wrong people when I was too young to know better." A wistful smile played at the corners of his mouth. "You seldom know better until it's too late."

"Thanks," said Billy, beholden. "I didn't think you'd be hard-set against it. Not too sure about the others, though."

"Oh, they won't mind. They'll realize that it makes everybody else's cut that much bigger. Assuming we pull it off. And they trust you, Billy. But this gent here still bothers them."

Billy looked down at Tom, and Tom grasped at one slim hope for all it was worth. Billy had drawn the line at coldblooded murder. That was the only reason he was still alive. Billy wasn't all bad. He just wanted to cut corners, take a shortcut off the straight and narrow, looking for the quick and easy way to that pot of gold every man strove for. Maybe, just maybe, he had the mettle to stand up to these desperados.

"It don't matter to me what you do," Billy said, "as long as you wait until I've hauled timber." Tom let go of that last little fragment of hope.

Addressing Samples, Cajun said, "Mister, I don't much like the idea, either. But you fell into a nest of rattlers when you fell through that hole up there, and you can't expect to get out unbitten."

"Reckon so," said Tom stonily.

"I suppose I'm to blame for giving Hainey the idea," Cajun said apologetically. "I once tied a rock to my reata and dropped it in that pool, just to find out how deep it was. But I can guarantee you one thing. You'll be dead before they drop you in there. You've got my word for that."

Tom just nodded. He didn't trust his voice anymore.

"Where are you headed?" Cajun asked of Billy. "In case Jake or your father asks."

"I'm going as far as I can get. But I'll tell them myself."

"You're going back to Llano?"

"One last time."

Suddenly, the cracking boom of the rifleshot echoed deep and hollow in the cavern.

Billy spun around. Landon was standing frozen by the campfire. Sligo was running toward the stone archway that led to the sinkhole. And then Billy saw Hainey. The rewrite man was sprawled on his back over by the Texas gate that stretched across the arch. Beyond, the stolen cattle were milling around and bawling up a ruckus.

On the east rim of the sinkhole, Calico Anne watched with sick fascination as Wolfhunter, standing casually hipshot, thrust the trigger guard of his Big Fifty forward, ejecting the empty metal casing. She was still bound hand and foot, and sat with her legs curled up underneath her. And she was precariously close to the brink—right where he had put her. Now, pulling another .50/90 cartridge from his bandolier, he grinned at her.

"What a way to say good mornin'!"

Annie looked down, through the arch, at the dead man. It wasn't Billy. But if Billy was down there then he was as good as dead.

Slipping the cartridge into the breech, Wolfhunter said, "Some hidehunters I know swear that the cleanest shot is a few inches north of the brisket. Now others will claim that you can't drop a buffalo in its tracks 'less you go for the brain. I always preferred a high lung shot. It does the job."

She could not bear to look at him. He spoke so offhandedly about killing a man! Like it was sport. Like it meant nothing to him. Like he enjoyed it, and was more interested in the technique than in the act itself.

Someone down below started shooting. Annie jumped as a bullet whined off the rock of the ledge right below them. More shots. Another bullet clipped the yellow-spined stems of a cholla scant feet to her left. Calico Anne cringed. She wanted to crawl away from the rim. But the coyote dog sat behind her, panting, tongue lolling, just waiting for her to make a move.

Wolfhunter laughed. Last night he had pulled the wolfskin over his head—now he swept it back from the long tangle of his auburn hair. The leaden gray overcast was breaking apart, and behind them the gold and plum-red colors of sunrise filled the gashes in the torn cloud cover.

"When you trade lead with a feller you try to put the sun in his eyes," explained Wolfhunter, bringing the Sharps buffalo gun to his shoulder and sighting down. "But we just couldn't wait on the sun today, could we? These boys were fixin' to pull up stakes, so we had to start the dance a mite early."

He squeezed the trigger. Reloaded and fired again. Then again.

Down in the arch the two halves of the Texas gate separated and writhed back against the iron stanchions. Wolfhunter's three shots had snipped the three strands of barbed wire. Billy and Cajun on one side of the arch, and Sligo on the other, stopped shooting and strove to elude the whiplashing wire. Landon was still back by the fire, crouching now, acting as if he had forgotten all about the gun strapped to his hip. Billy yelled at him to look out as the cattle began to come through the arch. The entire *vacada* thundered out of the sinkhole like whiskey pouring out of an overturned bottle, fanning out into the big chamber. Landon started to run one way, dodged the other way, then dropped behind the biggest boulder he could find. Some of the longhorns went off down the tunnel, smelling the way to freedom. Others wandered around the cavern, or stood stock-still and bawling. Tom had enough big rocks around him that he didn't have to worry about getting trampled, and the cattle stayed clear of the dead horse close by. Landon was unscathed, too. He got up and began an ungainly lope for the side of the arch where Sligo crouched.

Billy saw this, too late. "Landon, get down, you ignorant—!"

The Big Fifty boomed. The impact of the bullet threw Landon ten feet sideways.

"Damn!" breathed Billy, huddled in the shelter of rocks piled high on the east side of the arch.

Beside him, Cajun was reloading his short gun. "He was a good boy. But he's finished. And so are we if we don't get out of here, Billy."

Billy could look up and over the rockpile and see the horses on the stake rope under the west ledge of the sinkhole. They were acting up, aroused by the shooting and the stampede of the cattle, but they couldn't break free of their tethers. Outlaws like Sligo and Cajun knew how to stake down their ponies to eliminate any chance that they might bolt camp and leave their owners stranded afoot. But just this once it would've been nice if the horses had been able to come to them. Going to the horses meant running across open ground. It was no accident that the man with the rifle had selected a position on the east rim. At least, Billy thought, the mounts were saddled. A man on the dodge never knew if he'd have the leisure to saddle up.

"That gent is a crack shot," added Cajun, impassive. "Sounds like a .50-caliber Leadslinger to me. But that's the only gun I've heard from up there."

Billy looked at him. "You think he's alone?"

Cajun shrugged. "That's what it sounds like."

"Maybe the others are waiting in the creek bed for us to come runnin' out. Maybe this man is just trying to smoke us."

"Could be. If so, they'll eventually get tired of waiting and come for us. And there's no place to run in here. I say we take our chances."

Billy looked across the arch at Sligo, who had reloaded and was throwing lead at the east rim.

"Look on the bright side," said Cajun, smiling. "At least now there's no point in killing that Cyclone man back there."

Billy was heartened by Cajun's remarkable calm. Cajun was a good man to have siding you in a bad spot. His calm infected others.

"Sligo!" yelled Billy. "The horses!"

Sligo, reloading again, nodded, and Billy nodded back. Gathering himself up, he felt Cajun's hand on his shoulder.

"Billy, your brother's got nothing on you."

"Let's go."

They ran for the horses, all three shooting at the east rim.

Still standing on the brink, Wolfhunter watched them. He observed the muzzle flashes through the thickening pall of gunsmoke, and heard the shimmy of lead burning the air around him. He looked at Annie, cowering on the ground, and shook his head in mild reproof.

"Now girl, that's no fit way to live, with your face in the dirt. Come on, stand up." Stepping to her, he reached down to take a fistful of mouse-brown hair, and yanked viciously. With a gasping screech Annie came off the ground plenty quick. She did her best to stand on her own, but it was difficult with her feet bound. Wolfhunter pushed her to the very edge of the rim.

"Oh God!" she cried, strangling on fear, for only his cruel hold on her hair prevented her from falling.

Wolfhunter threw back his head and laughed. He lifted the Big Fifty high above his head. "Oh, God!" he roared at the sky. "This little lamb sure as hell has strayed, but she'd like to come home now!"

Almost to the horses, Billy stopped in his tracks.

That was Annie up there!

Sligo collided with him, cursed, slipped by and on to the horses.

"Come on, Billy!" yelled Cajun, running past.

Calico Anne screamed, "Shoot, Billy! Shoot!"

Billy heard the snicker of a rifle's action, spun as Sligo put the .52 Sharps carbine drawn from his saddle boot to shoulder.

Even as Billy shouted, the carbine spoke, jumped in Sligo's hands.

The bullet smacked into Calico Anne's midsection.

"I'll be damned," said Wolfhunter. "Sorry, darlin'. I guess you took one that was meant for me."

He let go of her hair. She disappeared over the edge.

Before Annie's body concluded its spinning descent to the sinkhole floor, Billy had fired the Dance. He shot Sligo at point-blank range, even as he lunged. It was reflex; he didn't even think about it. Colliding with Sligo, he bore the gut-shot man to the ground and laid the barrel of his revolver as hard as he could into Sligo's face. He struck again and again in a brutal, senseless rage, and before he knew it there was nothing left of Sligo's face. Springing to his feet, spraddling the dead man, he put one more round into Sligo for good measure.

"There, you sorry low-life sonuvabitch," he hissed, his tone fierce, his voice trembling. "How does it feel? You ain't smilin' now, are you?"

Cajun was mounted. "Billy, come on!" He hesitated one fatal instant laying spurs.

Billy looked up in time to see the bullet strike Cajun square in the chest. The boom of the Big Fifty filled his ears as he watched Cajun being thrown backward off the horse by the impact. Without conscious thought Billy leaped for the spooked horse as it went by, grabbing hold of the saddle's bisquit with his left hand and kicking his left leg up and over. He stayed low in the saddle as the horse galloped through the arch.

There was one escape: through the tunnel. But the tunnel was dark, black as the devil's heart. Pulling the long black muffler from around his neck, he checked the horse long enough to dangle the garment in the flames of the small campfire. It caught fire. Throwing caution to the wind, Billy quirted and gut-hooked the horse mercilessly down the cave tunnel, holding the burning scarf above his head. Hell-for-leather was no way to negotiate the tunnel, and several times the mount lost purchase on the slick stone, slipping and scrambling. But Billy didn't care. Calico Anne was dead. Bending low in the saddle, his face in the horse's mane, he felt something wet on his cheeks. So much for dreams. He would never amount to anything, so what did it matter? He was dead, before he'd even had a chance to live.

Emerging from the tunnel, the horse finally did fall, its legs sliding sideways out from under on the water-smoothed stone beneath the overhang. Billy kicked out of the stirrups and fell, hitting the rock hard with shoulder and skull. The horse got up and trotted out into the deep gravel creek bed. It was standing out there, blowing and looking subdued, when Billy got up and stumbled forward, fighting a wave of dizzy nausea. There was something wet all over his face now. He lifted his hand, touched his face, saw the scarlet smear of blood on his fingers. Wait a minute. This was his right hand. Something was missing. He stared dumbly at that hand. The .44 Dance, that was it! He tried to turn around to look for it, but only the top half of his body turned, his legs entangled.

He heard the Big Fifty speak again. It didn't even make him jump. He just turned his head slowly and looked dumbly at the horse, which now lay dead in the middle of the creek bed.

He kept looking that way. He wasn't exactly sure why, or what he expected to see, but he kept watching all the same. It was too hard, trying to think. He was too tired. And hurt. Hurt bad. He wanted to go to sleep, just to escape the pain.

A little while later he saw a man in buckskins astride a shaggy steeldust, prancing in the gravel of the dry creek bed. The man was looking in his direction.

And then the coyote dog came at him, running low and fast, fangs bared. The sound that issued from its throat was what Billy imagined the howling lamentations of all the tortured souls in hell sounded like.

The coyote dog lunged.

Billy's wail was cut abruptly short as the fangs ripped his throat.

Chapter Twenty-Three

As it turned out, Cale couldn't pass the night in a cold camp under that limestone ledge. He couldn't shake the feeling that waiting until daylight to press on would be a terrible mistake. He couldn't explain it to Frisco, much less to himself. But he had learned in years of hard and dangerous campaigning to heed his battlefield instincts. And that was precisely what he had now: a battlefield instinct. It was time to ride to the sound of gunfire. Never mind that he couldn't actually *hear* the guns. Wait, and the battle might be lost.

So they traveled on, through the wet brush, across treacherous ground, holding their horses to a walk. Progress was slow, but Cale consoled himself with the sure and certain knowledge that if he lost his mount the progress would be even slower. It was too dark to look for landmarks in the *brasada*, and too overcast to read the stars. So they relied on another instinct, that strong sense of direction that experience had instilled in them both.

Daybreak found them only slightly off course, and they turned south, striking Whitetail Meadow just as the sound of distant gunfire came from a few miles west.

Frisco rode up to the door of the line shack, leaned in the saddle to work the rope latch, pushed the door open, and peered inside. He turned to Cale and shook his head.

Grim-faced, they sat their horses a moment and listened to the gunfire.

"Well," muttered Cale, his tone hollow, "let's get there."

It sounded to Frisco as if they were riding to a funeral rather than a fight. The anticipation was gone, replaced by dark presentiment.

Cale remembered what Tom had said a few days earlier about tracking Billy Yellen to the vicinity of a hogback ridge, about losing Billy's trail and hearing unseen cattle. He put two and two together. It would be just like Tom to pay no heed to Cale's warning and go off half-cocked hunting the nightriders. Could be he had found them. Could be the distant gunplay was the result of that discovery. And, reflecting on that hogback ridge, judging distance and time as he heeled Beau into a high lope, Cale also remembered the small cave entrance he had found when looking for dry kindling to build a branding fire. This country was honeycombed with caves. That was one reason the area around Llano was so popular with the dishonest element.

Tom Samples was tenacious enough to hunt those rustlers until he found them, and foolish-brave enough to try to take them on single-handedly.

"By God," thought Cale, "I won't abide losing a half brother the day after I find out I have one."

The faint smile that played across his dark features was self-deprecating. He couldn't help wondering what he was most afraid of: losing his own kin and kind, or losing his best excuse for quitting the cattle business and going home to the cavalry. He sure wasn't chock full of brotherly love, but then again, maybe the reason he and Tom were at each other was because they shared the same nature.

They came across a few cows grazing the brush. Noticing the Bar Buckle brand, Frisco threw a querulous look at Cale.

"That's a new one, *amigo*. I don't know it."

"A new brand," replied Cale cynically, leaping to another conclusion, "for an old profession."

They came next to the dead horse in the creek bed, led to the spot by circling buzzards. Their subsequent discovery was the most gruesome of all: the savaged remains of Billy Yellen. Cale recognized the clothes—that was the only way he could say for certain that this was what was left of Billy. No man could have done such damage. It looked more like the work of a pack of rabid wolves. Frisco mumbled a quick but heartfelt prayer, and they moved on, to the mouth of the cave, where they found and lighted a lantern.

Up the tunnel they went, single-file, with Cale in front and holding the lantern. They led their horses. Eventually the tunnel emptied into a big cavern, with a natural stone arch to one side, and beyond the arch a huge sinkhole. Bright sunlight broke through the clouds and slanted into the sinkhole.

Neither man spoke as they surveyed the carnage. Cale went to each body, and each time breathed a sigh of relief. Tom was not among the dead. He noted that three of the strangers had been killed with a big-caliber rifle. What appalled him was that the ears of all four dead men had been cut off. *A hundred dollars an ear.* That was the deal struck by Wolfhunter and the Association.

Kneeling beside the body of the half-clad girl, he frowned, wondering what part she had played. She had been shot; just as obviously she had fallen from the rim of the sinkhole. Standing, he stepped back and craned his neck to scan the rimrock, trying to piece it together. It was clear that these men had been ambushed, most likely from up there. He went to the four horses still securely tethered to the stake rope. All of them wore that Bar Buckle brand. There was no doubt in his mind that this had been the hideout of the rustlers.

Frisco's shout brought him back into the cavern at a dead run. The *caporal* was in the rear of the big chamber, over by the steep slope of rock and debris that ascended to a smaller sinkhole in the ceiling.

"Tom's mare," said Frisco glumly.

Cale stared at the dead horse. He had missed it at first, hidden as it was behind a pile of large rocks. Its foreleg was fractured, and someone had put it down with a bullet in the brainpan.

"Look," said Frisco. He was walking away, pointing at the cavern floor. Cale saw the marks gouged into the stone, two parallel lines about three feet apart.

"What do you make of it?" he asked.

Frisco, grimacing, shook his head. "*No se.* But something tells me we should follow it. Maybe it will lead us to Tom."

Cale nodded. Walking back to the ground-hitched chestnut, he saw the gray longcoat lying on the ground. He picked it up, carried it with him out of the caves and paused to cover Billy Yellen's body with it.

"We should bury them," said Frisco.

"The dead will wait. We've got to take care of the living first."

They had not gone far from the caves before several things became clear to them.

"These marks are made by a travois," said Frisco.

Cale nodded. Somebody was hurt. Hurt bad enough that they couldn't ride. Was it Wolfhunter, or Tom? He could only hope the former, but the trail they followed led away from the Cyclone into rough country. There was no town or ranch nearby in this direction, nothing but the big wide-open. Seemed to him an unlikely course for Tom to set if he had an injured man in his keeping.

It became immediately evident that they were not the only ones tracking the travois. The marks of shod hooves here and there obliterated the travois sign.

"Looks like somebody has invited himself to the fandango," observed the *caporal.* "Maybe one of the rustlers escaped. Maybe he intends to even the score."

"There you go again with your damned maybes," said Cale crossly.

It was a simple task, following the sign across the rain-softened ground. As they pushed on, Cale's thoughts turned time and again to the Comanches. They had arrived in the vicinity about the same time as Wolfhunter Geddes. Was that more than just coincidence? Wolfhunter claimed he had killed them, but there was at least one left alive—the one who had ambushed Abner and taken his horse. Could the lone rider be the last of the warriors?

If so, that put Tom Samples between a rock and a hard place.

He touched spurs to the chestnut and picked up the pace.

Riding on the travois, feeling every jounce and jolt in his busted leg, Tom Samples wondered where in hell the tall man in buckskins was taking him. The cloud cover had broken up and the sun was shining, and by its position in the sky Tom could tell that they were traveling in a southwesterly direction. Casa Piedra and Llano happened to lie in the opposite direction. He couldn't figure out what their destination might be. Far as he knew, there was nothing but miles upon miles of *monte* ahead of them.

At least, he thought, he wasn't going to end up at the bottom of the sinkhole pool. At least he was alive, out here in the open, breathing cool rain-freshened air.

He went back over it in his mind. The shootout—most of which had been hidden from his view. Watching Billy's escape on a fast horse. Only one more shot after that. The voice of the big-caliber rifle again. Then the man in buckskins had appeared in the cavern. He had seen the Diamond C brand on the dead sorrel mare, and asked Tom his name.

"Samples. I work for the Cyclone. Whoever you are, I'm glad you came along when you did."

"The Association hired me. Sit tight, boy. I'll be back."

And the man had departed the cavern, leaving Tom with the impression that they had met before. But he just couldn't quite remember where.

It wasn't long and the man was back, hauling a rope-bound bundle of stout tree limbs. He used two catch ropes gleaned from the belongings of the dead rustlers and in no time at all had a travois put together.

"I can ride," insisted Tom. "I don't need to travel on my backside like some pregnant Indian woman."

The man had smiled faintly and finished his task, lashing the crisscrossed top ends of the two long poles to the saddle on the steeldust. While this was going on Tom noticed that the yellow dog which accompanied this man was having a fine old time chasing the few cattle that lingered in the cavern.

"Did you kill them all?" asked Tom.

"It was their time."

The man went off to kneel beside the bodies of Hainey and Landon, and then proceeded into the sinkhole and out of Tom's sight. Returning, he tied a small, blood-soaked pouch to his saddle. Tom felt his spine crawl.

"What do you have there?" he asked.

"Markers. I'll turn 'em in for hard money. We're about done here. You want I should tie you to this contraption, or do you think you can hold on?"

"You taking me back to the Cyclone?"

"I'm taking you."

The man helped him settle on a couple of blankets spread across the travois.

"The crosspieces are mesquite," the man informed him. "Good and sturdy. The poles are cottonwood. Nice and limber. Makes for a smoother ride."

"I thought I heard a woman scream," said Tom, feeling less relieved and more apprehensive by the minute. "Was there a woman out there?"

"You ask a lot of questions," said the man as he climbed aboard the shaggy steeldust.

Now they were miles away from the sinkhole, proceeding slowly through the *brasada*. A pair of mockingbirds came swooping down out of a post oak tree as they passed, raising cain. The yellow dog leaped again and again, jaws snapping as it tried to catch one of the birds in flight. Tom pulled for the mockingbirds. The way they were acting, he figured they had a nest in that post oak. Anything that came too close to that nest was going to get this kind of attention.

They moved on, and the mockingbirds went home, and the yellow dog, looking disgusted, fell in behind the travois, flinging slaver from its lolling tongue.

Facing backwards, Tom didn't see the granite dome until the brush fell away and they began the ascent up a steep slope of barren, coarse-grained rock. The man in buckskins angled one way and then cut back the other to make it easier on the horse. Tom had to hold on for all he was worth. The travois bounced over broken sheets and tent blisters. There was precious little foliage up here: a wind-gnarled cedar surviving in the shelter of a rock pedestal, sparse tan grass growing in the crevices between sun-whacked slabs and in the weathering pits where, compliments of the recent rain, water had collected. As they neared the summit, Tom could look out over the brush country for what had to be at least fifty miles in every direction.

At the summit they stopped, and the man in buckskins dismounted and relieved the steeldust of the travois burden.

"Hey," said Tom. "I don't mean to sound ungrateful, but you mind telling me what the hell we're doing way up here?"

The man stood with hands on hips, gazing all about, a satisfied expression evident on his bearded features.

"You can see forever up here. Always liked this big rock. For one thing, you don't have to worry about Injuns. This is a sacred place to them, chock full of spirits, and they'll go out of their way to avoid it."

"Who are you?" asked Tom.

The man sat cross-legged, the Indian-sheathed rifle across his lap. For a spell he watched the yellow dog chase a lizard across the top of the dome. The lizard dove into a crevice and the dog, furious, tried digging rock. Finally the man fastened squinty, sun-faded green eyes on Samples.

"They've called me Wolfhunter for so long I done honestly forgot my Christian name."

"You're the one my mother ran away with."

Wolfhunter's smile was one of mild reproach. "I am that, and more. Ain't you even gonna say hello to your pa after all these many years? I gave you life, boy. And I'll wager I just saved it, too."

"You're not my father," denied Tom sharply. "My father was a horse trader named Ira Samples."

"That may be what your mother told you, but it ain't true. I dislike saying bad things about the dead and departed, but it's true."

"Dead?" echoed Tom, his voice hollow.

"I hate to be the one who deals you a low card, son, but I come a long way to tell you that your mother has met her Maker."

Tom swallowed the lump in his throat. Many times in the past, moved by discontent and self-pity, Tom had cursed his mother. Cursed her for leaving Sam McKeller. And for sending him away at a tender age. But she had been, for better or worse, his mother—no getting around that—and her passing dimmed the light of the sun.

"You'll be an orphan before long, I reckon," observed Wolfhunter.

"I have been," said Tom stiffly. "My father died. My mother sent me away. There was no place in her world for me. So I made my own place. You've told me what you came to. Now why don't you leave me the hell alone?"

"Sounds like you hold a grudge against me, boy," said Wolfhunter softly.

Tom didn't say anything. What scared him was a gut feeling that maybe, just maybe, this man *was* his father. He had been eight years old when Ira Samples was killed. He remembered the man as being very reserved, and in moments of indiscretion brought about by severe drunkenness, Ira had denied any part in bringing a "half-breed bastard" like Tom into the world. Oh, he had always apologized later, at Susanna's insistence, but had never really behaved like a loving father.

"Shouldn't have pulled that on you, boy. I hope I can make up for that mistake by doing a little something for you before I die."

"Don't do me any favors."

"Oh, but I insist. I got a good bit of money stashed away. Made a good living hunting shaggies, and wanted men, and Injuns, too. Got well paid, though I confess I didn't do it for the money. Now, it's all yours, boy. Got trophies on that saddle that'll bring you even more. Enough to buy you a fair-sized piece of this ranch you love so much."

"The Cyclone belongs to Cale and Katy McKeller."

"I can take care of that little problem. I aim to kill Cale McKeller for you, son. And I'll take Katy away with me. She'll be a real comfort to me in my last days."

Incredulous, Tom looked hard at Wolfhunter, and saw that the man was serious.

"You'll have to kill me first," he said.

Wolfhunter heaved a deep sigh, set aside his long gun, and stood up, slow and stiff. "I can do that. At least we'll be together in the next life, like we shoulda been in this one."

He pulled the Colt revolver from its holster.

Tom had had about enough of looking up into the barrel of a gun.

Kicking out with his one good leg, biting down on the pain this sudden and violent movement cost him, he caught Wolfhunter behind the knees. Wolfhunter lost his balance and fell. He rolled down the steep curve of the dome about twenty feet, losing his grip on the Colt. It went clattering downslope. Tom crawled for the sheathed Big Fifty. But Wolfhunter leaped to his feet and came at him in a low, running crouch, and sunlight flashed off the blade of his knife. Tom stretched desperately for the rifle. It was just out of his grasp. He wasn't going to reach it in time.

The gunshot came from behind him, and he saw the splash of rock dust and splinters between himself and Wolfhunter. More curious than alarmed, Wolfhunter looked past Tom, and Tom twisted around to see Cale on the chestnut, not thirty feet away along the line of the summit. The gelding was standing steady. A veteran cavalry mount, Beau was trained to stand fast around gunfire. Cale had the hammer back and the Colt Cavalry aimed at Wolfhunter.

"Stay away from my brother, you sonuvabitch."

"I knew you'd come," said Wolfhunter, sounding awfully pleased. "Sooner or later. I was counting on it. I'm sorry I missed Ol' Sam, but I didn't aim to miss you."

The coyote dog came charging at a dead run from directly behind Cale. He heard the beast snarl. Beau was already pivoting to face this new threat head on. The dog leaped before Cale could line up a shot. The jaws came down on his right forearm. He cried out as the fangs struck deeply into his flesh, laid the barrel of the Colt against the dog's chest and fired. The bullet struck high on the inside of the dog's left hindleg. The jaws released and the dog fell, writhing on blood-smeared stone. Snorting, Beau danced away. Cale fired again. The coyote dog yelped, spasmed, and died.

As the coyote dog lunged at Cale, Wolfhunter started for Tom again. But Frisco came over the summit on a hard-charging horse, yelling at the top of his lungs. Wolfhunter, flashing a grin, changed directions and ran right at the mounted *caporal*. Frisco had his pistol in hand. He fired, but Wolfhunter dodged directly into the path of Frisco's horse. Driving the knife to the hilt into the animal's throat, he grabbed the bridle with his other hand. The horse shrieked and collided with Wolfhunter. Both men and the horse went down.

Frisco, kicking out of the saddle, hit, rolled, and came up staggering. He had lost his gun in the fall. The horse struggled to its feet, blood spurting out of its neck, gave a shrill whinny, tottered sideways, and fell once more. This time it didn't get up. Stunned by his fall, Frisco stared dumbly at it, and then saw Wolfhunter hurdle the dying horse and bear down on him, bloody knife in hand and howling like a banshee. What shook Frisco was that Wolfhunter had just been run over by a galloping horse and looked none the worse for the experience.

It was reflex that guided Frisco's hand to the handle of the knife in his belt—the Comanche knife he had taken days before from the body of the young Penateka warrior Cale had done for. He tried to clear the cotton out of his head, tried to come to terms with the problems of balance and timing, for as Wolfhunter's knife slashed toward him he drew the Comanche knife in a quick upward arch. Steel clashed against steel. Frisco bent his knees and twisted away as Wolfhunter's body struck his. Both men fell, Wolfhunter rolling away. Frisco drew his own belduque from his boot. Wolfhunter started to close in again, saw that Frisco now had a knife in both hands, and pulled up short. He barked a harsh and scornful laugh.

"You bean-eaters like the blades, don't you?"

"Come and get it," urged Frisco.

Wolfhunter knew that a man with two knives would draw blood. It didn't matter what the man with only one blade did, or how well he did it. Frisco had every right to sound confident.

But Wolfhunter lunged, anyway. He threw himself at Frisco, grabbing the *vaquero*'s wrist, felt the Comanche blade, a cold bite of white agony below his rib cage, and thrust his own knife deep.

The two men stood braced against one another for one trembling moment, then broke apart.

Frisco took one step back, turned toward Tom, and fell.

Only seconds before, Cale had put the coyote dog down, then turned to find Wolfhunter and Frisco locked in mortal combat. He had hesitated, waiting for a clean shot. He had waited too long.

He fired.

Wolfhunter doubled over. He dropped to one knee, heaved back onto his feet, and raised his head slowly to leer at Cale.

"You better spend the other five, if you aim to keep me down, hoss."

"Only two left," rasped Cale. "But they're yours."

The Colt spoke twice more.

This time he aimed higher. The bullets threw Wolfhunter backward. He landed spread-eagled, and his body slid a few feet down the slope before coming to a stop.

Cale threw himself out of the saddle and ran to Frisco's side.

The *caporal*'s eyes were open. He lay there with knives in both hands, looking up at the clouds drifting lazily in the sky. Cale put his own hand against the wound, feeling hot blood running through his fingers. Wolfhunter had thrust his knife into Frisco's left side. He had aimed high under the arm, going for the heart.

Frisco managed to focus on Cale's face. "This is one grave I won't have to dig," he whispered.

Cale shook his head. He could tell that Wolfhunter's aim had been off. The knife had entered too low to do fatal damage to heart or lungs. Frisco had a chance—which was all a toughened *brasadero* needed.

"I've seen a lot of men die, *amigo*," he said. "Too many. But you're not going to be one of them."

He looked up to see Tom dragging himself across the rock, his face etched with pain.

Cale said, "Take it easy, Tom. He'll pull through."

The clacking of steelshod hooves brought Cale's head up sharply. He caught only a glimpse of the mounted Comanche warrior on the summit, silhouetted against the bright morning sun. He saw the shape of the war lance, and dove as the warrior kicked the horse forward. The Colt Cavalry was in Cale's hand. He pulled the trigger, pure reflex. The hammer fell on an empty chamber. Swearing, he rolled in a frantic attempt to avoid being trampled. Then the Comanche was past him, uttering an ear-splitting war cry seasoned with a ring of savage triumph as he drove the lance into Wolfhunter's body, arresting Wolfhunter's loping run at Cale and the others. The impact picked Wolfhunter up off his feet and thrust him backward. The warrior released the lance and turned the horse away from the precipitous curve of the slope. Cale saw Wolfhunter's body tumble out of sight down the steep granite grade, heard the clatter of the lance as it came free of the body and rolled away.

Lone Dog checked the roan. He, too, watched Wolfhunter's body fall away, jubilation mixed with a strong dash of astonishment. Then he turned the horse to face the three men up near the summit. Only one of them was standing. This one he recognized as Long Blue Coat, the killer of Watchful Fox. And he remembered giving Bow String his word; he had promised to avenge Watchful Fox, upon his honor as a Penateka warrior.

As Lone Dog drew the rifle from its securing loop in the rope-saddle, Cale took a few long strides, stooped to heft the Indian-sheathed Big Fifty. A sideways fling of his arm sent the sheath flying away.

Lone Dog thought of She Walks Softly. "There is only so much that one man can do. Bow String, if you *are* my good friend, then you will understand."

He threw the rifle down with disdain, as though the weapon were a vile and unclean thing, unworthy of a warrior.

With a sharp, exultant cry he whipped the roan about, contemptuously turning his back on Cale and the others, and walked the horse at an angle down the granite dome, his eyes drawn to the far western horizon.

Cale lowered the buffalo gun and watched him go.

"You just going to let him ride off?" asked Tom. "That horse is wearing a Cyclone brand, you know. You're just going to let him steal one of your horses?"

Cale gave him an exasperated look. "One of *our* horses, dammit. And yes, he's welcome to it. If you don't like it, why don't you get up and run after him?"

"Well, somebody's got to look out for the stock."

Cale went over to hunker down alongside Frisco again. "Look at you two. All stoved up. What a pair. Guess I'll have to hang around and see to things until you boys are healthy enough to start running the ranch."

"Where are you going?" asked Tom.

"Back to the cavalry," said Frisco weakly, answering for Cale. "Back to fighting Indians."

"Better load your gun first," remarked Tom.

Cale had been looking around for the steeldust. But Wolfhunter's horse had vanished. Now he peered bleakly at Tom.

"Don't start on me," he warned.

"You two," sighed Frisco, "sound more like brothers every day."

Tom just smiled.

Look for these reissued ebook titles by Jason Manning:

HIGH COUNTRY SERIES
- High Country
- Green River Rendezvous
- Battle of the Teton Basin

FLINTLOCK SERIES
- Flintlock
- The Border Captains
- Gone To Texas

TEXAS SERIES
- The Black Jacks
- Texas Bound
- The Marauders

MOUNTAIN MAN SERIES
- Mountain Passage
- Mountain Massacre
- Mountain Courage
- Mountain Vengeance
- Mountain Honor
- Mountain Renegade

FALCONER SERIES
- Falconer's Law
- Promised Land
- American Blood

ETHAN PAYNE SERIES
- Frontier Road
- Trail Town
- Last Chance

THE WESTERNERS
- Gun Justice
- Gunmaster
- The Outlaw Trail

TIMOTHY BARLOW SERIES
- The Long Hunters
- The Fire-Eaters
- War Lovers

APACHE SERIES
- Apache Storm
- Apache Shadow
- Apache Strike

OTHER TITLES
- Showdown at Seven Springs
- Texas Helltown
- Texas Gundown
- Gunsmoke on the Sierra Line
- Revenge in Little Texas
- Robbers of the Redlands (originally titled Texas Blood Kill)

www.ingramcontent.com/pod-product-compliance
Lightning Source LLC
Chambersburg PA
CBHW070648100726
47907CB00007B/2140